PRAISE FOR

# THE WALKING TOUR

"Brilliant . . . The intrigue is splendidly teased out."
— Lorna Sage, *New York Times Book Review*

"I enjoyed it for its stupendous beauty. *The Walking Tour* is a book that you keep picking up because . . . it is so ambitious, so smart, so beautifully written that it is a pleasure to stand in its light." — Ann Patchett, *Mirabella*

"Entrancing . . . every sentence uncoils with supple grace."
— *Los Angeles Times Book Review*

"Davis's approach to novel writing is so original and the results so magical . . . I don't think I've ever encountered a book that withheld so much crucial information and produced such a sense of satisfaction, even fulfillment, at the end." — A. O. Scott, *Newsday*

"Davis brilliantly captures that terrible sense of walking blindly through mist . . . Reading her book is a remarkable experience."
— Nan Goldberg, *New York Post*

"Davis is brilliant at depicting the manners and motives of her characters. There are great self-deceptions exposed and wonderful, small sly moments revealed in almost every scene among the four 'friends.'"
— Suzanne Freeman, *Boston Globe*

"Mysteries, bees, abandonment, jealousy, computers, and the ominous dominance of nature over humanity are all bound up in this hypnotic novel by Kathryn Davis . . . Davis's gorgeous writing makes the journey a pleasure."
— Kathryn Rhett, *Chicago Tribune*

"Every page brims with action, but the pathos is real and the cliffhangers end with actual falls." — *The New Yorker*

"The work is so distinctive and fine that one is almost content simply to step back and admire." — Edwin Frank, *Boston Review*

"Some of the finest prose around. None of the poetical pyrotechnics that pass for style these days, just sentences and sentiments as meticulously shaped as pretzels, each echoing the shape of the novel as a whole."
— Dale Peck, *Book Forum*

ALSO BY KATHRYN DAVIS

*Labrador*

*The Girl Who Trod on a Loaf*

*Hell*

# The
# Walking Tour

—◆—

## KATHRYN DAVIS

A MARINER BOOK
*Houghton Mifflin Company*
BOSTON    NEW YORK

FIRST MARINER BOOKS EDITION 2000

Copyright © 1999 by Kathryn Davis

Visit our Web site: www.houghtonmifflinbooks.com

Library of Congress Cataloging-in-Publication Data

Davis, Kathryn, date.
The walking tour/Kathryn Davis.
p.   cm.
ISBN 0-395-94541-0
ISBN 0-618-08238-7  (pbk.)
1. Title.
PS3554.A934923W35          1999
813'.54—dc21    9-35547  CIP

Book Design by Anne Chalmers
Type: Janson Text; display: Centaur

Printed in the United States of America

QUM 10 9 8 7 6 5 4 3 2 1

*For Louise*

PART ONE

# Quick & Dirty

The end of all things is nigh: be ye therefore sober, and watch unto prayer. And above all things have fervent charity among yourselves, for charity shall cover the multitude of sins.

—1 PETER 4:7–8

Time passed. Or at least that's one way to get from *there*, my famous mother's infamous summer in Wales, to *here*, the ruined house and acreage she used to call home. "darling," begins a postcard of vine-draped Tintern Abbey in the moonlight, "as u can see, despite dr minton's dire warnings, i haven't left behind what bobby calls my *horror vacui*. the faces should be recognizable tho disguised as bees."

Her name was Carole Ridingham even after she married my father, Robert Rose, or Bobby, as he liked to be called, the way Napoleon preferred the Little Corporal. Bobby was the founder and original CEO of SnowWrite & RoseRead, a powerful man and hot, in the vernacular, unlike my mother, who eventually swelled up with the Change and never came back down. But she was a genius, it didn't matter. As for the faces (deliriously inked into any leftover space on the card, front and back), they include Ruth Farr's and her husband, Coleman's (the Snow of SnowWrite), and owe a lot to the portraits Blake drew of his friends, with flea heads, etc., that my mother made a point of seeing at the Tate while Bobby flirted with waitresses, and my so-called Aunt Ruth recorded her every move in her journal, and my so-called Uncle Coleman snapped photos covertly like a spy. The women's agendas may have been more overt, but don't be fooled, the men had agendas too, not the least of which was to figure out what to do with all the money they made five years earlier when they sold the business. Everyone has an agenda, me included, though we've been repeatedly reminded that the past's off-limits except to seers. Eyes straight ahead, let the dead wake the dead, as the saying goes.

The "dire warnings" refer to my mother's mental condition. At thirteen she was diagnosed borderline schizophrenic, and was put on drugs that made her thrust her tongue from her mouth in a way that looked less like a tongue than a nose, especially when she was trying to concentrate. My poor doomed mother—either sailing away from me across the meadow in her white beekeeping gloves and veil, in which case I couldn't see the tongue, or painting in the garden house she used as a studio, in which case I could but just barely, my view hampered by the gooseberry bushes outside the window and Bobby, who usually tried to keep me out. He said he was protecting her, but we all knew better; he was keeping her to himself, which I think was how he thought he could make sure she'd be his forever. Aside from the tongue, I almost never saw signs of what was referred to as "inappropriate behavior."

Later we'd have dinner prepared by Mrs. Koop, our humorless cook, and served by some cute-faced and inept maid —deluxe treatment even then. A long honey-colored table polished with beeswax and lit with beeswax candles, at each place one of the ever so subtly unmatched Blue Willow plates, and above the sideboard the plangent reds and golds and deep umbers of *492*. My God: *boeuf en daube*, mushrooms and pearl onions, *petits pois*, *crème brûlée*. In those days we ate like kings. Eventually *492* (the number of objects in the painting) got confiscated along with smaller and darker *53* that used to hang above my parents' bed. My mother said I was counting like a bank teller when I told her I couldn't find more than forty-nine.

I'll never forget the smell in that room: witch hazel, honey, wet dirt. Out the window the silver light of the Maine seacoast and on the bed Uncle Tony sitting with his head in his arms, sobbing. But that came later.

∽

The idea for the walking tour began with Ruth Farr, whose urge to follow in the footsteps of the legendary Manawydan on his journey through Bronze Age Wales was yet one more doomed attempt to seem as interestingly compulsive as my mother. Ruth was always saying things like *au fond I'm a dancer* or *fashion is my passion* with a perfectly straight face, her idea this time having been to write the kind of historical novel where fact vanishes in a haze of myth and romance. *A Fall of Mist* it was to be called, or maybe *The Fall of Mist*, and based on an ancient tale about Manawydan found in the *Mabinogion*.

A plan doomed to fail, if ever there was one. Like you could ever hope to block out your own dull self and with it the present—a gang of Strag boys with measuring cups—going bang bang bang on your door. Sometimes four or five of them, sometimes only the one, banging away in that preposterous dust-caked wig . . .

Ruth was about the same age as Manawydan when he made the trip, though he was sent by his father and ended his days in the Otherworld, while Ruth & Co. bogged down on the Gower peninsula. Also, while Manawydan was known as one of the "Three Ungrasping Chieftains," and took discretion for the better part of valor, Ruth never had a problem appropriating someone else's property. Like many weak people, she was obsessed with the idea of fairness and, consequently, litigious. Without her, there'd have been no trial after the disaster at Gower.

According to Ruth's journal, she and Carole first met in Mrs. Hecht's second-grade class at Henry Clay Elementary School, where Carole (a new girl and good at memorizing) got the part of Miss Springtime even though she was fat and couldn't act, while string-bean Ruthie (the former apple of Mrs. Hecht's eye) was stuck playing a worm. Naturally they weren't friends. Actual friendship, if you could call it that, came thirty years later, when Carole's good-looking husband chose Ruth's clever husband to be his right-hand man, and the next thing Ruth knew she and Coleman were walking up a long driveway bordered on both sides by acres and acres of grass, and there was a large blond woman sloping toward them, at her heels a dog so tall and with legs so long and thin it looked like it was going to tip over.

"Heavens," the woman said, "little Ruthie Farr," but Ruth didn't actually recognize her childhood nemesis until the dog began to bark, and in place of a total stranger there was seven-year-old Carole Ridingham, eyes fierce with apprehension as Mrs. Hecht handed back the spelling tests. Odd, Mrs. Hecht remarked, they'd both made exactly the same mistake. C-A-W-T. You'd almost suspect . . . and she shook her head, unable to entertain such a sinister idea.

Meanwhile it was as if no time had passed at all: Carole and Ruth still couldn't take their eyes off each other, like serial holders of the same title vainly trying to figure out what they had in common. Maybe they were hampered by their jealousy, a key element under the circumstances. Nicest looks? Most famous? Best husband?

In those days Ruth did everything she could to play up her naturally snow white skin, ebony black hair, and blood red lips. Women wanted to look like dead young girls; it was the style, meaning another way to put Death on the wrong track. I remember being afraid of her, particularly a large beauty mark on her upper lip that I mistook for a bee, and I remember the frail hippie gardener doing a trick with a hollyhock to calm me down. The glowing pond, the humming bee boxes, the thrillingly insane smell of heliotrope. Out on what my mother called the piazza, in the good old summertime.

That's where they met up with Bobby. He stuck a drink in Coleman's hand and said there was more on the way. No one smoked; a drink was the best you could hope for after having been forced to watch your husband's jaw drop open at the sight of the girl you thought you'd seen the last of years ago, when her parents mercifully shipped her off to boarding school. Pudgy Carole Ridingham had turned into the kind of woman men put on a pedestal, though I'm sure it was less to worship than to observe safely from a distance.

"Cawing crows," Ruth wrote, "drifted through the vapid blue like cinders from the furnace of my jealous heart." Except really there was no cause for jealousy. What interested Uncle Coleman in my mother never had anything to do with sex; it had to do with power. He knew that if he could win my mother, he could win anything.

That was her talent, to make people feel that way — I should know.

But "vapid"? Ruth must have been thinking of someplace else.

BOBBY FOUNDED the business, as he iconically liked to refer to it, the same month my mother called him from Venice to ask him to give me a birthday hug and kiss, which also happened to be three months after she'd won the Prix de Rome, and one month before my actual birthday. I put it this way on purpose to make it sound like everyone was too confused and distracted to realize what was going on, though of course that's a lie. Bobby was a genius at business like my mother was at painting. With them it was a fight to the death, and if I give her the edge it's not so much because I think she was better at what she did than he was, but to balance the moral fallout of his actions, the way they still poison every breath I take.

According to company mythology, the idea first came to him when he was reading a "melon-headed" critique of Ronald Reagan's supply-side economic policies in *The New Statesman* and couldn't stand not being able to share his thoughts with the author (ditto the reading public) "immediately." Though at the time it may have looked like Bobby was lost in contemplation of the snow falling past his office window, in fact his eye was trained as usual on the main chance, which is to say he knew that fortunes were about to be made, and not by admissions directors of small liberal arts colleges in northern New England. He knew this because he understood not only that the cowboy in the White House was planning to rob all the stagecoach passengers blind, but also how he was planning to pull it off. He also knew that anyone who happened to see Bobby Rose sitting by his window would think "poet," not "shark."

There was a knock on the door: in sidled Bobby's future partner looking for a stick of gum. Men, denied plumage by the fashion industry, nonetheless remain attuned to displays of power. It took Bobby and Coleman years to see each other clearly. Maybe they never did.

"You planning to waste your life in this dump?" Bobby asked, turning his dark gaze toward the decomposing ceiling, and Coleman, who was accustomed to lying about his commitment to progressive education, hesitated. He didn't especially like Bobby, who struck him as clever and vain and vulgar, and who, though he'd only recently gotten the job, already spent most of his time lodged in one of the college's cozier nooks or crannies with a winsome coed. On the other hand, a job caretaking audiovisual equipment in a school whose students were too proud to listen to directions and consequently were always wrecking the projectors was enough to drive even a patient person nuts, and Coleman, despite his geekish looks—tall and skinny and balding, with prematurely white hair and corrective lenses so strong they made the part of his face you could see through them contract weirdly like the middle of an hourglass—was, if possible, even less patient than Bobby. In his lifetime he'd already watched the first three generations of computers come and go, making his own progress seem sluggish by comparison.

They climbed into Bobby's VW and crept through the snow to a roadhouse on the coast just north of the town of

Pallas, where they got drunk and began making plans. Bobby was surprised not to be bored in Coleman's company; Coleman was surprised to discover that Bobby wasn't a total jerk. They both found it interesting that they'd chosen "artistic" wives, though Bobby and Carole had been married for over a decade and already had me, whereas Ruth had finally and somewhat sourly agreed to marry Coleman only that September, and was a known child hater. Bobby wondered whether the women would take to each other; Coleman didn't care. This was because there was nothing hidden about Ruth's emotional life and therefore no need to monitor her every word or gesture for clues, while Carole kept Bobby guessing.

"I hate John Dewey," Bobby's reported to have said. "I hate getting stuck with the losers at the college fairs. This place is a loser magnet." Coleman started drawing on the napkin that for several years would hang from a post in what Bobby liked to call his office, but was in fact a derelict pavilion on the old chautauqua grounds that define the eastern border of our property.

"Something like this?" Coleman said, drawing a series of branching and looping lines. "It wouldn't be that hard to program." But by now Bobby had lost all recollection of the particular train of thought that had sent him out into a blizzard with a man he barely knew.

The sky over the Atlantic turned a murkier shade of gray; from within a clot of cloud the moon released a dull yellow-gray beam. I'm adding this detail at my own discretion, but it was an undeniable aspect of the period: night would fall, people would sense the approach of bedtime, of sleep. They were sleeping less, but hadn't stopped altogether. Also they paid attention to Nature, though not so much as their parents and their parents' parents had. ("How oft, in spirit, have I turned to thee, O sylvan Wye!") They paid attention to it the way Coleman paid attention to Carole: to make sure it wouldn't get a jump on them while they were looking somewhere else.

People were only just beginning to learn how to do several things at once. That's why two years elapsed between Bobby's and Coleman's first fateful meeting and the actual incorporation of SnowWrite & RoseRead. It wasn't an idea whose time had come: you could still talk on the phone and not hear the sound of running water or food being chopped or antic keyboarding. Almost no one had a phone in their car, though sometimes you'd see someone reading the newspaper as they sped past you on the Interstate.

＊

COLEMAN DROVE BOBBY HOME that night; he could hold his liquor and Bobby couldn't, a fact I find touching, just as it touches me to imagine my big strong father putting his fate in weakling Coleman's hands, watching his new friend downshift into each tricky curve along the coast road, accelerate through each skid, manipulate the VW as if it were a delicate racing mechanism and not the piece of crap it was. The snow in the driveway was knee-deep, and the driveway itself almost a quarter of a mile long. "I can't just leave you here," Coleman said, blinking rapidly behind his thick snow-flecked lenses. Far off through the fast-falling snow he could barely make out the yellow porch light; somewhere closer at hand Bobby was floundering in a drift. Together they plunged forward. "I'm going to have to borrow your car to drive myself home," Coleman said. "Keep it," Bobby said, always a genial drunk. "It's yours."

All along the East Coast the power went out, trees came crashing through roofs, eighteen-wheelers jackknifed. With hyperbole typical of the period, newscasters called it the Storm of the Century, though of course they hadn't seen anything yet.

Dry and sparkling, the snow billowed around the two men; when Coleman tried hitting Bobby in the head with a snowball, it fell apart midair. But Bobby could have cared less. Unlike Coleman, who seemed to be thoroughly enjoying himself, Bobby was lapsing into a deeper and deeper melancholy the closer they got to the front porch.

The family story held that Carole was an insomniac who could be wakened by the sound of a falling feather, and that Bobby always made an unholy racket whenever he came home late, like a husband in what used to be called the funnies. As far as I know I'm the only one in the family to have inherited my mother's tendency; everyone else is or was a famous sleeper. She claimed to be a throwback to a time before civilization arrived with its alarms and bells, when you had to wake at the faintest sound, to know the difference between a guilty husband and the delicate footfall of a saber-toothed tiger, when you didn't need Freud because fear was always right there on the surface of your brain, waiting to be examined.

As a rule Bobby *wanted* to wake Carole, to feel her gaze rake him clean of the day's morally questionable detritus. Only then could he tell her what he'd been up to; only then could he sleep like a baby, secure in the knowledge that she'd be tossing and turning for both of them. The night of the storm was a rare exception: Bobby managed to keep his conversation with Coleman a secret for almost a year, until his melancholy had evaporated and it was too late to change course.

By the time it was over the blizzard had buried the entire state of Maine under six feet of snow, and Bobby was holed up less like a cartoon husband than a cartoon mouse with the cat he couldn't live without. For an ambitious woman, Carole had indolent ways, padding around like a whore between tricks in her graying long johns and cream-colored peau de soie bed jacket, paintbrushes stuck into her loose blond pincushion of hair. Dahling this, dahling that. I think maybe in the parlance of the times she was a sex addict, except addicted exclusively to Bobby.

School would've been canceled because of the blizzard, putting a crimp in her plans, but the house was (well, *is*) huge and Bobby routinely hired and fired au pairs from the college, ostensibly to keep me occupied, but really to keep him company in the bomb shelter cum bachelor pad out past the chautauqua grounds. Weeping Lotte of the faithless boyfriend, shy Li Fon and her origami chicks, Pia who made me eat raw fish —my mother would expunge their names from the family annals only to immortalize and mutilate them in her Calendar Series. Exquisitely rendered, the faces luminous in the style of Giotto, it was the girls (i.e., "Miss Maim," "Miss Dismember") she punished; she forgave Bobby almost everything.

She was an amazing painter. The art world in those days may have been fickle, but it couldn't seem to get enough of Carole Ridingham, who in turn couldn't seem to get enough of anything, hence her mania for covering every surface in the house with her work. Some of the pictures are still there, like the ghostly white wolfhound (Gretchen? Minnie?) on the pantry door, or the by now even harder to see hexagons crawling with bees around the kitchen window frames. Of course the actual dogs and bees are gone, though in an early memory (or was it a dream?) I'm sitting beside one of those windows in a red highchair, its tray loaded with lots and lots of little jars. Open wide, my mother's saying, spooning honey into my mouth. The bees made that with thyme, she informs me. Okay? Or do you prefer this? Her face very close and big, so big you can't believe it, like the moon some nights, filling the sky. She was an imposing woman, my mother. Her eyes were a light blue verging on white, and they were extremely wide-set and round, making you disturbingly aware of the eyeballs. Also I remember the smell coming through the window, a wet fresh smell of melting spring snow, gone forever along with the bees and the dogs and the paintings.

The snows of yesteryear—where are they now, oh where oh where? I suppose it's possible a private collector still has some of my mother's paintings locked away in a vault. Though it's just as possible nothing remains but the memory of them, shadowy as 53's fifty-three overlapping shadows of game pieces, like the jack and the die and the bishop and the hotel and the checker and the rope and the marble, and if the titles have hidden meanings as she implied she never let on, but mainly couldn't stop herself, shoe and queen and car and egg timer, and it's not hard to understand why, since God knows there's comfort to be had in endlessly filling the intolerable void with familiar objects, though anything will do, anything at all . . .

༄

Before Bobby came along Carole's interest in sex was more a matter of idle curiosity than anything else. She didn't take it personally; it didn't move her, like art. According to Uncle Tony, if it hadn't been for Bobby, she'd never have given a shit what Bobby did. It was like he turned her into a creature whose heart he could break.

They met (assuming anyone's still interested in stories like this) on the *Stella Maris*, a student ship plying the cold gray waters of the North Atlantic in the early years of the First

Great Denial, when the world's fate was in the hands of a superpower that liked to think of itself as a dear sweet baby. The *Stella Maris* was bound for Le Havre and had about three hundred students on board, most of them totally out of control. Initially Bobby couldn't get anywhere near Carole: he was overweight in those days and sported a crewcut that showed off the anvil shape of his head, while she looked like a movie star, something along the lines of Anita Ekberg in *La Dolce Vita*.

And then the ship encountered rough seas, and my parents turned out to be among the hardy few with cast-iron stomachs. On a blustery and overcast afternoon Bobby's self-imposed role of brooding outcast was interrupted by the sight of Carole reclining in a lounge chair, all by herself in her dark glasses and trench coat and leopard-print bikini, irritably fighting the wind to turn the pages of *Artforum*.

She'd figured out long before that a philistine will reveal himself immediately. My six-year-old could blah blah blah even a blah blah blah monkey . . . But when Bobby glanced over her shoulder at an Andy Warhol he's supposed to have said, "I like it. It's like money; it skips the middle step."

"What do you mean?" Carole's supposed to have asked in return.

"When a painting's already turned itself to money," Bobby explained, "you don't have to sell it. Like being a counterfeiter."

"Do you think it's art?" Carole asked, testing.

"Well yeah!" Bobby replied. "But it isn't as beautiful as money."

"Money's beautiful," Carole agreed, her voice softening. "I

love money." She relaxed a little, a fact that Bobby, who had perfect sexual pitch, quickly registered: now he'd be permitted to graze the nape of her neck.

"Business has to break the law to grow," he told her, grazing. "If it doesn't it'll die."

When did she notice the almond-shaped hazel eyes, the long black lashes, the fine bones of Bobby's face? He saw right away that she chewed her fingernails to the quick and that the dark glasses were prescription. He kissed her on the mouth and then eased her to the damp splintery deck, kissing her again, deeper this time.

Back then, despite her sex goddess looks, sex probably still made Carole nervous. For most of her childhood and right through her teenage years she'd always secretly wished she was a boy, or at least not encumbered with the same peevish female body she'd watched enslave her older sister, Doe, its trappings and leaks and hidden compartments just begging for trouble. Whereas Bobby, even before he'd left his ugly duckling self behind, was an enthusiastic lover. We're going to dock soon, Carole thought. The ship rocked wildly from side to side; Bobby undid the top of her bikini. A gull made off with the apple core she'd deposited on the arm of her chair. She was still a virgin—not so very shocking in those days but no doubt a surprise to Bobby. I don't think she ever slept with anyone else.

They were so young: he'd just finished his junior year at Princeton; if all went well she was going to begin Cooper Union in the fall. Afterward he told her he was majoring in economics and planning to do graduate work at the Wharton School. He didn't tell her he'd almost flunked out of Princeton, because he knew he was destined for success and the information would be misleading. She told him she'd gotten the only perfect score in the history of Cooper Union on the entrance test where you guessed how many blocks of a variety of sizes went into making a variety of structures of which you could see, say, only a part of a side. She didn't tell him about her mental condition, figuring he'd either deduce it for himself (from the information about the blocks) or else didn't care about such things. In this way they set the tone for all subsequent pillow talk: suppression disguised as candor.

Soon enough the weather turned; the ocean changed to glass. Bobby caught a glimpse of Carole at the farewell dance, her black sheath inching up her thighs as she did the twist with one of her no longer sick admirers. Then he went out on deck and watched the trail the moon made, from it to him, like an omen. There was the ghost of music, which was always the way he preferred it: Bobby, alone, smoking a Lucky, overhearing the sounds of human gaiety. He felt strong, as if he could pull the plug at any moment . . .

When the ship docked, Carole set off for Paris, where she would have a chance to paint from the model; Bobby headed south to study French and pick up *jeunes filles* on the Côte d'Azur. They both insisted they never gave their shipboard encounter a second thought until five years later, when they ran into each other at the opening of a group show in Chelsea. Carole's first show, in fact, it included the rondel Bobby would eventually buy, in which minuscule self-portraits peeked from the folds of her mother's black velvet opera cloak, as modeled by her brother, Tony.

Bobby asked her for a light and her first instinct was to pretend not to remember who he was, a pose that she quickly discarded as being shallow rather than nonchalant, given the fact that since she'd last seen him he'd turned into a truly handsome guy.

Instead she decided to flirt a little. She lit his Lucky for him and blew out the match, depositing it in a nearby ashtray that was actually the mouth of some kind of insane howling animal sculpted by Dottie Harmer, Bobby's bride-to-be.

"You're going to *marry* the person who made *that*?" Carole asked.

Some days the past seems so poorly lit I feel like Isabel Archer before her eyes adjusted to the dim light of the Old World. When I try reading the court transcript, for example, I feel naive and spirited and curious, as if inspecting Mr. Osmond's "bibelots" for the first time with no sense of how dangerous they are. "There was never any question," Bobby's again and again recorded as saying, by which he seems to mean: "Curiosity killed the cat." Of course no one ever said that who didn't have something to hide.

Then I look out the window. Then I try to see all the way to the end of a driveway no longer white with snow but overgrown with gray vegetation and I feel my curiosity transformed from girlish vice to unspeakable horror, which is what it becomes when you sound the depths of another living soul merely in order to locate something there to justify your own position, which is to say, to promote your own happiness.

The walking tour. A group of adults paid money to go on a walk. I'm sure when Leon Edel wrote his biography of Henry James he had so much material at his disposal he had to leave things out. What I have is a stack of court transcripts and a gray metal box that's actually the computer containing Ruth Farr's journal, as well as a pile of unlabeled photographs, and the postcards and letters my mother sent me from Wales, her handwriting overlaid with curlicues and inexplicable symbols, star shapes and spirals and things like blacked-in crescent moons, her spelling weird and her choice of subject matter particularly inappropriate given the fact that I'd only just turned thirteen, which also happens to have been her age when she began going mad.

We're told history is a pack of lies because it is. Lock the door and throw away the key. Though isn't it the strangest of reversals to be urged to see *those* days as dark and debased?

"There was never any question whose idea it was," Bobby says in response to "Mr. Rose, I wonder if you could help us understand what motivated you to go to Wales in the first place."

Ruth is less cowardly: "I wanted to get away. I wanted to get away from my dumb job at the reproductive clinic, and I wanted to get away from my ugly house, and I wanted to get away from my so-called literary career and my marriage, but the only way I could was to take everyone with me."

Wordsworth's lines were composed "during a Tour," after all. "More like a man flying from something that he dreads, than one who sought the thing he loved . . ."

THE WALKING TOUR was the brainchild of Mr. and Mrs. David Fluellen, their first step down what would prove to be a dead-end road to retirement. Headquartered in a charmingly restored inn on the banks of a tributary of the Wye called the Black Brook, the tour was managed by Brenda Fluellen, who mixed elements of Giraldus, Arthurian legend, Wordsworth, and the *Mabinogion* to create for her guests her very own brand of New Age Romantic Welsh Nationalism. Meanwhile David Fluellen, a genuinely inspired cook, packed the basket lunches.

My impression of Brenda Fluellen is by no means clear. I'd like to write her off as a fool, but then there is her face. In addition to my actual vaguely charged memory of it, I have two other views: one photographed atop a steep bluff overlooking an ashen strip of sea; one drawn on the back of the postcard my mother sent me not long after arriving in Wales. The face in the photograph is dark-browed, dark-eyed, the lips full yet the mouth compressed, scowling. It isn't exactly a beautiful face, but you suspect all it needs to take your breath away is to be set in motion, the way it was that day I saw it partly hidden by a flowering bush outside the Royal Courts of Justice, the lips moving inches from Bobby's ear.

The summer of the tour Brenda Fluellen claimed to be thirty-five, somewhat younger than she actually proved to be, though in the photograph she looks younger still. There's something unsettling in the sight of such a tan healthy face disturbed by such obviously grave thoughts. It's like the Strag boy who's taken to camping on my doorstep, when he isn't diced or drunk—that same combination of youthful health and a misery you can almost smell, possibly due to animal oils in the unwashed hair, the sweat of panic. Whereas in my mother's drawing (*b. fluellen, 4 june*) Brenda appears in the guise of the Beast carved over the door of a nameless village church, taking a bite of the Tree of Life. ("up rainy hill to see big stone laid atop smaller stones," she wrote in a lame attempt to reassure me I wasn't missing anything, "then down again to see church made of same stuff as hill.") The drawing shows every last one of Brenda's teeth, and all the checks on her shirt—their perspective adjusted to indicate the generous size of her breasts—before they turn to dragon scales or whatever. You can tell my mother was interested in her, though you can't tell whether she liked her or not. ("brenda's sneaky says coleman. bobby says no, no imagination. ruth's analysis too complex as usual to fit on postcard. i say *triste*.")

With David Fluellen it was easier: apparently everyone liked him. He doesn't appear in any photographs since when he wasn't in the kitchen punching down dough or chopping shallots, he was angling for salmon or floating around in his collapsible kayak or hoeing the bean rows or grocery shopping. Ruth describes him as being somewhat older than Brenda, "one of those weakhearted men built like tops, very wide around the middle and tapering delicately at the head and toes, contributing to your feeling that under the right circumstances they might spin wildly but gracefully out of control." She goes on to explain that the Blackbrook Inn had been in David's family for hundreds of years, and then speculates about Brenda's motives. But he's so *nice*, Ruth sighs, he'll never see what she's up to. That's why the nice men always marry witches.

Before heading to Wales, my parents spent a week in London, where, in addition to visiting the Tate, my mother sold a painting and immediately blew most of the profits on the insanely expensive mechanical beehive music box she never got around to sending me, while Bobby schmoozed at the Groucho Club. Then, as soon as Ruth and Coleman arrived, the four of them drove in a rented Ford Fiesta across the Severn Bridge and through Chepstow to the village of Teg Morwyn (Comely Maiden), where David Fluellen met them on his bike.

"I dreamed the place the night before we left London," Ruth wrote in her journal. "It was as if I dreamed it into being. A steep narrow road climbed steadily higher and higher, bordered on one side by tall dark hedges, dripping wet, swooning away on the other to a darkly raging brook. We kept passing children with perfectly round coal-smudged faces, carrying fishing poles over their shoulders, and one tall weedy boy who cradled a gigantic pink whalelike fish with big cartoon eyes. We were going up the hill, they were coming down, suggesting we'd arrived too late. A signpost pointing in the direction we were headed said FISH INN (fission? am I anticipating an explosion of some kind?). In the dream our guide hovered a little in the air a little ahead of us, which captures exactly the spirit of David Fluellen on a bicycle, right down to the orange high-tops. Sort of like he was flying (or maybe I was just picking up on the fact that Coleman's so hot for fly-fishing)." [3 June]

The road leveled off before forking in three directions. The right fork dipped to cross a stone bridge, then vanished into a moss-draped and unwholesome wood. The left fork rose even more steeply uphill toward a place called (interestingly, given Ruth's dream) Llangleisiad, or Young Salmon Land. Straight ahead was the inn, an unprepossessing loaf-shaped building of native stone painted white. It sat on a rise on the left-hand side of the road, its many small-paned windows squinting disparagingly down at the valley and brook where every surface exhaled a fine mist, meeting the rain halfway. "While the Blackbrook cannot lay claim to Arthur or Giraldus," admits Brenda Fluellen's brochure, "there is ample evidence J.M.W. Turner graced our halls sometime during the summer of 1794. In Cymru time has no meaning."

"I'm not a hundred percent sure," Bobby's transcript says, echoing the sentiment. "It was the beginning of the month, late afternoon. The second? The third? I'm guessing. Pouring rain, though, as usual. Fluellen got us there in time for dinner. He could even make you want to eat laverbread, poor guy. Excuse me? Laverbread."

∽

In fact they arrived at the Blackbrook on the third of June between four and four-thirty, just in time for tea. The heavens opened, according to Ruth, who also records the temperature as being unseasonably cold. Luckily there was already a fire blazing in the big stone fireplace at the far end of the lounge, in front of which reclined Mr. Tadeusz Kopecky, a fifty-something bridegroom, ardently chafing his new bride's wet hands and feet. In their native Poland Mr. Kopecky had been a pork butcher with a tendency to hypochondria, Mrs. Kopecky a nurse with a taste for kielbasa. They were both addicted to skat, an arcane card game they would have played nonstop if it didn't require at least three players, ideally four.

"You can tell they're either insanely devoted or jealous," writes Ruth. "They watch each other like hawks." She goes on to describe the man as big-headed, heavy-chested, proportioned like a dwarf only larger, with doll-like blue eyes and a doll's sweet rosebud mouth; his wife as tall and wide-hipped, with a goosey neck, gooseberry eyes, and a weak chin. Both of them friendly enough, and also no doubt quite intelligent, though the mistakes they made in English—the man referring to a movie as "perfumed" rather than "dubbed," for instance—led Ruth to think of them, no matter how hard she tried not to, as dimwitted and babyish. Which is precisely why, she goes on to say, she had such a rotten time on her honeymoon trip to Tuscany, though try telling that to Coleman.

For tea David Fluellen offered Caerphilly cheese and currant loaf and smoked trout. Nor does it seem likely he'd ever have dreamed of subjecting his guests to laverbread, which isn't real bread at all but a kind of seaweed indigenous to the Gower peninsula, served with oatmeal and bacon.

Upon arrival my mother pleaded exhaustion and went upstairs to take a nap; Ruth insisted on going for a run "to see just what a land of young salmon looks like"; Coleman loaded his camera and was thus able to document Bobby and Brenda's first encounter, though several of the shots are ruined by a blur that bears an uncanny resemblance to the elongated skull in Holbein's famous painting *The Ambassadors*, but was no doubt Major, the Fluellens' Irish setter. *Remember that you too are going to die*, Holbein reminds his ambassadors. Morbid, like most subliminal messages—an effect the painter's technique of anamorphosis is perfectly suited for, using tricks of perspective to so distort an object, to so radically flatten and stretch it that it can be comprehended only from an unusual angle or through a special lens. It also happens to have been a technique favored by my mother, who'd put it to good use in *Hive #11*, a painting renowned less for its artistic merit than for the part it would play in the trial.

Of course once you know something's there it's impossible *not* to see it. After the fact it's hard to look at that first batch of photographs and not find hints of memento mori everywhere: Brenda gesturing with a knife at a whitewashed segment of wall where Millais's Ophelia drifts deadly by. Coleman's shadow landing on the flagstone floor at Bobby's feet. Bobby looking up at Brenda from under his thick black lashes as she bends to remove a plate littered with cheese rinds and fish bones from the gateleg table under the Millais, where he's been sitting.

By the time Ruth got back from her run, Coleman had driven off in the Fluellens' Land Rover to fetch two "girls" lost somewhere on the outskirts of the Forest of Dean, the Kopeckys were shuffling cards at the dining room table, Bobby had moved to the armchair nearest the fire, David was busy washing up in the kitchen, and Brenda had vanished into thin air.

"Where's Carole?" Ruth asked, collapsing onto the sofa and unlacing her shoes. She was understandably anxious, having given my mother the opening pages of *A Fall of Mist* right before leaving for her run, during which she started to have second thoughts. Poor little book, she'd found herself thinking. Forgive me. She saw a hurricane bear down on the pages and rip them to shreds.

"Still napping," Bobby replied. "The title of Carole's biography." He tossed a smallish leafy branch on the fire. "Day one and bored. Not a good sign."

Ruth told him he should get more exercise. She extended her thin well-muscled legs for his inspection. People who exercise are never bored, she explained.

"Except if they're bored by exercise," Bobby pointed out.

It was getting dark in the room, the fire dying down. The rain had either stopped altogether or was a mere drizzle.

"Is either of you by any chance skat player?" asked Tadeusz Kopecky, and when Ruth and Bobby both told him no, he sighed and continued shuffling. From within the kitchen came the whooshing sound of a dishwasher starting up, the high whine of an electric mixer, the smell of garlic cooking in oil. David Fluellen was singing to himself: lalala lala lala Bamba.

"I told Bobby people who were bored with exercise were usually bored with themselves," Ruth wrote. "Don't go blaming the world, I told him. He just sat there staring at the embers, soulful but soul-less in that Bobby way. I prayed Carole would wake up." Or as Bobby says in the transcript, "Well, Carole first, then Coleman a close second. Ruth last. I mean, that's *my* order of preference. Ruth never approved of me. Go ahead, Ruthie, stick out your tongue, see if I care. Isn't that contempt of court?"

The sound of cards being dealt onto a wooden tabletop, scooped together, studied. Fabric rubbing against fabric. A sigh, a kiss. And then all at once the rain started up again, falling so hard they couldn't hear anything but the sound of it beating on the lounge windows, reinforcing their sense of isolation and intimacy. Bobby broke his silence to ask Ruth how her run had been. Did she see any infant salmon? Fry, weren't they called? "Unlike the flabby fish in London sold," he read from an antique guidebook he'd found on the coffee table, "a Chepstow salmon's worth his weight in gold."

But Ruth was in no mood for Bobby's humor. She'd been feeling out of kilter ever since handing the pages over to Carole and the run hadn't helped a bit, the way the road shot straight up for at least three miles through dense plantings of trees, all dark, all wet, mainly willow and ash and oak, not a single house or driveway or car or *anything* except trees and more trees and every now and then a telephone pole with a buzzard sitting on it. In those days the idea was to be in constant motion; if you stopped moving you might realize the pointlessness of your activity.

"They're in the guidebook too," Bobby said. "Buzzards."

"After a while I heard ringing," Ruth told him. "I thought it was my ears, but the next thing I knew there was a phone booth, the fancy bright red kind you see in London, all by itself in the middle of nowhere."

"Did you answer?" Bobby asked, and Ruth shook her head.

"No way," she said. "What if it'd been for me?"

Outside, from where what remains of the porch leaves off, over to the edge of the meadow and then down to the road, there's a sea of grayish weeds, tall things with knobby tops towering over thorny tangled bushes. When I was very young, my mother used to teach me the names of plants. She had a whole shelf of field guides (birds, rocks, trees, clouds, stars), and when we walked through the meadow she was always stooping to show me this flower or that. Nothing was ever the same as anything else: there were hundreds of different kinds of flowers, and you could tell them apart by the number of petals or the shape of a leaf or where they grew or when. There weren't so many that you gave up, though. Black-eyed Susan, I remember (like me). Buttercup. Bishop's-weed. You gave up only when you tried counting stars, and even then my mother said they were really suns shining on other worlds, also different, with their own names (only not called "names") for whatever lived and died there. "Lived" and "died" weren't called that either, but it hardly mattered. Death was the one thing you could count on. Stars died just like flowers.

When I heard that I cried and my mother rocked me in her warm freckled arms. I cried a lot, I think; it was a sad time, though outwardly the house was a beehive of activity, my mother occupied with painting and me, Bobby with the business. SnowWrite & RoseRead, my brilliant siblings. So what if they put food on our table and clothes on my back? I hated their guts.

At night, after Mrs. Koop had tucked me in, I'd sneak back downstairs from my lonely third-floor room and climb into my parents' bed, which was shaped like a sleigh and smelled like both of them: equal parts talcum powder, mowed grass, and turpentine; Lucky Strike, Chivas, and sweat. Bobby always griped when he found me there, but what could he do? "People like your father, who want to be young forever," my mother once said, "miss the point. Dying's the most important part of the plan. It keeps us alive." She'd wait until he'd wandered off before turning on the lava lamp she kept on her bedside table. The seductive orange blobs would begin taking form, and we'd both lie there, unable to sleep, as usual, but vastly entertained.

∽

Nowadays pointlessness is the point. This is what happens when you barricade yourself against the past; the minute you forget what's been lost you also forget what it's like to feel desire.

Of course Bobby, being a capitalist, would have put it a little differently. He would have said making money was like making love, sufficiently exciting in and of itself, not to mention the exciting by-products, specifically his family, his business, and his real estate, including a hundred acres of prime farmland and forest, a sugar bush, two well-stocked ponds, a trout brook, a bomb shelter, an elegantly sprawling white clapboard house and various outbuildings, as well as the chautauqua grounds. It's hard to say which parent would be most devastated to see what's become of the place. Or to imagine what advice they'd give me now that winter approaches with its coastal ashblow, its packs of whining Strags. Besides, my parents are dead, their advice a thing of the past, obsolete and bad.

"You think if you let one of them in," I hear Bobby saying, "you won't know where to draw the line?"

"Maybe the windows should be shut and the blinds closed," says my mother.

How clearly their voices come back to me! Except these aren't figments of my imagination but real voices adrift on waves of yellow sunlight, linseed oil and oil of cloves glowing in jam jars, a steaming pot of China tea, and out the window a sprinkler fanning its rainbow of water from side to side. Everyone knows that to get rid of the past completely, the part of the brain that remembers must be surgically removed—an extreme measure, though not unheard of.

I was sitting on the floor in my mother's studio, applying Magic Markers to the "coloring book" of Dürer engravings she'd provided for my amusement. An angel with a golden trumpet and violet wings, only it was hard to stay inside the lines since there were so many of them. Meanwhile she stood at her easel in her huge white smock, squinting through her glasses at the love seat on which she'd just posed a pale red-haired woman wearing a white chenille bathrobe amid a squirming pile of naked red-haired infants. *Ch. Mrs. Renfrew and Whelps*—my mother's response to what she referred to as the "obscene" multiple births caused by in vitro fertilization techniques. I think somewhere along the line her practice of stealing models' names from confidential files at the clinic cost Aunt Ruth her job.

The usual hot summer morning, a big yellow sun shining into my mother's eyes, Bobby and Uncle Coleman arguing just beyond the open window. Oh, we had summers in those days! Blue sky that went up and up and up—you could tell where Dürer got his ideas.

"I'll be the wimp," Uncle Coleman was saying. He sounded angry, and before my mother closed the blinds I had a perfect view of him in profile, the dilated nostril and rigid jaw, the pink glasses frames, the faded baseball cap, the floury white skin. "You be the hero."

"Business doesn't have heroes," Bobby replied pleasantly. "Besides, I'd rather be a villain."

"When you say villain you mean hero."

Eventually their voices died out as they wandered off beyond the sprinkler; my mother poured cups of tea for herself and Mrs. Renfrew. "Oops," she said. "Poor Susan—I forgot all about you. If you want something to drink you'll have to go up to the house and ask Mrs. Koop. Maybe you can catch Bobby before he and Coleman disappear."

Mrs. Renfrew had been as quiet as a mouse, but now she cleared her throat. "How about a Gummy worm?" she asked, going for her bathrobe pocket.

"No you don't." My mother squeezed some green paint onto her palette, mixed it with a little clove oil and some red paint that was already there, dabbed it on the stucco wall, then stood back and squinted at it. The clove oil was to keep the pigment from drying too quickly. She was a famously slow painter, my mother—the Renfrew babies would be in college by the time she was done with them. "Susan has legs," she pointed out, glancing down at me to make sure that this was still the case. "An orange sky with red clouds. I like that, darling. Maybe you could introduce a little black around the edges? But . . ." and then suddenly she was on her way across the room, a white mountain momentarily blocking the sun, having forgotten me completely. "That left hand wasn't always so limp, was it," she was saying to Mrs. Renfrew, "not so . . ."

By the time I found Bobby, he and Uncle Coleman had already crossed the brook and made their way through the woods and to the chautauqua grounds, though I knew I was on the right track when I saw a Little Debbie snack cake wrapper shivering near the bank—the only one of Bobby's addictions I think he actually succeeded in keeping from my mother. It used to be that hemlock trees grew on the far side of the bridge, white-flowered mousy-smelling hemlock, more delicate than spruce or fir, and casting mysterious blue-gray shadows. A seemingly endless trail through the trees, and then just when you thought you'd left civilization behind forever, you found yourself in an enormous clearing filled with trim white cottages, an ornate pavilion, a no longer plashing fountain, an entire grass-lined amphitheater.

The first time I remember seeing the place I must have been about six or so, certainly no older: back then everyone was still alive and kicking, the walking tour not even a vague bosky shape in Ruthie's mind. She liked planning her projects while she ran, which is what she did while my mother painted and Bobby and Uncle Coleman fought about the business. Dripping sweat and panting, she'd come running up to me and grab one of my markers, terrified she was going to forget some crucial detail she'd been repeating to herself like a mantra for the last two miles. "Gussets," she'd gasp (or "Rabbits" or "Soffits"), madly scribbling, not so much oblivious to my presence as dismissive of it, which was worse.

At my approach, Bobby left the pavilion, where he and Uncle Colemen had been sitting, and took my hand. The place was like a magical city whose true inhabitants, being fantastic, were invisible to the naked eye. White buildings, green grass, blue sky—the three colors I miss most. From nearby the sound of a woman singing a song from *The Gondoliers*, the sole record that came with the wind-up Victrola Bobby bought at a yard sale, and standing in the fountain a beautiful naiad, her arms raised above her head to show off her large breasts . . . *and o my darling o my pet whatever else you may forget in yonder isle beyond the sea do not forget . . .*

"Your mother will kill us when she finds out you crossed the brook alone," Bobby said, nuzzling me, the heavy growth of beard he referred to as his three o'clock shadow scraping my cheek. "But it'll have been worth it, right, Suze?"

He smelled like he'd been smoking and drinking whiskey, also forbidden. "A hundred years ago people really knew how to live," he said, and his voice trembled slightly, as if he might be about to cry. With Bobby you could never tell whether he was putting on an act, genuinely moved, or, as Aunt Ruth claimed, moving himself with his own acting.

Every summer, he told me, families used to pack their bags and stay in these cottages for weeks at a time. Sort of like the Lazy River Campground out on Route 12, except you could attend lectures, concerts, readings, plays. A hundred years ago, there were no televisions or computers. People were better then, smarter, more resourceful. Little children like me knew how to read Latin and Greek.

Little children like me were dead of cholera, Uncle Coleman remarked loudly from within the pavilion. "For Christ's sake, Rose," he yelled. "You'd've gone nuts. You can't sit still for five minutes, and you hate being lectured to."

Of course he was right. It isn't as if the world was so idyllic, even then. But how far back do you have to go? Does paying attention to the past create a kind of competitive spirit in you, vis-à-vis the time in which you live? Or is it just another way of killing time?

o you shall go
into a hare
slow to tame
and quick to scare.

hare watch out
for the devil's hound
who harries you up
these fells and down.

she'll crack your bones
in jesus' name
and so you will be
fetched back home.

cunning and art
you do not lack
but always the whistle
will fetch you back!

—c.r.

THE WALKING TOUR officially set forth at one o'clock in the afternoon of Thursday, June 5—not immediately following breakfast as originally planned. This was due to the late arrival of Mr. Hsia (pronounced Shaw), who showed up around midnight the night before, pounding on the door to be let in and ruining everyone's sleep. "5 June," Ruth wrote. "A cold wet day, not exactly raining but the air thick and moist like a damp washcloth on my face, like being sick at camp. I kicked off the covers before I knew what I was doing and was surprised to find Coleman sprawled on his back beside me, fists clenched. Still pleading for an heir, someone to carry his genetic snapshot into the twenty-first century, as if I haven't explained a million times that my uterus is as laced with blood vessels and tissue as the inside of a pumpkin . . . We made love (his idea and a trifle on the rough side), after which his mood improved and mine took a turn for the worse. Homesick for N.J. childhood? The familiar sound of female chatter in the next room, except not my sister's voice but Carole's. Bobby silent as the grave. He'd been listening to us, I just know it."

The transcript lists the members of the tour as having been Robert Abrams Rose, Carole Ridingham Rose, Coleman H. Snow, Elena Ruth Farr, Tadeusz Kopecky, Magtil Laan Kopecky, George B. Hsia, Paula Herne, and Naomi Grace Westenholtz. With the possible exception of those last two, whom

I never saw in the flesh, I have no trouble matching the faces in Uncle Coleman's photos or my mother's drawings with the people in the transcript, though I'm guessing Paula (identified as "Veterinary Surgeon's Assistant, The Rookerie, Spithead, Hants") must be the tall young woman with spiky yellow hair, cable-knit sweaters, and binoculars, who's usually pictured slipping food to the dog, making Naomi ("Potter, Isle of Wight") the short young woman with thick eyeglasses, unlaced combat boots, and a camera.

Brenda Fluellen intended the first day's walk to be an easy one, approximately five miles to Tintern Abbey, where they'd eat a picnic supper amid the ruins and stay to hear Vivaldi if the weather held. Before setting out, the entire group stood for a photograph, posing formally on the south terrace like nineteenth-century explorers, their expressions mostly solemn as if contemplating death by starvation, though on close inspection a few inconsistencies appear: the ghost of a grin on Bobby's face, his one arm around my mother and the other around Mrs. Kopecky, who's beaming gaily, showing her gums. Everyone's wearing some kind of rain gear; Mr. Hsia brandishes an umbrella. All the women are in pants except Ruth, who's been knocked slightly off balance by the wild-eyed, exuberant dog.

Generally they'd be on their own, Brenda explained, but since they were getting off to a late start and needed to walk a little faster than usual, today she was going to join them. She set the pace, striking off ["like my camp counselor, right down to the whistle hanging from a lanyard around her neck, but with way more hip action"] in the direction of Teg Morwyn, taking the first fork left across the stone bridge and heading briskly downhill into the woods. For a while the road ran along the far side of the Black Brook ["moss on the trees, on the boulders, on the walls of ruined houses and their ruined gardens, its color that Day-Glo shade of green that's Nature's way of warning us she can't be trusted"], when suddenly it veered to the right, climbing gradually through woods to arrive on a windswept hilltop crowned with a handful of stunted bushes and several recently shorn sheep, where it met up with the road to Trelleck.

Ordinarily they'd have made a short side trip to Trelleck's famous well and druid stones, but today they were in a hurry, Brenda explained, taking pains to reassure everyone (when Mr. Hsia objected and Paula Herne boldly reminded him it was his fault) that there'd be plenty of druid stones in their future. She pointed south, indicating the Wye Valley, the Devil's Pulpit towering over the village of Tintern Parva, an easy three-mile walk from where they stood, with excellent views of the Wye and downhill all the way. After taking tea in the Beaufort Arms Hotel they'd continue along the river, arriving at the abbey around five-thirty.

"But Mrs. K must urinate," Mr. Kopecky announced, and his wife concurred. "I burst," she said.

"Go behind a bush. Or a sheep. That's what they're there for," Paula snapped at Magtil, who looked a little bushlike herself in her tent-shaped coat of boiled green wool.

Brenda was more sympathetic. "Relax," she said. "We'll just walk on ahead to give you some priv-a-cee." Naomi produced a sheet of Kleenex, explaining the leaves looked pretty scratchy.

"Priv-a-cee," Bobby echoed, admiringly. "*Privv*-a-cee."

✦

By the time David Fluellen arrived in the Land Rover with their picnic supper, the group had already developed at least two factions. The "cooperators," led by Brenda, included Naomi, Magtil, Bobby, and Coleman; the "rebels" consisted of Paula and Ruth and Mr. Hsia, all of whom were chafing under Brenda's leadership, though for different reasons. Tadeusz Kopecky's feet hurt, causing him to drift anxiously from camp to camp; my mother fell into neither, being basically a loner.

Tea had been substantial, but it had been hours ago and many of them had walked farther in one afternoon than they normally did in a week; at the sight of David bearing a huge wicker hamper toward them, his orange high-topped feet delicately picking their way among the other concertgoers seated on the darkening grass within the great stone cage of Tintern Abbey Church, a little cheer went up.

"I could eat a horse," said Mr. Hsia, "if I weren't a vegetarian." "Like Paula!" exclaimed Naomi, who was eager to make peace and prematurely hard of hearing.

The sky must have finally cleared. My mother's pastel sketch shows a beet red light filling the west window's famous Gothic tracery; the same light Coleman captures on Ruth's pinched face as she rummages in the hamper, her elbows sticking out like chicken wings, and that turns Magtil, unflatteringly shot from behind and glancing over one shoulder, into a red-eyed demon. Bobby sits in her shadow, his profile that of a bored Abyssinian king, shirtsleeves rolled, forearms resting on bent knees, hands dangling loosely in front of him, the posture of a smoker without a cigarette. Except for his eyes, which are the unearthly blue of certain now-extinct alpine flowers, and the moist bud of his lips, Tadeusz has completely disappeared into the larger shadow cast by the church.

Back then shrubs weren't permitted to grow on the buttresses and transept arches as they had been in Wordsworth's day, late twentieth-century taste in ruins tending to the ascetic, bare-bones look. Desuetude was fashionable only if it made you seem like you came from old money. Naomi had paid more for her "distressed" jeans than the Kopeckys had for theirs, which looked brand-new. Whereas the shawl collar of Coleman's navy blue sweater had started coming unraveled years earlier, when his father wore it crewing for Yale. Both periods romanticized ruin, even though their stories varied; what they agreed on was that something valuable, something infinitely desirable, had been locked away in the past where it would remain out of reach forever. Of course you only romanticize ruin when you don't have to live with it.

While the tour members fell on David's supper (smoked brook trout, prawns marinated in lemon and fennel, *pâté de campagne*, spinach terrine, Veuve Clicquot, etc. etc.), Brenda conferred with David, and Ruth eavesdropped. ["We were on the whole 'better than the last lot, excepting the Jew,' by whom for some reason (dark hair? aquiline nose?) she seemed to mean me, despite the fact that I'm not. I decided to stick by David Fluellen through thick and thin because he came to my defense. He's like that substance you use in chemistry experiments that turns murky liquid crystal clear. Of course we were ravenous, so food and drink alone could account for the change, but there's no denying the fact that our collective temper improved one billion percent the minute David Fluellen showed up."]

The concert itself either was or wasn't a success, depending on whose version you credit. In her sketch, my mother drew halos over the heads of the wild-haired young people perched on gilt chairs and holding odd-looking instruments; Bobby called them "a bunch of freaks sawing their way through the seasons." Aunt Ruth doesn't weigh in on the subject, except to say she guesses she dozed off around Halloween and woke up for Easter.

The stars came out, a cool breeze blew; moonlight poured on everyone from above, there being no roof to block it. My mother leaned into the seat Bobby made for her between his legs, her eyes closed, her glasses folded away in her purse, her lips faintly parted and not a hint of tongue. She loved him— I'll always believe that; she really loved him.

"By the way," she whispered, "I read it," but because she didn't open her eyes or turn her head, Ruth wasn't immediately sure who she was addressing. "Your book," Carole hissed. "*Lost in the Fog.* Out of this world. We'll talk."

"Thank you," Ruth replied. She settled back and groped for Coleman's hand, which seemed unusually soft and warm. The dew had fallen and was beginning to seep out of the grass and through the blanket, but Ruth didn't care. Indeed for the first time since leaving home she felt almost euphoric, drugged even, girlish and lovable, her mood partly due to the sweet mingling of praise and music, partly to a sense of herself and Bobby and Carole and Coleman as an enviable little group within the larger group, an exclusive club to which the others, no matter how hard they pleaded, would always be denied access—especially Brenda, who was lying with her head in David's lap and her knees bent, showing her underpants.

"We shall speak further of this?" Ruth heard Mr. Hsia whisper to Coleman, and then she heard Coleman whisper in return, "Better yet, I can show you. When we get back."

"Show him what?" Ruth asked, and Coleman gave her fingers a little squeeze before releasing them. "Nothing," he said, rolling over onto his stomach.

Ruth pushed herself into a sitting position. By now the Kopeckys were behaving more like the newlyweds they were, Tadeusz pretty obviously feeling Magtil up. Ruth could see his hands moving under the blanket, adjusting the expression on his wife's round white face like a percussionist tightening the head of a drum. "Get that," Bobby said, rolling his eyes at no one in particular, maybe the moon. Meanwhile the orchestra had reached midsummer; bees were buzzing above a grassy meadow as a storm began to take shape in the woodwinds. "Open wide," said David Fluellen, feeding Brenda one of his strawberry tarts; when a little of the kirsch-flavored custard oozed onto her chin, he licked it off.

David Fluellen—not only nice but handsome, Ruth decided, in a bigheaded noble way. Moonlight turned his thinning hair into a nimbus, and revealed his surprisingly good bone structure. She threw him a smile, since it seemed Coleman couldn't care less who she flirted with, as long as it wasn't Coleman. Apparently rigid with irritation, he was still lying face down beside Mr. Hsia, who was noisily paging through a guidebook.

(8 June) darling—do me big favor & have uncle tony send pills—green & blue ones i forget name but bottle's in sock in top dresser drawer. send express c/o fluellen blackbrook teg morwyn gwent uk zip dot com dot cosmos. don't worry i'm fine just having trouble sleeping, bobby's snoring worse than usual & also talking in sleep. dollars on brain i'm guessing, chinaman wooing coleman behind bobby's back. i drew him (chinaman not coleman) w/ long earlobes to show he's buddhist tho really his ears are small like apricots. takes umbrella everywhere (even up mt fuji!), smokes (!) & is bee lover tho maybe only acting nice. don't want to be cynic (but are buddhists *really* purer?). in any case he was crushed as i was guidebook lied about bee boles at beaufort arms hotel, tho tea helped w/ scones & best cream in world. (remember haunted garden story u loved when u were little? bee boles in wall where ghosts lived?)

DOING FINE & working hard as u can see. trust some in group more than others, especially sad-eyed mountain (david flu) & flowering plum (hsia). sweet-faced pond (magtil) wife of cloud w/ lightning (tadoosh?) who dotes on her & both basically ok, ditto fox curled in den (naomi westen-something). 4 of us u know so guess yrself. don't like paula herne but don't think she's harmful unless combined w/ ruthie. 2 of them together make single-minded harridan as women sometimes do.

magtil & naomi & paula all circle shapes, v. womanish. MISS BRENDA (crow w/ lips) another story.

friday a.m. set out less glum & better rested than day before, david flu depositing us in black mts 20 miles from inn as crow flies (& fly she did). day dawned gray & damp but mild. boringness of hiking like underpainting, climbing steep rocky slippery hills thru darksome chattery woods yr soul's ears can barely stand so active & suggestive of how yr doomed to fail & then all of a sudden beautiful valleys lay selves adoringly at yr feet. no idea where we were, up high in clouds, exact clouds turner painted big & smoky looking when just a youth! ate lunch in tiny graveyard atop moss cushioned dead then on to capel-y-ffin—ancient monastery turned hostel where we'd spend night.

tour supposed to provide food, lodging, also maps (enclosed) including "instructions & advice." follow sheep path, bearing right at cairn to lake celebrated (& i quote) for miracles, assuming sometimes greenish hue, or appearing tinged with red, not universally but as if blood flowed partially thru certain veins and channels. (giraldus cambrensis.) pause but don't linger. avoid temptation to swim or fish. cross stream at mouth of lake, aiming for stile in hedgerow. if you would avoid your fate / hurry past and bar the gate. da da da da da etc.

tour supposed to provide maps & food & lodging, yes, but NOT personal guide so what's miss brenda doing climbing out of small blue car at capel-y-ffin saying david forgot to pack dessert? saying, now i'm here, might as well stay. valley most beautiful in all wales. suggests hike to lake (sending questioning smile around group) or to llanthony priory (mr hsia) or pony trek for adventurous (bobby) or maybe just stay put (me) since place was artists' commune in 20's & great for painters. look, an eagle. bobby preening but i'm guessing miss b's just keeping her hand in u might say, practicing for future or vamping for husband who actually still seems in love w/ her despite her personality. then it started to pour & everyone ran for cover.

(dessert surprisingly bad tho later naomi showed me sales slip from abergavenny baker she found crumpled in grass) . . .

"THE HAUNTED GARDEN" was a horrible story. Not only did it leave me with an aversion to gardening, but it still shows up in my dreams as one of those sinister places you can't get away from no matter how hard you try. A pretty enough place, complete with blooming roses and dancing fountains, but ruled by a wish to assert its essential ugliness, like a premonition of things to come. Ugly cities, ugly houses, ugly people, ugly art. Making a virtue of the inevitable, the way a bird sucked into an oil spill keeps preening its ruined feathers, or that boy I saw yesterday kept throwing rocks at the garden house windows, trying to smash every last pane. Pausing to size the scene up, glancing back toward the house once or twice before stooping to mess with some typical Straggish bundle on the ground.

In the story there was a brick wall running the garden's perimeter with a door in it that came and went, depending on the ghosts' mood. I'd be lying in the sleigh bed, fresh from my bath, listening to my mother's voice as it went on, low and husky. "The builder took care to choose the sunniest corner for the hives of plaited straw, and plants of balm still grew along the haunted wall . . ." Watching her spotted hands turn the spotted pages, I had this idea then that mildew was catching. The window would be open, the nearby smell of the sea mixing restlessly with the cellarish smell of the book.

It's still readable, though the paper's rippled and damp, and if you aren't careful the pages tear off in thick clumps when you try peeling them apart. Bobby's whole library's like that, rows of books welded together, like the leather edition of Robert Louis Stevenson he shipped home from Hay-on-Wye before leaving for Gower. ["An entire town devoted to books," Ruth wrote, "every inch of it crammed with bookstores and plastered with posters advertising the recently concluded Hay Festival of Literature. After two nights tossing and turning on a pallet crawling with God-knows-what in a dreary monastery, I thought things couldn't get much worse, but that just goes to show how much I knew. The sun had finally come out and I was sipping a gin and tonic in a nice little outdoor café, tapping away at my computer and feeling cheerful, when up waltzed Carole. She'd been looking for me everywhere, she said, and I could tell from her expression that I wasn't going to like what came next. Nor was I wrong, though whatever I expected, it certainly wasn't the full-scale attack she proceeded to launch. She wanted to know how much more of that mist thing I'd written, and when I said not much, she let out a sigh. She'd caught me in the nick of time, she said. It wasn't just the writing, it was the whole idea, like a rowboat disguised as an ocean liner. Predictable, the same boat everyone had been drifting around the same pond in for years. Too many ribbons, she said, heedlessly mixing metaphors; too much jewelry and no oars. But hadn't she called it 'out of this world'? I asked. Only three nights ago while we were sitting on the grass at Tintern Abbey, waiting for the concert to start? Well, yes, she replied, and then sat there blinking at me, the implication being, You didn't actually think that was *good*, did you? She hated to be the bearer of bad tidings, she said, because she loved me, really she did, her eyes growing bigger and moister by the minute, as if they were turning to pure liquid and all I had to do was jostle her lightly and the meniscus would break and she'd never stop crying. Then she leaned across the table and hugged me and I let her do it, hampered as usual by our shared sense that as a person of character she's always been several jumps ahead of me, though it shouldn't actually count as character, should it, if you're immune like Carole is to temptation? Surely there must be some chink in the armor. But I don't have to love her back just because she's so fucking sad."]

First comes day, then comes night, night and day, day and night. *Night and Day* also turning to pulp, ditto *Mrs. Dalloway*, etc. etc. It's like the books are trying to revert to what they were before getting mixed up with writers—Bobby's library, a ruined monument to human pride and hope. My parents used to have friends in New Hampshire and sometimes they'd take me along when they went to visit. A long drive with nothing to look at but fir trees, our car stuck behind logging trucks headed for the border towns of Rumford and Mexico, where the paper mills were. Once we decided to stop in Mexico for ice cream cones, and the stench was so bad it made me sick. Bobby pulled over; my mother held my head. It's okay, darling, she said, don't cry. She would've been a young thing, much younger than I am now. I remember a dress with tiny blue-and-white checks, white sandals, and red toenail polish on duck feet exactly the same as mine.

Believe me, Ruth, I'm sad too and you don't have to love me, either.

&

At some point every day the sun actually rises, dragged from under the horizon by a net of clouds and then left there to seep through the sky's spongy grayness in a halfhearted version of morning. While this is happening I feel jumpy, like I'm hearing "the still, sad music of humanity" that drove everyone mad back in the good old days: the rooms seem emptier than usual, my parents and their fellow tour members having rustlingly vanished overnight into thin sheets of paper. Effect precedes cause; answers, questions. Smoke comes drifting from the Strag encampment beyond the chautauqua grounds and with it a yipping sound like ravenous coydogs make, or frenzied human beings. Though there hasn't been a gale in weeks, not even a little rain shower, everything feels foggy and close and still, like being stuck inside a giant's mouth; the only thing to do is get up and go somewhere, usually downstairs or more rarely out the door, motion giving the illusion of purpose. Today I hot-wired the no longer quite blue Volvo wagon and went to town.

Pallas used to be a fishing village before it got usurped by the college where Bobby met Coleman; these days it shelters a depressing community of fly by night storefront operations, their fate more or less in the not so very reliable hands of the power station. Perched on a high bluff overlooking the ocean, the whole town and everything in it—the narrow streets, the frame buildings with their sagging porches, the packs of short-legged yellow dogs and footloose young people—feels like it's draining into the harbor. At some point, in a touching attempt to attract tourists, strands of Christmas lights were strung from building to building and draped from feeler to feeler and claw to claw of the two-story-high statue of a lobster that still looms above the harbor front, monitoring the comings and goings of small boats at all hours of the day and night, as the foghorns toll and the seagulls clamor around it. The pervasive smell in Pallas is one of tide pools, but also gasoline, with an undercurrent of something else, burnt rubber maybe, or wiring. "Meet me at the lobster," people used to say. They probably still do, though not for lunch or romance but to conduct some dubious transaction.

My mother, a first-class speed demon, was known to make the trip to town in twenty minutes; now, even on a good day, it takes more like two hours to get to the intersection of Pallas and Water streets, where the old IGA continues to pretend to do business, its shelves piled one month with industrial-sized cans of tomato sauce, and books like *The Satanic Verses* or *The Scarsdale Diet*; the next with tiny jars of apricot jam, wrapperless tins of what might be sardines or smoked mussels, and display cases of Pez dispensers. An everchanging tribe of young women appears to be in quarrelsome possession of the place, lounging around in the manner of bored courtesans until you force them to ring up a sale, at which point they become coolly businesslike, despite their hit-or-miss method of assigning prices.

Of course it's not like you have a choice; they have you, as Bobby would've said, over a barrel. According to Bobby, the consumer only enjoyed a position of advantage in a free market economy. Anyone who wanted to make a killing should keep their barrel hidden. It was as simple as that.

No matter how quickly you finish your shopping at the IGA, you're always forced to wait. In this case it was for a tall young woman with big teeth and wide-set superstitious eyes like a horse to examine my purchases (a sack of rolled oats, six yellow bug lights, a bushel of rutabagas, an assortment of shampoos and sewing kits and shower caps and soaps and shoe buffers from a variety of long-gone hotel chains, as well as— amazingly—a dozen eggs and a pound of butter) in such a parody of slowness it could only have been intended, which is to say hostile. Naturally, when she asked if I needed help with my bags, I refused.

Suit yourself, she said dully, then reached into a carton filled with what looked like trash and removed a dirty envelope, a gold crown printed on its back flap, which I couldn't help noticing had been taped shut. Yours? she asked, handing it over and pausing to watch as I checked the name and address and tore it open. Not really, I said. It was Aunt Ruth's long-awaited wrongful death settlement, about thirty years late and many hundreds of thousands of dollars short, though clearly someone had replaced whatever had originally been inside with a handful of wrinkled and filthy bills. Ms. Ruth Farr (addressee unknown), and before that SnowJob Inc. (ditto), Mr. and Mrs. Hamilton Snow (Coleman's parents, deceased) etc. etc. Of course Ruthie had given up hope of ever seeing a penny of the settlement money years earlier—but who knows whether that was because she was dead herself, or merely living in New Jersey.

When did you get this? I asked, but by now the young woman had rejoined her companions at the rear of the store; I could hear them breaking into gales of laughter as the door banged shut behind me.

Conditions had improved since the trip in, and traffic was moving along at a steadier pace, but fog still draped itself in thick brown folds where least expected, and even under ideal circumstances the road is awful, wildly leaping and swooping and curving with the coastline; most of its guardrails having long since plunged, as would so many subsequent motorists, straight into the sea. Fogland, veiled and still, land of unearthly vapors. Stunted trees, faded billboards. Cap'n Billy's Deep Sea Fishing. Davy Jones Clambake. The intermittent flash of Penniman's Light and the strangely withheld sound of the surf, nothing for a few moments and then a hushed smash, like someone waiting to speak until they're sure they've got your attention. Like the hypnotist's gold watch, here one minute, gone the next, lulling your eyelids closed as the steering wheel turns to a snake in your hands . . .

By the time I finally got home it was late afternoon, the same net of clouds that dragged the sun up from under the horizon hours earlier having dragged it back down. Down down down into the pit where Apollo and his horses supposedly tumble when day is done, though probably it just falls into the void—one of several words, including *good* and *nice* and *existence*, which Bobby knew could be counted on to torment my mother because she insisted they were meaningless. I made my way along a barely visible stone pathway through what had once been the herb garden, weaving between the big flannelly plants that grow here now, dusty plant towers crawling with the latest in flies, wingless and tirelessly buzzing.

The flies were creating enough racket, and I was preoccupied enough with watching my step in the growing dark, that I didn't realize I wasn't alone until I'd come around the corner of the garden house, where I was at first alarmed and then angry to find the same boy who'd been smashing windows yesterday sitting on what remained of the stoop, bundle in lap, staring into space with his mouth hanging open and a pale thread of smoke drooling from it.

Or at least I was relatively sure he was a boy—a young man, in fact, about nineteen or twenty—though it was hard to tell. The loose clothing didn't help, or the mud-caked face, or the usual Strag wig, an insane affair of straw and wool and fur, elaborately curled in some places and braided in others, the whole thing dusted with dry mud and a grayish green powder that looked vaguely familiar, and hacked off at the nape by some once sharp object, possibly the garden shears I was planning to use on him if he gave me any trouble.

As it turned out, I needn't have worried. Despite his appearance the boy seemed basically mild, shy even. When I asked him what he was doing trespassing on my property, he looked at me in surprise. Forgive us our trespasses, he said. A soft pleasant voice, slightly thick, indicating genetic failure or sickness or a major tea habit. Forever and ever amen, he added thoughtfully. Of course I've seen the poppy fields out beyond the chautauqua grounds, a flesh-colored and clearly resilient strain, producing just the right kind of big hairy pods. Escapees from our defunct garden, the seeds blown every which way by sino-gales.

I told him this was private property. The building he'd been demolishing used to belong to my mother, I added. It was her studio. Carole Ridingham? MOMA retrospective, Venice Biennale? I think I was angrier that he hadn't heard of her, or of any of these things—that there was no longer any way to impress him or to impress anyone, that accomplishment meant absolutely nothing—than that he'd broken the windows in the first place.

She was a great painter, I said.

Tra la, the boy replied. He kept staring into space or at something in the distance, the house maybe, certainly not me. Then he took a last drag on whatever it was he'd been smoking, stubbed it out with the sole of his apparently rock-hard foot, and began to stroke the bundle with his long weedy fingers, smoothing its mud-caked folds. Mickey Mouse, I saw. Red and white stripes. Blue plaid. ARD OCK. A patchwork of what looked like old T-shirts and dishtowels held together with rusty safety pins. I told him that as much as I was enjoying our little conversation, it was time for me to be heading home, and I urged him to do the same.

At first it seemed as if he was going to comply. He shifted position slightly and readjusted the bundle, the airiest specter of a smile flitting briefly across his lips. Then he scooted his thin butt over, making room for me on the stoop, and peeled back a corner of the patchwork to reveal a small fist, a wiggling nest of fingers. Netta, he explained. With enormous delicacy he handed me the bundle.

A dust dervish blew past, followed by the sound of grit sifting through bushes, the squealing of the goose weathervane on the garden house roof as it shifted to the east. Otherwise it was perfectly quiet, the boy on the alert for my slightest false move, his dirty fingers tensely gripping his kneecaps. When I asked if the baby was his, he seemed exasperated, once again directing his gaze out across the plant towers; even all that mud couldn't hide the fact that he had an unusually fine profile, not unlike the Charioteer of Delphi's, one of my mother's "crushes."

Is it your house? he asked.

The bundle felt light as a feather and I began worrying that something was wrong. Suppose the baby died while I was holding it? I've never been exactly what you'd call maternal. Its little chest seemed to be rising and falling, but it was hard to tell, and its face was a mask, caked like the boy's with dried mud. I'm sorry, I said. I really don't know what you want. Is he sick?

For the briefest instant the boy looked furious. Net-tah! he spat, I think implying "girl." Then, without any warning, he leaped up and yanked the bundle away. Give us a kiss, he directed, pursing his lips, sticking his face in my face. By contrast with the surrounding grayness of his skin, the gray of his eyes seemed supernaturally brilliant, like a doll suddenly infused with life. Payne's gray, my mother's favorite color. I could hear my breath rush into my body, penetrating all those small dark rooms where I never went. One in particular, far far off at the very end of an endless cobwebbed hallway, a graveyard for broken appliances, mismatched shoes, steamer trunks whose locks were rusted shut.

But by the time I'd been there and back, the boy was gone, a tall hunched shadow threading its way among the taller towers of the plants, a quickly moving shadow trailing a baby's howl behind it.

I returned to the house. *My* house, I thought. Keep out, keep out, keep out. Trespassers Will Be Shot. No boys allowed. "Alas, Almighty God, woe is me," laments Manawydan in the Third Branch of the *Mabinogion*. He and his brothers have just finished carrying their beloved father's head hundreds of miles in an ancient version of a walking tour, and he's understandably exhausted. "There is none save me without a place for him this night," Manawydan goes on to complain.

And what exactly does he want? His own land and territory, despite his reputation as one of the "Three Ungrasping Chieftains."

Then and now, property's always been the issue, even if these days we're supposed to be too enlightened to believe in it. That's the legacy of SnowWrite & RoseRead, a business built on the idea that no one owns anything, especially not an idea, while simultaneously gobbling other companies up. It was Bobby's contention that you could remove the *idea* of owning a thing as long as you didn't relinquish the thing itself. Enlightened ownership, he claimed—the only way to keep the water free of sharks.

At some point during the trial he actually offered Capel-y-Ffin by way of explaining this philosophy: after the monks abandoned it, it stood empty, meaning it could be defiled by any common thief or low-life. And then along came Eric Gill, an idealistic artist who bought the place and made it hospitable to other artists and dreamers, or to wanderers like themselves.

"By the mercy of geographical accident," Bobby insisted on quoting Gill into the court record, "all the valleys are cul-de-sacs. Let the industrial-capitalist disease do its worst—the Black Mountains of Brecon will remain untouched and their green valleys lead nowhere."

Whereas according to Bobby it wasn't an accident of geography that made paradise possible. It was capitalism.

ROBERT ROSE: No sir, you've got the order wrong. Hay-on-Wye *before* Brecon. And Brenda—Mrs. Fluellen—never meant for us to climb the mountain.

QUEEN'S COUNSEL: We take it you're referring to Pen-y-Fan? But we were under the impression that the defendant had by now joined the group. Do you mean to suggest that you were acting in flagrant disregard of her instructions?

ROBERT ROSE: Flagrant? Come on. You know what it's like with groups. Brenda was doing the best she could. It was so foggy you could hardly see the nose in front of your face, for chrissakes.

QUEEN'S COUNSEL: Bear with us, Mr. Rose. We know how very difficult this is for you, but it's essential that we establish a clear picture of group relations prior to the events of 15 June. Would you agree with Ms. Farr, that after Mr. Fluellen dropped you at the Visitor Centre, a "screaming match" ensued between Mr. Kopecky and Miss Herne?

ROBERT ROSE: Ruthie tends to exaggerate. The parties in question had a disagreement. Paula complained that Magtil— Kopecky's wife—was a wet blanket. They were standing in front of a trail map, and Paula was saying    not screaming— that if it weren't for Magtil we wouldn't be stuck on a trail designed for babies and people in wheelchairs. If I remember correctly, Ruthie was the one who suggested climbing the mountain, and Brenda said that even seasoned climbers would have trouble seeing the cairns in such heavy fog. That was when Hsia said he had eyes like a needle, whatever the hell that means, and Magtil announced that speaking of babies she was sick of being treated like one.

QUEEN'S COUNSEL: Could you describe for us the defendant's behavior at this point? Did she attempt to step in and take charge?

ROBERT ROSE: For all the good it did her.

QUEEN'S COUNSEL: May we accept that as a reply in the affirmative?

ROBERT ROSE: Like I said, Brenda did the best she could, but she had her work cut out for her.

Gradually a picture emerges of Brenda Fluellen giving in to what Bobby calls "typical sisterhood bullshit," with Ruth and Paula and Naomi closing ranks around an increasingly self-assured Magtil. At some point Mr. Hsia called everyone's attention to the window, where a wan ray of sunlight was breaking through the mist. The world was full of danger, he said, but to live in fear was not to live. Exactly! Paula concurred. She went on to say there was nothing a woman couldn't do once she put her mind to it, and Mr. Hsia pointed out, grinning, that on the top-ten list of dangers, pride was number two. What's number one? Coleman wanted to know. But because the group was already preparing to disperse—Brenda distributing David's lunch among their various packs, checking to make sure they had enough water and what she called "sticking plasters" before taking a final look at the trail map—my mother's reply to Coleman's question seems to have been lost on almost everyone except Ruth, who overheard her say "a woman's mind," and Mr. Hsia, who "stiffly nodded his head." As for my mother, I'm sure she didn't care what they did, given her theory that on a spinning globe you could never tell which way you were tilted. "up down it hardly matters," as she said in one of her letters. "gravity, ha."

And Bobby? "It was exciting to me," he says in the transcript. "The thought of climbing the mountain?" asks Queen's Counsel, hoping to pin him down. "Everything," Bobby replies. He leans forward, hands outspread, in what Ruth describes as a misguided attempt to appear wide-eyed and innocently eager, while at the same time sneaking a meaningful glance at Brenda.

But Brenda's not having any of it. Dressed in a white linen suit, her hair pulled into a knot at the nape of her long tan neck, she maintains throughout an expression of utter seriousness, occasionally consulting with her solicitor, more often staring grimly at the judge. Doing her best to look incapable of negligence, Ruth observes.

According to the journal, by the time they actually set out the sky had partially cleared, though the rain-sodden earth continued to exude great clouds of mist, hiding the peaks of the surrounding mountains. Brenda insisted they choose "buddies." Like Noah's Ark, she explained, Carole and Bobby, Ruth and Coleman, Magtil and Tadeusz, Naomi and Paula. And of course she and Mr. Hsia, because they both were dressed from head to toe in the same yellow rain gear.

"Since when did we become a couple?" Paula wanted to know; Naomi, clearly hurt, replied, "Don't worry, I'll do fine on my own." "You be *my* buddy," Magtil said, linking arms with Naomi and giving her a peck on the cheek. "Tadeusz only slow me down. Last one to top is rotting egg." Meanwhile Paula sidled up to Ruth, who because she found Paula's assumption they'd pair up annoying, in turn wandered over to where Tadeusz was struggling with the straps on his pack. "Let me give you a hand," Ruth said. "I was a Girl Scout, you know." "Ouch!" Tadeusz replied, and Coleman let out a cheerful little laugh. "The only badge Ruthie ever got was Jogging," he said, then fell into step beside Bobby, leaving Paula and Carole, an unlikely duo. "Just don't touch me," Carole warned. "I hate to be touched." "What makes you think I want to touch you?" Paula asked.

At first the path was red and muddy, slippery in places with disintegrating sheep excrement—you couldn't see the sheep but you knew they were there from an incessant baaing, as well as the presence of big tufts of wool snagged on the gorse. Brenda's plan was to take the longer but "quieter" route that led from a pair of late Victorian reservoirs Ruth describes as "seething with unearthly vapors," following the steep ridge line that would eventually deposit them at the summit of Pen-y-Fan.

Brenda and Mr. Hsia led the way, setting a moderately brisk pace, down through a soggy gully and across the grass-choked and slippery wall of a dam, then up a long hill with a patchy planting of fir trees to the left, more sheep—visible at last, the sun having come all the way out—grazing among bluebells to the right. Everyone's mood improved during this stage of the climb. Naomi, who had a nice voice, began teaching Magtil, who didn't, "Green Grow the Rushes, Ho." Bobby and Coleman ambled along side by side, their hands shoved deep into their pockets like schoolboys, Coleman occasionally stooping to pick up a stone and throw it at a sheep. Ruth discovered that Tadeusz came from the same part of Poland as Bruno Schulz, and was trying to draw him out on the subject. "When I asked if he lost family during the war, he said yes, but not how I was thinking. Then Carole, who'd sort of snuck up behind us, asked if I had a safety pin since her bra had come apart, and before I knew it I was rummaging through my stuff and she was unbuttoning her shirt and the others were starting to vanish over the brow of the hill."

By now it was probably close to noon. The voices of Naomi and Magtil came drifting back: "Two two the lily white boys, cloth-ed all in gree-een-oh, one is one and all alone and ever more shall be so." On closer investigation Carole's bra proved to be fine, and Ruth realized that the whole thing had been a ploy, a lame attempt to make sure she harbored no hard feelings for the conversation in the café. Don't hold your breath, she thought and was just turning to leave when, exasperatingly, Carole urged her to go on without her. They'd have to stop for lunch soon, right? Besides, Carole added, she really ought to wait for Paula, who'd skulked off *feeling sorry for herself*—nor was the intended effect of those last four words lost on Ruth.

The sun was still shining, though less brightly; when Ruth crested the hill she looked back and saw the reservoirs they'd left behind like little bowls of water set out for pets, and ahead in the distance the two tallest mountains—Pen-y-Fan and its twin, Corn Du—sticking up side by side in the configuration the ancients called Cadair Arthur, or Arthur's Seat, but which made her think of the ears of an enormous celestial beast come down to drink.

It was getting windy and the ridge was narrow. Ruth picked her way carefully, singing as she went. "Five for the symbols at your door and four for the gospel makers"—another dumb relic of Girl Scout camp. She seemed to recall a plump girl with glasses belting out the descant. "Three, three the rye-eye-vul-ul-ul-uls." Or maybe she was thinking of Carole, who seemed finally to have made it to the top of the hill, though she couldn't be sure, scarves of mist having once again come loose in the air, tangling together maddeningly, making it hard to see.

The farther Ruth walked, the more small streams there were to be crossed; the sandstone path was simultaneously slick and crumbly. Up ahead someone in yellow arose from within a cluster of hunched forms, blowing a whistle, then pointing and calling out to her, the wind tearing the words apart into nonsense syllables.

Ruth paused, suddenly uncertain. Off to the left heavy black clouds were rolling in fast; the ridge seemed razor thin, the land draped over it as insubstantial as gauze and plummeting straight to the valley floor a million miles below.

"Wait up!" she heard, and she was immediately relieved. Carole, she thought, thank God. Generally when you've been wishing your best friend dead, the last thing you want is to get your wish. But when Ruth ran back to greet her, she saw it was Paula, studying her through the same pair of binoculars she usually had trained on some poor unsuspecting bird.

 ⁓

ROBERT ROSE: No, I wasn't worried. I got over worrying about Carole years ago. Frankly, I was more troubled by the discussion I'd been having with Coleman. Money matters, assuming you're interested—nothing to do with this mess. Anyway, by the time Ruthie and Paula showed up, we'd decided to turn back. It was already raining pretty hard. Yoda—that is, Mr. Hsia—was running the show, since Brenda had her hands full. Kopecky was limping—a bunion, I think. That was Wales for you, someone always limping. And Paula was in hysterics. She kept saying it was her fault we'd lost Carole. I tried reassuring her, but she looked at me like I was some kind of monster.

COUNSEL FOR THE DEFENSE: Let us decide what is or isn't relevant, Mr. Rose. The "money matters" to which you refer, for instance. Perhaps it might be helpful were you to describe to the court the nature of yours and Mr. Snow's "discussion."

ROBERT ROSE: You want to know what we were talking about? Well, sure, if you think it'll help. We were having the usual argument about whether we'd made a mistake selling the business when we did. If only we'd held out a little longer, I was saying, given today's market. Then we'd be *really* rich, rich enough that it wouldn't make a difference how big a fiscal idiot a person was. Of course Coleman didn't want to talk about it—like anyone who comes from old money, he found the whole subject embarrassing. And there you have it, the problem in a nutshell. Give the guy a computer and he could do anything, he was absolutely intrepid. But with the business end of things? No guts at all. Though naturally he didn't see it like that. Coleman always said that as far as the business was concerned, he was the conscience and I was the balls.

COUNSEL FOR THE DEFENSE: Would you describe the

company's financial holdings as having been divided with similar equity between yourself and Mr. Snow?

QUEEN'S COUNSEL: Objection. We fail to see what bearing this line of inquiry has on current charges.

COUNSEL FOR THE DEFENSE: May it please the court, we hope to prove that Ms. Farr's motive for bringing suit may have less to do with getting financial recompense than with getting even.

BENCH: Overruled. You may answer the question, Mr. Rose.

ROBERT ROSE: Okay. But wouldn't it depend on the relative weight you attribute to conscience and balls?

COUNSEL FOR THE DEFENSE: Say they're equal.

ROBERT ROSE: Then, yes.

COUNSEL FOR THE DEFENSE: Meaning, the balance of power between yourself and Mr. Snow was evenly distributed?

ROBERT ROSE: No, that isn't what I said. Coleman and I both owned equal shares of the business; so did Ruthie and Carole. The shares were divided in four equal parts, ditto the profits from the sale.

COUNSEL FOR THE DEFENSE: Making yours and your wife's interest equivalent to Mr. Snow's and Ms. Farr's?

ROBERT ROSE: That was the plan, yes.

COUNSEL FOR THE DEFENSE: And would it be safe to say that the success of such a plan rested on an assumption of marital accord?

ROBERT ROSE: Safe? You've got to be kidding. Besides, you can't slice power in even pieces like a cake. You of all people should know that.

COUNSEL FOR THE DEFENSE: Mr. Rose. Did you ever

suspect that your wife's tendency to exercise her independent spirit might have repercussions not merely on the trail?

QUEEN'S COUNSEL: Objection. Counsel is leading the witness.

BENCH: Sustained.

COUNSEL FOR THE DEFENSE: Allow us to rephrase the question. Were you ever concerned that your wife's mental instability might severely limit your own ability to act autonomously?

ROBERT ROSE: No. No I wasn't. Like I said, I wasn't worried about Carole. In fact the only thing I suspected her of exercising was good sense. I mean, by the time we got back to the car park, we were like a pack of drowned rats. And there she was, sitting toasty and dry in the Rover with Mr. Fluellen, the two of them eating chicken, drinking Chardonnay, and laughing at us. I guess we must've looked pretty bad. Kopecky could hardly walk, Ruthie'd been crying her eyes out so her mascara was a mess, and Brenda'd had to give Paula Herne a Valium.

⁓

To the story of the failed ascent of Pen y Fan, Ruth adds her own typically personal final note: "I was so relieved to see Carole I burst into tears," she confesses. "I don't think anyone could tell; it'd been pouring the whole way back to the parking lot, a cold pelting rain, the worst yet. My reaction surprised me; I'd thought I was furious with her. Plainly, she had no idea of the trouble she'd caused, but then Carole never did. In fact she looked like the cat who ate the canary. Or who ate *some*thing, and not just David Fluellen's chicken, which she was polishing off as the rest of us came limping into the lot.

Even through the streaked windshield you couldn't miss those big sky blue eyes of hers. Her hair was totally dry. Eventually everyone piled into the car except me. I hung back for a moment. I wanted to separate myself from the group the way Carole had, and see if anyone would give a shit, but they were all too busy fawning over her to notice.

"That was when I found the mouse skeleton. I was kicking through some rubbish at the edge of the lot, and I was thinking of the game Carole and I used to play during recess when we were girls. 'Breezing,' we called it. We both had a huge crush on this older boy, Tom Savage, and we'd sort of amble over to where he'd dropped his jacket on the ground while he was playing baseball and start kicking it along ahead of us, hoping to get his attention. Naturally he couldn't have cared less—we were big-time losers, and he was the cutest boy in the sixth grade.

"So there I was, shuffling through a wet heap of balled-up potato chip bags and cigarette wrappers and road grit in a Welsh parking lot—the same old Skinnybones Ruthie Farr I'd always been, overwhelmed by a feeling of deep betrayal, Fattypants Carole Ridingham having abandoned me to a future of endless lonely breezing—when the mouse caught my eye. I didn't even know what it was at first, only that it looked different from the surrounding rubbish. A tiny skull, the front portion of a smashed rib cage, two wire-thin forelegs, the whole moldering thing clinging to a clump of dead leaves. An enchanted mouse, like the one Manawydan catches stealing his wheat, and uses as a bargaining chip in his negotiations for the safe return of his wife and friend. All of it the same brownish color save the whiskers, which were long and delicate and perfectly snow-white.

"Heartbreakingly white, I thought, but I was in a state to begin with. It killed me that the friendships formed by little girls were powerless to resist the ravages of adult envy and desire. No matter that when we were little girls, Carole and I hadn't really liked one another. It was as if I'd lost a friend, though who that friend was, I wasn't really sure."

*o you shall turn*
*into a mouse*
*and hurry to*
*the miller's house*

*to eat your fill*
*of grain and corn*
*from dark of night*
*to yellow morn.*

*mouse watch out*
*for the white tomcat*
*that never lost*
*its mouse or rat.*

*for he'll crack your bones*
*in jesus name*
*and so you will be*
*fetched back home.*

*cunning and art*
*you do not lack*
*but always his whistle*
*will fetch you back.*

—c.r.

SNOWWRITE & ROSEREAD (Ruth's name, by the way) began as a drawing on a paper napkin, the result of two men caught in a bar during a blizzard, and eventually became a sinister tool that changed how people saw the world. Though maybe I'm being overly dramatic. Better to say that Bobby and Coleman didn't single-handedly change things any more than the author of the *Mabinogion* did. They all just took what was in the wind and gave it shape: a business and a story, both ventures having at heart an alliance between two marriages. ". . . and as they wandered through the country, they had never seen a land more delightful to live in, nor a better hunting ground, nor a land more abundant in honey and fish. And therewith such friendship grew up between those four that no one of them chose to be without the other, day or night . . ."

Bobby's original idea was relatively simple, the logical offshoot of computer technology then available, coupled with his own famous impatience. "When I'm reading, why should I have to wait to express my opinion?" Bobby's supposed to have asked Coleman, in what was to prove a momentous conversation. I imagine them sitting together at a window booth overlooking the coastal highway, snow piling higher and higher on the sill, empty glasses on the table between them; by now they're the only people left in the roadhouse.

"Why can't I just send my opinion directly to the writer?" Bobby demands. "It's only a matter of time before I'll be able to call up anything I want on my computer. The *Wall Street Journal*'s already there, also the *Times*, the *Christian Science Monitor*, even *Rolling Stone*, for crying out loud." He's still young, my father, fidgety yet languid, the picture of arrogant, inebriated youth.

"You can," Coleman reminds him. "You're describing e-mail. But suppose the comments could be made to appear in the appropriate place in the text?" Interested, he begins drawing on the napkin. "A kind of gloss, a sort of New Age textual exegesis."

To which Bobby replies, "Too slow. I want it quick. Quick and dirty. I mean, while you're at it, couldn't you fix it so I could actually *change* the text to reflect my opinion?" And the rest is, excuse the blasphemy, history.

Four friends, two married couples, embarked on a journey. That's the *Mabinogion*. Pryderi and Cigfa, Manawydan and Rhiannon. At some point they were enveloped in a "fall of mist"; when the mist cleared, everything was different. Click on the names and make them COLEMAN and RUTH, BOBBY and CAROLE.

Of course I have a computer, or at least I have Ruth's old gray notebook, but aside from occasionally scrolling through her files to read her journal entries, I never use it. It's hard for me not to think of computers as tools of the devil, like whatever that long ago enchanter used to turn his subjects, most notably his pregnant wife (click, BRENDA), into mice.

I've given a lot of thought to this subject, since without Bobby's business I certainly wouldn't be who I am now, living where I do, in this nice big house he left to his beloved daughter, Susan R. Rose, whose loyalty (so he thought) knew no bounds.

But how did it work, I wonder? By which I mean morally, not technically. What came over people that they'd let other people fool around with their words, their sentences, their ideas, their dreams? Was it because the human wish to be innocent is stronger than the wish to be original? Maybe it really was a fall of mist.

When Bobby's business took collaboration as its model, insisting that every great idea had its roots in many minds, what it meant was that you couldn't write a single sentence without watching it get tampered with, "improved," "perfected." And of course the minute you ceased to own your ideas, you could no longer be held responsible for them. The dish ran away with the spoon, as my mother said, by which she meant, when art went out the window, morality went along with it.

"And afterwards, lo, when they looked to see the flocks and the herds and the dwellings, no manner of thing could they see: neither house nor beast nor smoke nor fire nor man nor dwelling, but the houses of the courtyard empty, desolate, uninhabited."

༄

The young man from yesterday was back again today. Definitely a young man, though he acts like gender's the same as property, subject to infinite reversal. He appeared just after breakfast, weaving through the plant towers, still in that preposterous wig but plainly bundleless this time, then stumbled onto the porch, where he came to a halt, staring at the door and assessing it, almost as if he'd never seen a door before, or didn't know what he was supposed to do with it.

I was at the kitchen table, trying to unstick page 44 from page 45 of the *Mabinogion*—by the time I'd seen him it was too late to hide. *Let one of them in, and you won't know where to draw the line.* I shushed the voice, feeling Bobby's immense disapproval. A man's home is his castle, he used to remark, like it was an idea that had just come to him. According to Bobby, kindness and generosity never flourished under pressure. That's how he could maintain a view of himself as a kind man, generous to a fault, even while driving Jehovah's Witnesses off at gunpoint.

Eventually the young man pressed his face and palms against the pane, the look in his eyes weirdly vacant and purposeless, given his importunate stance. In fact he looked so drained of life and motive that when I opened the door and he shoved his way in, dusting me with more of that gray powder as he elbowed past, it took me completely by surprise.

How do you do, he said, the words marching from his lips as if he were speaking a foreign language.

I'm fine, I said. And you?

I can't complain, he said. Then he pulled out a chair and sat down stiffly, without being asked.

It reminded me of long-ago tea parties with Mrs. Koop, though she was always jumping up to fuss at the stove, and I was the only one properly dressed for the occasion, generally in my mother's neglected Donna Karans or Manolo Blahniks. The same fundamental inequality of position, the same awareness, nonetheless, that birthright wouldn't help a bit. Do you mind? the young man asked, sliding a long gray cigarette of some kind from where he'd stowed it behind his ear, and I told him if he wanted to kill himself it was all the same to me.

He said his name was Monkey, and he came from "the west." One day he started walking and just kept going until he was stopped by the ocean. It took him by surprise, he said, though he'd known it was there. When he lay down to sleep on the shore, it tried to "get" him. You mean the tide came in? I asked, and he glanced up sharply. There, too? he demanded. For the first time I saw something like interest animate his face: he seemed smart, grown-up almost, and I suddenly realized how starved I've been for company.

It turns out that Strag culture, if you could call it that, owes whatever it has in the way of ideology to the old geek lingo. Probably inspired by "surfing the Net," a whole vocabulary developed with oceanographic origins (coring tubes, waves, trenches, shelves, currents, sediments, etc. etc.), though it was Bobby and Uncle Coleman who gave tidal phenomena pride of place. In their system, for instance, "slack water" (the exact moment of change from ebb tide to flood and vice versa) was also the moment of greatest vulnerability. If your file was "slack" you could expect to see your text drain away, a line at a time, until nothing was left, and then alien text creep in to replace it, a line at a time, lapping against the frame.

For Monkey, on the other hand, "slack water" seems to have had purely psychological connotations. When he was a little boy, he said, it wasn't so bad. Then he could "drift" (precursing slackness) to his heart's content, though he never went far. He described a house surrounded by desert. Enormous blue mountains in the distance. His hair was very long and his mother pulled it back for him in a ponytail. She used a ponytail holder, he told me. Not a rubber band. She didn't want to hurt his hair. Where he lived the earth's surface was so thin that underground streams were always breaking through, sending up hot smelly fountains; also you had to watch out for sinkholes. Monkey knew enough to be careful, but that was his own good sense. At least it was neap, he said. So long as he was little the tide was neap.

Only when he got older did he encounter the spring tide's stronger pull. By then the wind had started—you couldn't stay put. If his mother and father refused to face facts, he said, that was their problem. Or so he thought till the morning came when he was at last ready to leave, headed across the sand toward an immense hazy sunrise "like a bomb," and he felt his brain filling with their furious denials. The worst garbage, he said. He wanted to pull his head off. The farther east he went, the worse it got.

At first Monkey tried explaining it to himself in terms of Newton's law: force increases proportional to size and distance. Only later did he realize it was because he was slack— that his parents had been able to get to him because he was slack. Nowadays, he said, things were so much better. Nothing could change you, because "you" was all one thing.

At some point he'd left the table and begun circling the room, picking up objects (cup, knife, teakettle, book) and examining them listlessly—everything that is, except the book. Can you read? he asked, and when I nodded, he held it out to me. Go ahead, he ordered tensely, like someone bracing for a blow. I read him the section about the fall of mist; when I was done he let out a deeply held breath. Okay, he said. Okay, okay, and paused briefly, his hands—and who knows what else—stealing into his pockets. Then he cocked his head from side to side like a dog listening to a private muffled signal and bolted for the pantry door, plainly having arrived at a decision. Of course we never act from a single motive—the least twitch is the result of a hundred warring drives.

The pantry, the long room, the Blue Willow room—it had many names, though its main use was as a dark airless conduit between the kitchen and the back staircase.

Hey! I said, where are you going? But he'd already started up the stairs, moving lightly on the balls of his feet, his long fingers delicately tracing the banister. When I finally overtook him he'd gotten to the third-floor landing, come to light near the hexagonal window where the ocean used to show before the haze set in, and above it the sky, an endless pour of space and possibility.

The window's panes were chattering faintly: the season was changing and a storm was brewing. Or at least that's what the commotion in the plant towers should have meant, the clotted greenish look of the air, as well as the grit shower ticking against the glass.

No luck, Monkey said, turning from the window. Then he wrapped his long gray arms around his chest and fixed me with a stare. You don't belong here any more than I do, he said, and I felt like I was being stared at by a statue. By the Charioteer of Delphi, its face of stone made stonier still by the presence in it of pale glass eyes. We might as well go back down, the statue said, and its eyes blinked.

But how long had it been—one month? two? Or even longer, a whole year even, because without a calendar, how can you tell? How long had it been since we'd last felt it, that familiar sensation of being dropped from a great height straight to the center of the earth, the house inhaling every clotted greenish air particle, making room outside for the storm, a series of surprised popping noises at first, then louder and louder, building to a finale like the fireworks Bobby used to set off over the chautauqua grounds every Fourth of July but with no beautiful result, because that's the way we live these days, in an endless state of cause without effect, which is to say endlessly waiting, waiting, waiting.

(10 june) everyone mad at me but david fluellen, even mr hsia, ruthie livid. didn't know til they got in rover & it was angry tongues licking me all over, tho saying SOOOO glad to see me. asking why why why? but just try explaining (got turned around in fog, also cold & bored) & next thing u know bobby's rolling eyes & brenda's draping self over seat to warn me never do that again (but really to show off butt). ruthie's wrong as usual, applying own complex motives to everyone. brenda's exhibitionist & nothing more, basically dull with exhibitionist's tendency to dramatize self & act indignant. DE-TEST groups. had only finished telling david how group rejects parts of self til mixed, like fingerpaints end up awful brown/gray/sludge tho colors bright enough to begin with. yes, he said, food also. sadly, chewing. so sad, david, but nice as pie & HE was glad to see me. said he didn't get it, bright orange fish on green bed of lettuce goes in blah person's mouth & turns to more of same. said it was bad system & i apologized (sadly, chewing salmon) but he said not u mrs rose, yr never blah & i felt flattered i confess (only to u my darling). didn't even correct mistake with name, feeling so happy & then whole picture changed like lousy painter making shadows opaque, globby & dense & light too thin to register as light—that foul rossetti knock-off in stairwell bobby dotes on & is for yr information exact image of miss brenda all gussied

up for hateful party finally over thank god. can't sleep. hot milk & honey don't work, ditto yoga, trollope, nothing. bad case of jumpy legs, jumpy soul. wish u were here to rub my back or i was getting drowsy rubbing yrs like when u were my dear little baby a million years ago . . . tho probably just as well yr not since believe me darling sometimes world turns to a dish, white dish of an open valley filling with fog where u mustn't go, unless u swear 1) not to let thing into yr soul that makes its nest & calls itself mother to fool u or 2) to forget all mothers who tuck in yr bed, who tuck folds of fog round u while u sleep since yr real mother's name is panic & her beak's a mile long & she'll tear u in 2 like making paint rags out of sheets or cut u in 2 like a delicious sandwich she eats all alone while clock strikes 1 & 2 & 3 & 4 . . .

Following the group's failed assault on Pen-y-Fan, David Fluellen suggested they return to the Blackbrook, rather than spend the night at the Castle Hotel in Brecon, as planned. "Maybe we could have a party?" Naomi added. "A nice little party to celebrate Carole's safe recovery?" Both ideas met with no argument, everyone feeling immense relief to be off the mountain, as well as eager to shed the wet clothes that were making the inside of the Rover almost as foggy as it was outside. "I wasn't *recovered*," Carole told David in a loud whisper. "I got back on my own." "I know," he said, nodding once to let her know he understood perfectly. "Listen, love, do you think you could wipe the windscreen until the fan starts working? I can't see a thing."

They were headed toward Abergavenny on the A40, moving along at what Ruth describes as an insane speed, given the total lack of visibility. David and Carole were sitting up front, Carole "hogging the best seat, as usual"; Naomi and Ruth, being the smallest, were jammed on Bobby's and Coleman's laps with Brenda pinned between them; the rest were tumbled together in the way back, Tadeusz on one jump seat, gripping Magtil, Mr. Hsai perched on the other, Paula at his feet. "I teach you all to polka," Magtil announced. "Like Poles." "I can't wait," Paula replied grimly. Brenda meanwhile hunched over a map, dispensing advice: "Slow down or you'll miss the turn"; "Didn't we want that last exit?"; "Oh my God, look out!" The roads were slippery and fog-shrouded, hedgerows hemming them in on both sides, the Rover hurtling blindly through traffic that reminded Ruth of "marbles released down a marble shoot by a retard whose idea of fun is one big collision at the bottom."

By the time they arrived at the Blackbrook, she could almost see the bad mood that had overtaken their earlier high spirits piling out of the Rover with them, all of them shuffling along like Naomi in those goddamn boots. "Down, Major. Bad boy," Brenda said, but so halfheartedly that Ruth ended up covered with muddy paw prints. "That dog's a menace," Carole remarked. Meanwhile David repaired to the kitchen to fix supper, Bobby enlisted Tadeusz's help building a fire, Coleman and Mr. Hsia discussed the Internet, and the women quickly dispersed, each hoping to beat the others to the showers. "For the money, you'd think the least they could provide would be plenty of hot water," Ruth wrote, "but guess again."

She goes on to compare her own toilette to Brenda's: "I managed to squeeze about a teaspoon of tepid brown sludge from the showerhead, just enough to foam and rinse. Fortunately I've gone for the waif look, unlike our guide, whose hair, when she made her appearance in the dining room, resembled coonskin. Well, okay, I'm exaggerating, but at least *I* gave some thought to *my* make-up, and finally got to wear the tight red T-shirt and flippy little black skirt with the black ankle socks and evil red heels I've been saving for just such an occasion. Unlike Miss Brenda, whose dress combined all the worst details fashion's decreed and then rejected over the last thirty years. That dress! A particularly unfortunate shade of yellow, the skirt pleated and the pleats stitched down to an unflattering place right below the hips, its sleeves, in weird opposition to the pleats' austerity, ballooning wildly from the waist, the overall effect that of a luffing sail. Not to mention the scalloped eyelet lace at the collar and cuffs, and the three huge concave pearl buttons deployed along the bodice like dinner plates."

The party got off to a slow start like a junior high canteen, the boys in a lump on one side of the gym, egging each other on, the girls on the other side, pretending to be deep in conversation. Of course after a while a boy always comes detached; tonight it was Ruth's own charming white-haired husband who broke the ice, wandering over to ask Magtil, girlishly attired in some sort of native costume, if he could take her picture.

The room was cold, the kindling damp. Bobby kept blowing on it, wadding up sheet after sheet of newspaper until Tadeusz told everyone to stand back, and squirted it with lighter fluid. "Do you want to kill us?" demanded Paula, but a giant whoosh drowned her out, and the next thing she knew the Duprees were inviting her to watch the sunset from a tropic isle, David was handing round shots of Prince of Wales, Mr. Hsia was doing the box step with Ruth, and the fire was burning brightly.

A half hour or so of self-conscious merriment ensued, until the drinks kicked in. Coleman continued to amuse himself by taking pictures (Bobby filling Brenda's glass, Paula playing tug-of-war with the dog, Ruth blowing a kiss at the camera over Mr. Hsia's shoulder, making a face I actually remember, eyes half-lidded and slightly crossed). David produced a basket of hot rolls and a steaming pot of soup, then removed his apron and asked Carole, who insisted she didn't know how, to dance. "David could make an elephant look graceful," Brenda remarked.

Ruth describes her standing propped against the mantel, darkly watchful and putting away whiskey at a healthy clip, her eyes becoming blacker and blacker, her body more and more languid, eventually flapping loose like a vengeful moth to join poor Naomi at the soup table, berating her on the subject of British reservoirs, most notably one made by submerging an entire Welsh village in order to supply the people of Liverpool with drinking water. Initially Naomi tried to sympathize, but Brenda was too wound up to listen. Water, coal, what wouldn't the Brits steal to fuel the engines of empire? One day Tryweryn Valley, the next, Aberfan. A hundred and sixteen children buried when a mountain of mine waste slid from a coal tip and landed on a school. "No one wants to see *those* graves," Brenda said. "Oh no. It's just Arthur this and Merlin that and goddamn Dylan Thomas."

"In Poland—" put in Magtil, who'd been hovering near the table, but she was drowned out by a loud clang as Naomi dropped the lid back onto the pot.

"Ouch!" Naomi yelped, sucking her fingers dramatically in an obvious bid for Paula's attention, though by now Paula was crouched on all fours growling at the dog. "It seems to me people don't go on vacation to be depressed," Naomi said. "It seems to me life is depressing enough."

"In Poland," Magtil persisted, "is exact opposite. Who cares we have beautiful mountains and lakes, Copernicus, Chopin?

We be so glad to move on, build new lives, show the world our beautiful country, but everyone want to see Treblinka." As she spoke she took Naomi's hand, studied her fingers, and jammed them into the ice bucket, remarking that it was never a good idea to fool around with a burn. "The flesh is compromised," Magtil said, but it wasn't clear if this was another mistake like "dubbing" or an actual medical term.

"And you're complaining?" Brenda asked Magtil. "That's how it ought to be. You should be relieved the world hasn't reduced where *you* live to one big Disneyland. Oohing and aahing over the sheep and thatched cottages, behaving like ostriches, pretending the whole history of human nature isn't one vile bloodbath after anoth—"

"I live with my mum," Naomi interrupted, pointedly addressing Magtil. "She has Alzheimer's. I change her diapers and I feed her. Of course I know I'm no saint—the fact is she drives me mad—but I like to believe there's a little goodness in me even when I'm at my worst, you know, when I'm wedging clay with a vengeance and thinking vile thoughts."

"Is so sad," Magtil replied. "Your poor mother. She is very lucky to have daughter like you." She put her arm around the young woman and led her to the gateleg table, where Tadeusz was sitting alone beneath water-logged Ophelia, glumly shuffling cards.

"We play skat," Magtil said. "Is best."

"I don't know how," Naomi wailed.

"No matter. My honey show you."

By now the music was slower, moodier, Carole and David the only couple left dancing. Her large blond head rested heavily on his shoulder as he ferried her across the floor in a lethargic fox trot. Muted horns, lightly brushed cymbals, a plaintive female voice: "Bewitched, bothered, and bewildered . . ." Ruth reclined on her side on the sofa, ostensibly watching Mr. Hsia stir the fire, while continuing to monitor the conversation at the table. "Your husband," Mr. Hsia was saying, "has done me the honor of inviting me to fish with him tomorrow." "*Passt mir nicht,*" Tadeusz was instructing Naomi. "Say after me. 'It do not suit me.' " Mr. Hsia jabbed at a log, releasing a noisy fall of embers, then scowled ("for the first time ever") and asked Ruth if she thought Coleman was merely being polite. Not about fishing, she reassured him. Coleman could be as hypocritical as the next guy, but never about fishing. Never. "I admire your husband," Mr. Hsia informed her, his tone, Ruth notes, like a rebuke.

"He was staring at me, hard, in that way spiritually evolved people have that makes you feel both invisible and utterly carnal. I tried staring back, but I knew I couldn't keep my eyes from sending all the wrong messages. Then the music stopped, or the tape ran out, or the angel opened the seventh seal, and in the ensuing silence we heard Brenda say, You want sad? I'll give you fucking sad . . . And suddenly there was big soft David Fluellen rushing across the room, brushing past Naomi and Magtil and Tadeusz, stepping over Paula and the dog to envelop Brenda like a big white cloud; you could tell it wasn't the first time he'd had to do this. He didn't say a thing, but looped his arm around her waist and led her to the middle of the room. E*xcuse* me, Paula said. The music started up again ('Melancholy Baby,' ironically enough) and when David and Brenda began to dance, their performance was so sublime that everyone, including me I hate to admit, was totally transfixed.

"A queer match, Mr. Hsia observed, given the fact that Mr. Fluellen was an old soul, and Mrs. Fluellen brand-new. When I asked him how he could tell, he came up with some nonsense about the whorls on David's fingers forming complete circles, one for each life. You're kidding, I said, and he laughed, going on to explain (I'm paraphrasing) that David had ceased to crave, which was driving Brenda crazy. What about Carole? I wanted to know, trying to steal a glance at my own fingers while he wasn't looking. Carole, too, he said."

By this point Ruth seems to have grown bored with the discussion. She rose to her feet and went off in search of a stiff drink and a livelier companion, ideally someone even more profane than herself. Mr. Hsia continued to poke at the fire, David and Brenda to dreamily circle the dance floor, the Kopeckys and Naomi to play skat; everyone else was gathered around the table, ravenous and smashed. Everyone, that is, except Bobby, undeniably Ruth's best choice. She asked, but no one seemed to know where he was. Carole suggested maybe he'd already gone up to bed; Coleman said he'd seen him drinking alone in the kitchen. Paula reported hearing a door slam, and seeing a white shirt she thought might have been his through the window, only that was hours ago.

It was like a game of Clue, Ruth complains. One minute Colonel Mustard was right there with you in the ballroom, and the next thing you knew, he'd vanished. People were constantly vanishing, swooped by an enormous ghostly hand from room to room (or mountaintop to car) in the twinkling of an eye. Plenty of weapons too (knives and pokers and candlesticks), but without a dead body to give the whole thing meaning. She wasn't hungry, and had consumed enough whiskey to no longer feel its effect. Also she was bored and resentful and sorry she'd ever wanted to come to Wales in the first place.

Ruth Farr, all dressed up with nowhere to go. I can picture her so clearly—even summon a little sympathy for her—as she steps out in her finery into the moist Welsh night, momentarily blind and susceptible to every little noise, the nearby scuffling as some creature even smaller and more vulnerable than she is runs to hide, the constant drip of water from the eaves, and far away on the other side of the road the Black Brook, swollen after the storm, insanely thundering, a sound which, being in a morbid mood, she likens to the approaching hooves of the Erlking's horse. When she takes a step onto the rain-soaked lawn her "evil heels" immediately sink in, and she kicks them off. This is a measure of how far she's come, that she doesn't even care about her shoes, her darling shoes she loved so when she bought them. "Bobby?" she whispers. "Is that you?" She's caught sight of a tiny orange light across the road, moving erratically downhill in the direction of the brook. A cigarette, for sure, but when did he manage to buy a goddamn pack of cigarettes, since everyone's always watching everyone else like goddamn hawks, and Carole would have a fit if she knew.

The black ankle socks are getting ruined yet Ruth keeps them on, hoping they'll protect the soles of her feet, which are unbearably tender, and the surface of the world studded with sharp, cruel objects. It's no longer raining, but wet wet wet, the air clinging like drenched curtains, every tree and shrub ready to release its store of cold water as she brushes past.

"Bobby!" she calls, louder this time, and finally she can see him, a solitary figure sitting on a big rock beside the brook, smoking and drinking and looking so forlorn that the self-pity she's been feeling instantly attaches itself to him, a transaction that restores her sense of control, propelling her down the hill at a run, faster and faster, heedless, almost happy.

"Ruth?" Bobby says. He rises to his feet unsteadily and turns to greet her, the expression on his face hard to read but *interested*. "Ruthie?"

⁖

As for what happened next, their accounts vary. Ruth, not surprisingly, takes pains to establish a flattering view of herself. Bobby's ego had been wounded by Carole's attentions to David, she claims, and it took all her feminine wiles to convince him otherwise. They sat together on the rock and shared a cigarette — the one fact on which they agree. She reminded him that as far as he and Carole were concerned, *he* was the more desirable. Women were always going out of their way to impress him, she said. Brenda, Magtil, even "that Naomi," who, though Bobby probably wasn't aware of it, had practically shoved Ruth to the ground in her eagerness to sit on his lap during the ride home. Just as any fool could tell that David danced with Carole to get back at Brenda. And for what? For the same reason Carole was punishing him, namely Brenda's infatuation, though it certainly wasn't his fault the bitch couldn't leave him alone. When Bobby leapt to Brenda's defense, Ruth merely sighed and said he'd proved her point. Brenda had obviously had her eye on him since day one — and if he couldn't tell, it was because as bitches went, Brenda, to give her credit, was pretty subtle. In Ruth's opinion, while Bobby might pride himself on his business savvy, his inability to be duped, when it came to women he was like a baby. Indeed if she's to be believed, she did everything she could to convince Bobby of his charm and his innocence.

It seems he needed a lot of convincing, and Ruth was happy to oblige. She offered several pointed observations (Brenda sitting closer than she needed to in the Rover, her not so very veiled glances), which Bobby "ate up" in what Ruth seems to have taken for a mood of mutual derision. Encouraged, she went on to ask if he'd noticed Brenda's anti-Semitism, and when he expressed surprise, told him what she'd overheard the night of the concert. They had to stick together, Ruth said, going on to suggest that if Bobby really wanted, he could get revenge for both of them. All he had to do, she said, was seduce Brenda. Assuming, that is, he could overlook the bad dress and the lipstick applied as if with a trowel—and she pursed her own lips by way of demonstration.

"I was being funny," Ruth insists, "but Bobby evidently misread my intentions, and the next thing I knew I was pinned to a cold wet rock on the bank of a raging river while my best friend's husband made a pass at me."

Bobby, on the other hand, claims he wasn't feeling even remotely neglected—*au contraire*. Pressed by Queen's Counsel to describe his actions, he says he left the party at about eleven o'clock, fed up with the political bullshit and bad music, and wandered down to the brook for a little fresh air. Indeed he was in a buoyant mood, having scored a pack of Woodbines when they'd stopped for gas in Abergavenny. Nothing made him happier, he said, than to smoke a cigarette outdoors, a pleasure he'd been denying himself much too long.

So there he was, sitting on a rock and smoking, minding his

own business, when along came Ruthie, obviously four sheets to the wind, whereas he, Bobby, was sober as a judge ("no offense, Your Honor"). After plunking herself down more or less on top of him, and removing the cigarette from his mouth to take a deep drag, she grabbed his hand and began studying his fingers. Not bad, she observed. Though it was too dark to be positive, it looked like Bobby was a middle-aged soul, unlike some people she could mention. Four lives, six to go—and here she let out her "trademark giggle," the breathy little *haaa* Bobby'd always found nauseating, given its basic message of 'What do you expect from a lovable ditz like myself?' when to know Ruth was to conclude she was anything but ditzy. "But that's her *modus operandi*," Bobby elaborates. "It's how she fools you into thinking she's harmless." Reminded to stick to the facts, he points out it was Ruth herself who taught him the importance of detail in understanding event. A hair on a wart, the Wife of Bath's red stockings, blah blah blah. He assumes they've all read their Chaucer.

"Hang in there," he says. "I'm just getting to the good part. Anyway, the first sign I had of trouble was she wouldn't give me back my hand. And she had this expression on her face like she was going to cry, or at least I thought that's what it meant until she kind of toppled over and started kissing me. I was completely taken off guard. I didn't want to encourage her, but I didn't want to humiliate her, either. I mean, this was *Ruthie* . . . we'd known each other forever; she was Carole's oldest friend. And to be honest, there was something almost —I'm not sure how to put this—fitting, well, almost a relief, about us kissing each other after all those years. As if we'd both wondered what it would be like, but had reached a tacit agreement we'd never find out, or at least not in this lifetime. Maybe we'd been lovers in a past life. Ruth had this fixation with some old Welsh tale she was always harping on; you'll have to get her to tell you about it."

"Perhaps later," says Queen's Counsel. "And then?"

"And then what?" Bobby replies. "I hate to disappoint you, but nothing else happened. After we kissed, we got off the rock and climbed back up the hill. We weren't even holding hands anymore. Ruth made me go on while she looked for her shoes. She wouldn't let me help; I think she was feeling embarrassed. By the time I got to the inn, the first floor was dark, except the windows nearest the fireplace, and even they were pretty dim. Upstairs a light was on in the Kopeckys' room; I knew it was theirs since I could see Magtil brushing her hair. Mr. Hsia also seemed to be awake; though his room was at the far end of the building, I saw light from it shining on the Rover. All the other windows were black. I had no idea what to expect when I went inside, certainly not what I found, which was the Fluellens going at it on the rug in front of the fireplace. I tried not to disturb them, but I guess I stepped on Major's tail. Major. The dog."

AND HOW ABOUT ME? Who do I believe?

The thing is, these people are the only company I've had for the longest time—unless you count Monkey. But he's a wild card, showing up unexpectedly and acting strange, in ways I can't understand, unlike my parents and their friends, who can always be counted on to stay right where I put them the day before. Their world's the one I was born into. Its rules are the ones I was raised to obey: a trust in the civilized virtues of kindness, honesty, hard work, and compassion, combined with a dedication to what everyone took for enlightened self-interest but was really greed. Back then money was the measure of success: if you followed the rules, you'd be rich and happy and gorgeous and live forever in a nice house like this one used to be. Poor people lacked motivation; their punishment was to spend their days in jail or on welfare, smoking and drinking and eating bad food, their bodies a mess, their chance at immortality nil.

So far, though, having been raised with the rules hasn't been much help. Instead I find myself wandering (literally) farther and farther afield, past the plant towers and into the so-called meadow, almost as if the truth's out there waiting for me to extract it from its comb, like honey, in a nerve-wracking process that always used to mean getting stung. My mother's bee boxes are still clustered at the meadow's edge. I stumbled on them just this morning, though these days they look as much like boxes as the meadow looks like a meadow, their white paint worn off, the wood eaten away in some places and in others sprouting big pie-shaped fungi or thick patches of moss, making them lopsided and shifty. No bees, just more of those awful wingless flies, and a poachy track of dust-caked weeds marching off in all directions.

In fact the only way I knew I was *at* the meadow's edge was because of the boxes—the whole idea of edge having become a thing of the past. And as I stood there, shivering in the left-over chill of the night before, watching a spotted beetle with tiny red horns creep sluggishly across a rotten board, and as I felt the endless shadows deepen around me, accompanied by that tightening of the air which heralds the approach of what we used to call *noon*, I had a sudden and overpowering memory of brightness, prompted maybe by those implausibly red horns, the way they seemed (if only for a fraction of an instant) to have been lit from without, to be actually shining . . .

My mother was walking through the meadow with Aunt Ruth, headed for the hives. They had their arms linked and were talking—the impression they gave was of girlfriends sharing secrets, both of them completely unaware of my presence. I was hiding in the tall grass, making a clover chain. The white clover the bees loved, so it must have been midsummer, hot and drowsy, a sizzling noise like frying bacon.

I wasn't afraid of bees, but Aunt Ruth was. She had on a black-and-yellow-striped halter top and black-and-yellow-plaid shorts. "They'll think you're their queen," my mother said, and Aunt Ruth said she wasn't going another step closer.

"You know I'm allergic," she complained. "What do you want to do, kill me?"

The sun poured over everything like honey, turning them both into giant golden statues. Two queens, I thought; for the first time in my life I remember actually feeling proud that I, too, would be a grown woman some day. And then my mother told Aunt Ruth not to be crazy, and Aunt Ruth tucked her chin into her neck, fakely meek, and said she was tired of being bossed, and who did Carole think she was to be calling *her* crazy? And my mother replied that she *thought* she was her friend.

A minute ticked lazily by—bzzzz bzzzz bzzzz chhchh ching, chhchh ching—the clover and the bees and the crickets and the grass.

"You don't need friends," Aunt Ruth snapped. "*You've* got your *art*, remember?"

"So do you," my mother reminded her, but Aunt Ruth wasn't interested in being condescended to.

She pointed back across the meadow in the direction of the garden house, where I was supposedly busy coloring in the Four Horsemen of the Apocalypse. "You've got your daughter," Aunt Ruth added, but even I could tell she meant it as revenge.

Bzzzz bzzzz bzzzz. Chhchh ching, chhchh ching.

That's as much of the conversation as I remember. The sun was still shining brightly, but it felt like a cloud had covered it. My mother was standing pretty near where I was hiding. I could see the yellow hair on her legs—she usually stopped shaving after one of what everyone called Bobby's "lapses." Meanwhile Aunt Ruth had stalked off in the direction of the hives, and suddenly I was reminded of another morning not long before when Bobby, no doubt bored out of his mind with slapjack, had tried teaching me chess.

That was what they were like, I realized, big powerful chess pieces, both of them queens just as I'd thought, but it was their position that was going to determine who was most powerful. And I remember thinking, where were the kings? I vaguely recollected fishing poles, hip-waders, Uncle Coleman holding up a bit of fluff and glitter for Bobby's approval . . . The kings could move only a little, one space in any direction, but Bobby had explained that was a sign of true power. Men didn't need to swoop around dramatically like women. Which also happened to be why women wore dresses—to accentuate the swooping.

Ruth was sniffling softly, peeking back at my mother over her bare shoulder. Less than a year later (after the kissing rock episode) she'd write in her journal: "Anyone who falls for the craziness theory about Carole Ridingham should have their head examined." And, truly, the role of innocent victim bored my mother, which I think is one of the reasons Bobby fell in love with her. Victims bored Bobby, too.

So there we were: Aunt Ruth sniffling, and the crickets chinging, and the bees buzzing, and the sweet smell of the meadow making me giddy to the point of fainting. I saw a pained expression cross my mother's face, almost as if she'd been stung. I saw her draw down her veil from where she had it tucked into the brim of her straw hat, pull on her gloves, and advance toward the hives. For a moment nothing happened.

And then I'm not sure whether what I remember is what I actually saw, or whether it became my memory after hearing it described so many times afterward, and by so many different people, including Ruth in her journal.

In any case there's no way a twelve-year-old would have recognized an alien "robber bee" skulking across the alighting board, or known that my mother's bees were in a bad mood due to the fact that an early-morning thunderstorm had dampened a clover flow of unprecedented vigor. "Idle bees are the devil's workshop," Bobby said, to which my mother replied, "I hate it when you joke about things you don't know anything about." This was much later, after she'd dispatched me to run "like the wind" back to the house and get Mrs. Koop to call 911, a measure that proved unnecessary since by the time I returned, so had the men. I found Uncle Coleman rummaging for epinephrine in the huge duffle bag Monkey would eventually steal from the hall closet, my mother wringing her hands, Aunt Ruth lying draped across Bobby's lap, her eyeballs exactly like peeled hard-boiled eggs. "Don't just stand there," Bobby said. "Jesus, Roo," Uncle Coleman added, holding the syringe aloft and expertly squirting a drop of serum into the sweet summer air. "What the hell were you doing?" You couldn't tell who either of them meant. My mother just kept wringing her hands, saying "no no no no" over and over.

"But hey, don't go thinking she was worried on my account," as Aunt Ruth went on to write. "Oh no. Carole's never wasted a minute of her precious time worrying about anyone except Carole. That robber bee was just the first sign of trouble. You could tell he was a robber because he looked sleek and black, all the usual gold fuzz having been worn away in countless battles. Sleek and black and furtive. Evidently there's nothing more depressed than an out-of-work bee, or a neglected husband."

                         *∽*

I suppose in the end the truth about the kissing rock episode has less to do with who I believe than what I believe in. Bobby is—*was*—my father, and though he hardly could be called a paragon of virtue, he always made sure I knew I was the apple of his eye, whereas Ruth tended to treat me like a worm. What's at stake here is bigger than Bobby's or Ruth's egos, though they were both pretty big; what's at stake is morality, or, more precisely, the place where morals and nature intersect—in that sense of the future, for example, that makes the bees kill their failing queen no matter how much they love her.

But even if I'll never know who to believe, one thing is clear: by the time Bobby had disturbed the Fluellens' lovemaking, the configuration that would play itself out in Gower was complete.

PART TWO

# Gower

This is a hard province . . . yet yesterday it was found too soft.

—GIRALDUS CAMBRENSIS

"A PLATEAU of carboniferous limestone folded in a rather complex manner," the geologist J. A. Steers says of the Gower peninsula, as if describing what an origami artist does with a piece of paper. First there's flatness, then the living forms emerge, breathe, walk, learn to love and hate, crown kings and queens, fight wars, bear young, build cities, dream, and die. It's a wild place, Gower, extending hunched into the Bristol Channel; to the north of its central rocky spine, treacherous pockets of quicksand lurk in the bogs and salt marshes; to the south, steep limestone cliffs tower over the sea. Many-cornered castles, they've been called—just unfold the rock and out pop the skeletons. In the caves along the south shore archaeologists have found the bones of lions and mammoths and elephants, as well as those of the Red Lady of Paviland, who's no lady at all but a young Cro-Magnon man, tucked in to sleep under his blanket of iron oxide.

Wake up! Wake up! Only this was a real young man and he's been dead for over twenty thousand years, unlike the Tylwyth Teg (or fairy folk), who are presided over by Morgan le Fay, queen of the Land of Gore, and can be waked without even trying. Watch out not to step into one of their circles or they'll whisk you away, and if you ever manage to find your way back home, at the first bite of food or touch of a loved one's hand you'll crumble into a thimbleful of black dust.

Of course Arthur visited Gower, and left behind the usual dolmen, high on a ridge over Rhossili Beach, that place Dylan Thomas called "the wildest, bleakest and barrenest I know—four or five miles of yellow coldness going away into the distance of the sea." Giraldus also stopped in Gower, it being a popular destination for pilgrims, many of them drawn to the shrine of the holy hermit Cenydd, who as a baby had been deposited by a seagull on one of the high-tide islands of Worms Head, and nourished by, of all things, a "breast-shaped bell."

Haunt of curlews and jackdaws, sea holly, polecats, cockles, adders, owls—at the time of the walking tour Gower still had very few roads and no rail service and was evidently a very easy place to get lost in.

A brutal landscape, dangerous and strange, but also enchantingly beautiful. I know this because even if Uncle Coleman was more interested in fish than in people and scenery, he couldn't leave the scenery out of his pictures: the rain-swept cliff Aunt Ruth is struggling up in her famous black-and-yellow-striped halter top ["easily a million steps, no kidding, and where there weren't steps there were rocks slimy with sheep shit, and the sheep themselves in their wigs judging your every move, as if *they* wouldn't have been so dumb as to leave *their* allergy kits behind in the car . . ."], and in the distance the serpent's gigantic neck and head, the flat silver sea, the clouds like pearls spilled along the horizon.

BUT I'M GETTING AHEAD of myself. The walkers haven't even left the inn yet. Most of them are still in bed, variously suffering from hangovers and trapped in their private nightmares: Magtil's skull cleft by an axe, a sour rag stuffed in Carole's mouth, and Bluebeard next door violating Ruth, who smiles for a change. The sun is just starting to turn the sky across the road a pale pinkish gold, as well as all the east-facing windows. Birds are singing loudly, the way they do after a rain. It's a nice day, Friday the thirteenth.

Of those with east-facing windows, Naomi Westenholtz seems to have been the first up, mildly hungover and roused by the smell of sausage, the noise of drawers opening, banging pots, and the annoying voice of Radio Cymru. According to her testimony, when she opened the window and leaned out to sniff the morning, she saw a pair of red objects in the middle of the lawn that she mistook for birds, until she put on her glasses and realized they were Ruth Farr's shoes. Paula was the birder, after all; Naomi preferred botanizing. Flowers didn't move and you could carry them home to stare at without getting your eyes pecked out. No doubt the shoes were ruined, but Naomi felt sure Ruth could care less. Or, as she told the court, "If *her* mother were suffering from Alzheimer's, Ruth Farr would've hired a hit man."

Six o'clock. A little wedge of sun was showing behind the

tangled woods on the far side of the brook, and the air was mild and fresh—a perfect day for walking, though walking wasn't in the cards, at least not today. Today they'd be stuck in the Rover. Naomi knew the itinerary by heart: the M4 more or less along the coast and then across the River Neath to Swansea, where they'd lunch at the Queen's Hotel, view the Lower Swansea Valley reclamation project (yawn), and then on to Gower and a night of grotesquely rich food, posh accommodations, wild ponies, etc. etc. at Fairy Ring. *Tomorrow* they'd be allowed to walk . . .

If you want to invest creatures from the past with life, you have to use "transplants": a nose here, a laugh there, a curious mannerism, a limp. Otherwise they're no better than dolls or zombies. When I try picturing Naomi Westenholtz, all I see is a girl I knew when I was growing up: Nancy Dickinson, a spanielish girl with floppy "ears" of hair, brown pleading eyes, and lots of pointless energy. I admit—I've got them mixed up, Naomi and Nancy. Two adolescent girls, awkward and unformed, though at the time of the tour Naomi would have been about twenty-six, a full-grown woman living with her invalid mother on the Isle of Wight, doing the laundry and pushing around the Hoover and throwing pots.

Yet even so, there *was* something of the adolescent girl about Naomi Westenholtz. Something tenderly sullen, druggily sarcastic. "Huh?" tends to have been her response to almost every one of the Queen's Counsel's questions. ("Huh? Oh. Well you know Gower's lousy with dolmens, so everything always had to grind to a halt to let the men [except Don Juan, there] take pictures. I thought a walking tour was for walking.")

In fact on the morning of Friday the thirteenth, as Naomi Westenholtz was stomping around upstairs, noisily searching for the bottle of aspirin her hangover demanded, and as David Fluellen was tiptoeing through the lounge below her like a big dainty pasha preparing to let out the dog, Mrs. Westenholtz was in the hospital having her stomach pumped. The visiting nurse Naomi had hired to look after her mother while she was on vacation had gotten delayed by a roadblock, and in the meantime Mrs. Westenholtz decided to fix herself a cup of Ovaltine and accidentally used Drano instead, thus consigning her daughter to a life of shame and guilt. Though Naomi wouldn't find this out until much later; for the moment the date's ominous significance left her unmoved. She was in good spirits, getting dressed with an abundance of energy, causing the goose-shaped ceiling fixture above the sofa to swing wildly back and forth. For a small woman, Bobby said, Naomi Westenholtz was extremely heavy-footed.

Maybe we're not supposed to look back because we're not supposed to horn in on places where we don't belong, like those time travelers in the old movies who do some inconsequential thing—eat a pomegranate, for instance—and ruin the future for everyone. In a photo showing the empty lounge a pale ray of the morning's first light points out a stain on the rug in what I imagine is the exact place where Brenda and David Fluellen made love the night before. Otherwise everything's spick-and-span, though I'd like to think this provided David small consolation—that sometimes the lives of the people who came on the tours were so sad they broke his heart. Those little birds embroidered on Mrs. Kopecky's black velvet bodice, and the way she'd laced it way too tight, like

Snow White. Or Ruth Farr at the edge of the dance floor, glancing around like a dog with its leash tied to a parking meter, but only when she thought no one was looking.

Not my mother, though. Nothing heartbreaking about that one. *Really* sad people never break your heart.

༉

I imagine thin light with a faint pink undercurrent, like tap water running over a cut finger. Eventually the bleeding stops and the water runs clean, by which time the sun's above the woods. David Fluellen floating cloudlike around the kitchen in a cloud of delectable steam (hot grease, sage and thyme, baking yeast and currants), busy fixing the typical Welsh breakfast he hopes will compensate for his decision to postpone the Gower trip until the following day. At some point he'd have heard the weather report on the radio and decided to keep it to himself. ("Sunny and mild all weekend, with a storm predicted to move in late Sunday," testified Brenda. "By the time he finally got around to telling me, it was too late.") Who knows? Maybe he liked the idea, since even I know there's nothing better than the thought of bad weather when you're sitting safe and sound in a warm fragrant kitchen.

Meanwhile Naomi had made her way downstairs and out onto the wet front lawn, where David eventually found her, in the usual beige anorak and corduroy trousers, teetering after Major on the thin heels of Ruth Farr's red shoes. She recalled her mother reading her the story: the vain girl danced and danced and danced until she dropped dead, Mrs. Westenholtz having taken the side of the shoes. In any case Naomi was embarrassed, since not only was it her brand of vanity not to appear to care about how she looked, but she also had a major crush on Ruth.

Six-thirty. By now Mr. Hsia had arisen. Wearing a bright yellow kimono embroidered with black dragons, he'd taken up position in the middle of the lounge, where he was balancing himself on one foot while pressing the sole of the other against the back of his head. Yoga, he explained, to offset the effects of last night's whiskey.

David put a log on the fire; the banjo clock ticked like the log before it burst into flame. He said he'd always thought the only reason to exercise a heavy hand with the bottle was to get the place to yourself the morning after, a remark that made Mr. Hsia break into peals of laughter, though Naomi found it rude.

Perhaps this is why their conversation lurched along, or at least until the others joined them. Naomi's theory was that David failed to register her existence because she wasn't "a looker," actually giving her a plate of sausages even though she'd told him time and again she was a vegan. Nor could she eat the currant buns he offered in exchange, since they'd been made with sugar, and everyone knew it was processed with horse hooves. Though it wasn't like he was such a prize himself—just let a woman who was as overweight as he was try to get herself a great-looking boyfriend. Pointedly, Naomi peeled a banana and began taking ridiculously small bites, like a person abandoned on a desert isle.

Quarter past seven. "yolk of sun broke across lawn, poured through window and onto bed, oozing by where bobby should have been and onto me, filling noseholes, mouth, eyes, ears, pores, etc. etc. with goo. dying of thirst & head pounding & damn bird whistling on and on and on: tweet tweet tweet." Rather than let it make her lose her mind, my mother evidently raced downstairs as fast as she could, not bothering to brush her hair or change out of her blue-and-white-striped pajamas. In the lounge she found Mr. Hsia, still gracefully posed on one leg like a stork, and she stood staring at him for several minutes, taking in the scene she'd later sketch ("like bird who brought u to me"). Then she entered the kitchen, plunging past David Fluellen and heading straight for the sink, where she gulped down three glasses of water without pausing to breathe. I love you too, David said, smiling. Shortly thereafter Paula arrived, her slicked-back yellow hair still showing the comb's tooth marks, and Naomi darkly informed her that while she'd been asleep their plans had been changed.

The water pump in the cellar kicked on: the Kopeckys were showering. By now Mr. Hsia had joined the group around the kitchen table, suddenly and mysteriously clad in a crisp lemon yellow sports shirt and a pair of wrinkle-free khaki trousers, his black hair pleasantly redolent of lime. Sausage? he inquired, sniffing, and when Naomi said she'd taken him for a fellow vegetarian, he replied, laughing, that to smell a thing was not to eat it. Paula asked Naomi if she had any aspirin. "Don't think I didn't see you, Gnome," she added, sotto voce. "On the lawn. Guess Who will be pissed off."

A scene composed of one part conjecture, one part fact— but how could it be otherwise, even for the five people gathered in that warm, fragrant kitchen? Could Paula's headache really have been identical, as Naomi assumed it was, to everyone else's? Everyone else's dry mouth to hers?

And where do I fit in, since whenever I picture that room ("warm" and "fragrant" being my own assumptions) it's not from an elevated observer's perspective but at eye level, like a sixth invisible guest, my head swiveling with everyone else's at the slam of the front door, Major bounding damply exuberant through the lounge and into the kitchen, and behind him my similarly damp yet definitely not exuberant father.

Suze, he says, what're you doing here? Or words to that effect. The usual display of surprise, really, at seeing me anywhere, though in this case what would've happened if I were to have said, I've come from the future, Dad. Leave for Gower now! Or better yet, Don't go at all . . .

He'd spent the night outdoors, Bobby told the court. Major could corroborate his story. He'd found Bobby lying there on the far side of the clethra hedge, minding his own business, when he came blowing by, hot on the trail of a shoe. Could a dog be subpoenaed? Of course Bobby thought he was being funny, but the truth is there actually used to be a tradition in English law that held animals responsible for their actions.

Two entire days of the trial seem to have been spent establishing contingency, the idea being that if they'd left for Gower on the thirteenth, as planned, nothing would have gone wrong. The kind of crazy reasoning that keeps sending you further and further back, trying in vain to get a foothold in that place where the seeds of future events first got planted, until you find yourself wishing no one had ever been born.

Bobby stood in front of the fire for a while, shivering. All walkers loved fires, he claimed—it was one thing they had in common, that and an abiding interest in meteorology. According to Naomi, his cheek was crosshatched "like a Zuni beaker" and there were grass stains on his shirt, bearing out his testimony. He pointed in the general direction of Ruth and Coleman's room, asked where the lovebirds were, and made a veiled reference to having greased *someone's* wheels, then said he didn't mean to be crude.

"I reminded everyone it wasn't even eight o'clock yet,"

Naomi explained. "Surely with a little effort we could've been on the road by nine, just an hour behind schedule. I addressed my remarks to Mr. Hsia, since in the past he'd tended to share my impatience with scheduling changes, but he was so excited by the prospect of a day fishing with Mr. Snow he didn't care. Mrs. Ridingham rolled her eyes at the ceiling and told him not to hold his breath."

Or, as Bobby put it: "If what you're trying to get at is who opposed the change in plans, that would have to be Miss Naomi Westenholtz. The rest of us were too hungover. Of course maybe she took that position just to be perverse. I don't know if you've noticed, but there's something about Westenholtz that makes you want to deck her. It's like she wants to get you in a fight so she can retreat to her little hole and lick her wounds and look at you out of those big near-sighted eyes."

o you shall go
into a trout
lithe with sorrow and
quick with doubt.

trout beware
the otter sleek
who charts your passage
down the creek.

she'll crack your bones
in Jesus' name
and so you will be
fetched back home.

cunning and art
you do not lack
but always a whistle
will fetch you back.

—c.r.

THE WYE VALLEY (*A Pictorial and Descriptive Guide with Notes on Angling, Boating, Cycling, Motoring, etc.,* Ward Lock & Co., 1929) says that the chief fish to be found in the river and its tributaries are salmon, trout, and grayling, "besides every other kind of coarse fish known." Salmon season runs from January 26 to October 26, trout from February 15 to October 1; the price of a license varies from a shilling for a whole year (coarse) to several pounds for a measly half season (salmon). Though the book's an antique, many of the recommended lures—cow dung, frog hop, yellow sally, hawthorn—were still in use at the time of my parents' trip, Uncle Coleman evidently having opted for the last, the day being unusually warm and sunny.

In the photograph, he's just come into the kitchen and is holding up a hawthorne lure for the photographer, whose shadow falls across his face. Naomi? Mr. Hsia? The face is narrow, clean-shaven; the white hair neatly trimmed and combed back from a high narrow forehead. A pale face in which the openings look more than ordinarily like holes, in particular the nostrils and the eyes, which suck you in, like the man in the photo's forming a judgment of you, rather than the other way around.

He was the last one down to breakfast if you don't count Ruth and Brenda, neither of whom put in an appearance until midafternoon. Mr. Hsia tried to hide his impatience while

Uncle Coleman fixed himself a sausage sandwich with excruciating slowness—it seemed to take him forever to finish his cup of tea, rinse his plate, locate his prescription sunglasses, clean the lenses, make his way to the door.

According to Naomi the two men were noticeably mismatched, Mr. Hsia with his Abercrombie & Fitch waders and Wheatley fly box; Uncle Coleman with his patched chinos, Hush Puppies, and margarine tub. Once on the road they headed south, taking the right fork uphill (past Ruth's red phone booth) to Llangleisiad, whose sole inhabitants appeared to be some sheep wandering in and out of the village's few lopsided houses, the tops of their heads spray-painted silver. After clambering down a steep hillside, the pair found themselves in a deep dark pool rimmed on three sides with rock, and bleeding on the fourth into the swirling light-flecked current of the brook.

My guess is Uncle Coleman hoped to give the impression that while he wasn't eager to have Mr. Hsia tagging after him, he didn't have much choice in the matter. In fact Uncle Coleman truly was anything but sociable, and never less so than when he had a fly rod in his hand. I know this though I went fishing with him only once, and that time by default, really: he'd finally convinced my mother to let him teach her how to cast, and when the big day came, she didn't want to go. Barking up the wrong tree, as Bobby would've said.

Instead, she put the moves on me, standing there in front of her easel and staring not so much at the canvas as through it —at some point beyond it or maybe even inside it where the molecules were seductively grouping and regrouping—pleading her case without once looking me in the eye.

"I can't leave now, darling," she said, stating the obvious, a surgeon who'd just slit open a patient's chest. "When have I ever asked you for anything?" she added, to which of course I couldn't reply *always*, since that would just serve to depress her, something we weren't supposed to do, though as far as I could tell she was the same as most people in that the only thing that really depressed her was when she didn't get her own way. Certainly it was depressing to have to hike to the chautauqua grounds over acres of baked arid meadow in the blazing sun.

By the time I arrived the sword grass had cut my ankles to ribbons and I was itching everywhere. "Hello, Susan," Uncle Coleman said, trying to hide his disappointment. He was sitting inside the pavilion, in the shade, his hands patiently clasped on the picnic table in front of him; as I approached he looked up and blinked. The sun was shining in his eyes, glinting off his glasses, but even so he could tell I wasn't Carole, and when I tried giving him her message, obsessively rehearsed, he actually put his hands over his ears.

"Not another word," he said, handing me a bamboo fishing rod. "Shhh. Consider me as you would one dead." The rod trembled in my hand like a new soul, trailing a piece of fluff called a popper. He told me to watch him carefully and imitate what he did, his teaching plan (encircling arms from behind, etc. etc.) no doubt having undergone major revision. We plunged through bushes and into a raging river. I caught a rock, a bush, my own leg. "Well, Susan," he said, "I can see you've inherited your father's touch"—an insult that's remained with me to this very day.

And yet when I think back on that afternoon what I chiefly remember is the huge brilliant river rushing by inside its banks with all those small brilliant fish rushing by inside *it*, both river and fish alike moved now and then to leap wildly into thin air—as if to be alive were to resist containment, to aspire to that condition of play between sunlight and shadow, the angler's hand and the fish's mouth, the vicarious thrill of feeling at once formless, weightless, and becoming suddenly whole, a coherent living creature snagging on a hook.

Of course Bobby didn't believe Uncle Coleman's display of diffidence about his fishing partner for one minute. Bobby had seen it all before, five years earlier to be exact, when Carole first let drop that Coleman was conducting secret negotiations with a group of Chinamen behind Bobby's back. She'd heard it from Ruth, who'd complained that Coleman was sick and tired of having his warnings fall on deaf ears.

According to Coleman, SnowWrite & RoseRead had grown as big as it could in its existing form; if it got any bigger it would no longer be a business but a sort of economic force, the equivalent of a country like France suddenly acquiring the international status of the United States. The business had reached the point of no return, Coleman said, explaining that his understanding of the problem had its roots in higher mathematics, specifically calculus, which provides a means of computing the size of objects or entities otherwise impossible to measure, and which has "limit" as one of its key concepts. The only thing to do was sell, he'd insisted, ideally to one of the Pacific Rim megacorporations, and the sooner the better.

Which is why, despite Bobby's assertion that he'd always been the balls of the operation, the idea of Coleman "going fishing" with Mr. Hsia made him deeply uneasy. Perhaps Coleman had an even more lucrative idea, only this time he was planning to hitch his wagon to an Asian star without any intermediary step, leaving Bobby all alone with a crazy wife and a seven-year noncompetition agreement. Hsia didn't exactly look the part, but then who did? One thing was certain, Bobby mused: a hawthorne wasn't the only lure that was going to get used that day.

Monkey says Coleman was greedy; I'm not so sure. Uncle Coleman never struck me as greedy, but maybe that's only because he was forced to adopt a strong antimaterialist stance to balance out his ultramaterialistic partner's appetite for things. Like a marriage, a business partnership often resembles a jar into which two apparently harmonious substances have been poured, and only when they've been thoroughly shaken together do you see them for what they really are, distillate and residue, one crystal clear and the other troubled, murky. For example, was Aunt Ruth's moral sense indeed deficient, or was it her response to Uncle Coleman's Eagle Scout mentality? Did my mother really need to have her head examined?

In fact Monkey's appetite for information about these people seems boundless and apparently self-serving, though I've noticed (to my great annoyance) that, like Naomi, he seems to have a "crush" on Aunt Ruth. He purposely misquotes her ("fish bone" for "fusion" as in "no fish bone for that star-crossed pair"), his mood uncharacteristically playful, his gray eyes flashing, like he's flirting with a dead woman.

In any case, the fishing excursion seems to have been a success, at least in the words of Mr. Hsia. (QC: Did you catch anything? GBH: Yes indeed. I caught the old man. QC: I'm afraid

we need more . . . GBH: [laughs]. BENCH: [prompting] And
the old man would be? GBH: [laughs again]. Ah! A big salmon.
[gestures with hands] The biggest.)

"It was getting late and they hadn't come back," wrote Aunt
Ruth, "so I thought I'd go for a run and see what was up. I was
feeling fidgety. That leg thing, you know? That thing where if
you don't move your legs you're going to go nuts."

By now the group had migrated to the terrace. The sun
was still shining brightly, the afternoon breezeless and warm.
Aside from the brook, churning away on the far side of the
road, it was very quiet, everyone's tongues thick and their
brains stuffed with moss and wool. The Kopeckys sat with
Carole and David at the wrought-iron table in the shade of a
dark green market umbrella, their skat game disturbed by the
antics of Major, tearing across the lawn in front of them as
Paula tried to give him a bath.

"He think it's duck," said Magtil, watching the dog snap at
the glistening braid of water spurting from the hose. Ruth had
spread a towel near the clethra hedge, not too far from one of
her ruined shoes, and was lying flat on her back in a lime
green bikini, working on her tan. "You'll get cancer," Naomi
predicted cheerfully just as Bobby sauntered around from
behind the inn, barefoot and overly casual, flipping open a
Guinness. "Duck," he echoed.

Carole scooped up a trick; Magtil blushed. "Always you
have the jack of clubs," she said, trying to hide her pleasure at
having made even the smallest dent in Bobby's consciousness,
though it soon became clear he'd meant it as not so much an
echo as a warning, for Paula had whirled around and ("accidentally on purpose," according to Ruth) squirted Naomi

smack in the face, knocking off her glasses, which Bobby proceeded to walk on, cutting his heel rather badly in the process.

Ruth goes on to explain how in the ensuing confusion she stepped into the pair of running shorts and Nikes she'd been using as a pillow, laced up her shoes, and took off. She wanted to get away from Bobby, who was looking at her "funny," and so she didn't bother to stretch, an omission which, combined with the heat and her sudden decision to stand, made her feel faint. As soon as she thought she was out of view of the inn she collapsed onto the grass verge and put her head between her knees. Church bells were tolling not too far away, peal upon peal upon peal in that tuneless descent called change ringing, their noise cruelly mimicking her blood's clamorous rush through her swooning brain. A black ant, laden with what looked like a big bread crumb, threaded its way through the dark forest of grass under the tent her bent head and knees made.

"I thought it was *his* fault," she says. "Bobby's. I thought everything was his fault, including the way those women were all over him like a batch of Florence Nightingales." At this point the logic of her testimony becomes a little muddled, since—while approving counsel's suggestion that Paula purposely blinded Naomi—she seems to have nothing but scorn for the idea that Bobby might have purposely cut his foot in order to provide himself with an excuse for subsequent lax behavior. (QC: No doubt we've misunderstood the connection you intended between "everything" and "fault." RF: I intended to explain how Bobby operates. He makes you dizzy. Well, not *you*, sir, per se.)

Mainly though, Ruth said, she wanted to be alone, running, no longer aware of each breath she took or each footfall, but like a young horse, full of high spirits and vitality, galloping down to the crossroads, down down down like those infernal bells and then, without so much as a single skipped beat, galloping up the steep hill past the gleaming red phone booth, alive and kicking, finally wrenched loose like a bright star from the gravitational stew of the group.

It was exactly three o'clock when she crested the last hill and arrived in Llangleisiad. She knew it was three because, having concluded in a frenzied din that resembled hundreds of pots and pans being hurled down hundreds of flights of stairs, the bells suddenly and with unwonted restraint tolled the hour. BONG (silence) BONG (silence) BONG. Three, a magic number, yet portending what? — likewise followed by silence, lingering and oddly openmouthed. The village would have been even emptier than when Coleman and Mr. Hsia ventured through it, since by now the silver-headed sheep they'd encountered hours earlier had made their way into the valley where Ruth could see them, a bunch of fluffy white dots milling around among the underbrush, not bleating for once but placid and dumb, the way sheep were supposed to be.

She stopped running and took several deep gulps of air. Across the valley the church spire arose, predictably phallic, from its tuft of trees. St. David's? Most Welsh churches seemed to be named for him, a man who subsisted on leeks and water and caused a hill to grow under his feet so he could address his disciples from a lofty position, more or less in the spirit of modern-day vegetarians. David the Water Drinker — though speaking of which, for Ruth had suddenly realized she was about to die of thirst, where the hell was it? At the inn the sound of running water was a constant backdrop, but ever since she left the brook behind at the crossroads, the sound had grown fainter and fainter, at some point vanishing altogether.

Indeed the village—organized around a single narrow street, dusty and gray and edged with tall tilty houses, likewise dusty and gray—gave the impression of having been left high and dry. Little stabs at decoration cropped up from time to time, a yellowing bay tree in a cracked iron kettle, a clump of Welsh poppies faded to transparency, a yew hedge painstakingly trimmed to resemble something utterly unrecognizable. At the far end of the street Ruth saw a sign hanging over the door of what she thought might be a public house, and as she walked up to get a better look, a weedy young man in a green T-shirt emerged, his hands in his pockets, whistling. THE DANCING FRY, said the sign, and there was a painting on it of an orange fish reared up on its tail in a black pan set over orange flames, its upper "torso" and "face" rendered in such a way as to seem almost human, though not entirely so, like those postcards where the picture changes when jiggled.

"Excuse me," Ruth said. The young man had been heading away from her toward the place where the street began once again to dip downhill and out of sight, but now he turned and stood stiffly as if to let her know he was in a hurry, though to go where or to do what was anyone's guess. He looked vaguely familiar. "I'm trying to find my husband," Ruth added, since it had occurred to her that the sudden materialization of a small brunette, scantily clad and dripping sweat, might have caused him alarm. "He and his friend came up here to fish?" Because the young man just stood there, she mimed fly casting, where-upon a sea of gibberish poured from his mouth and he struck out in a slightly different direction, slipping through a narrow gap between the two houses directly across from the pub, tak-ing short inflexible strides like he was on stilts.

Ruth didn't know if he meant for her to follow, or if he was trying to get away. In any case she decided to go after him down what turned out to be a paved alley, a foul-smelling place where she was again met by the noise of water—surpris-ingly loud—and which led to a linked row of shallow back-yards festooned with fishnets and wash lines draped with limp gray underwear. The whole area had been broken into a patch-work of untidy garden plots sprouting vegetables, mainly cab-bages, likewise limp and gray, and dropped off abruptly in a snarl of woodbine, beyond which she could just make out sun-light glinting off a dark sheet of water. There was no sign of the young man anywhere.

The bank was rocky, and laughably steep; Ruth was so busy watching her feet she didn't notice Coleman until she'd reached the very bottom. A sinister-looking pool, swarming with midges and clouded with tapioca-like larvae, stretched in front of her, at the far edge of which her husband stood, up to his thighs in water and facing Mr. Hsia.

Ruth could tell they were involved in an animated discus-sion, possibly even arguing. Mr. Hsia was making chopping motions with his hands, and Coleman was reaching back with his arm to rub the nape of his neck, up and down and with in-creasing vigor, a clear sign he wanted something and was afraid someone else was going to get it first. It couldn't be a fish, since neither man held what Ruth persisted in calling a fishing pole, though God knows she'd been corrected often enough.

She had just removed her shoes, having decided to wade out and join them, when Mr. Hsia suddenly twisted an invisible key in the pursed lock of his lips and threw it as hard as he could, up into the air and then out across the pool, where it twirled around and around, bright gold in the late afternoon sunlight, before landing with a splash. Sunlight, Ruth thought. The village had been so gray it seemed like the sun had only just come out, even though it had been shining all along. Coleman seemed confused; Mr. Hsia pointed. There on the rim of the bank above her, his face melodramatically lit by that same sun, posed the weedy young man.

Now for the first time she got a good enough look to realize where she'd seen him before. Of course. He was the boy in her dream, the one who'd been carrying a little pink whale with cartoon eyes.

Ruth knew something bad was about to happen, but by the time she'd screamed to warn him, it was too late. As she watched, helpless, the dream boy spread his wings and flew.

ME, MONKEY SAYS. The dream boy was me. She dreamed me up and now here I am, at your service.

I know he means it seriously, including the service part, which is his explanation for why he refuses to listen when I tell him to go away and stop bothering me. The same message I've been giving him ever since the day he forced his way inside and then wouldn't leave until I promised he could come back tomorrow and tomorrow, and the next day and the next, and so on and so forth until yesterday morning, when I went to the garden house looking for the good scissors and not only didn't find them but also found the room ransacked, bags of pigment strewn here and there and all the drawers of the little chest where my mother kept her brushes and jars of varnish and oil sticking out like tongues, most of them empty, and all but one of the panes that hadn't been broken earlier, broken, and Monkey standing there in the wreckage, a bolt of the expensive linen my mother liked to paint on tucked under one arm, smiling. Well? I prompted. Well, he replied, then bent to pick up a rock, which he threw at the last unbroken pane. There was a crash, a delicate shower of glass. Sparkling pieces of glass joined the dull ones that already made the floor treacherous to walk on, or treacherous if you were, as he was, barefoot.

Strag culture is a triumph of the virtual: the very legacy Uncle Coleman foresaw but couldn't forestall. The more material objects that fill the space around you, the less mobility you have, like a computer disk filled to bursting. Just one fact too many—a perfect pane of glass, for instance—and the entire system jams. Of course you'd want to get rid of things. Only then could you be free to fly through time and space and into a strange woman's house.

And it's true he's *gray* enough to be Ruth's boy, who also seems to have had his origin in grayness. Gray laundry, gray cabbages, gray houses—the world as we know it, our poor little world, though in those days there were only the faintest hints, like the barely visible bubble of paint on a car, the precursor of things to come, at first nothing more than a pockmark of rust and then a growing patch of it, a whole door turning insubstantial, lacy, its metal flaking away to leave a huge hole and, finally, no car at all, a complete absence of car, nothing.

When I ask Monkey what about Netta, he says—slyly, almost as if he's trying to test me or trick me—Netta's my little whale.

We're at the kitchen table, where Monkey's "helping" me sort through piles of paper and photographs, filling the room with a sweetly disgusting cloud of smoke. Just the two of us, because ever since that first so-called visit he hasn't brought along the baby, and all my attempts to find out where she is have been met with dull menacing stares.

Carole, Monkey's saying. Ruth. Patting the gray metal box that was her computer the way I remember Bobby patting the knee of whatever attractive woman happened to be sitting next to him, his manner offhand yet braced for action.

Meanwhile in a tall carton near the door crouches the rabbit Monkey says he's brought me as a gift, one of those enormous dun-colored hares you sometimes see at dawn, rigidly posed along a murky horizon, bigger than rabbits used to be or maybe they only look that way because there really isn't much to measure them against, a rabbit next to a bush naturally seeming larger than a rabbit next to an oak. The rabbit's nibbling something Monkey put in the carton with it, some leafy plant. Its flanks moving rapidly in and out, and its pupils unnaturally enlarged, huge and reflective and terrified.

Who are you? Monkey asks, poking my upper arm with his index fingernail, which for some reason he keeps uncut and pointy like a mandarin's.

I think he's goading me, so I don't answer.

Who are you? he asks again. Then he exhales, and for a moment—maybe because he's sitting there tailor-fashion in that long gray garment like a long gray worm of a boy—I can almost see the words forming in the smoke above his head.

Alice, I reply, and he bursts out laughing.

Of course his "sense of humor" is as hard to fathom as everything else. No, he doesn't get the allusion. It turns out his mother's name was Alice. You're not my mother, he reminds me, still convulsed. My mother was fat. She wore an apron. He puts on a pair of Mrs. Koop's bifocals and peers at me, fakely stern, over the rims. My mother knew how to cook.

All right, I say. Easy now. Easy. Just suppose you were that boy in the village. Then maybe you can explain to me why he —I'm sorry, you—jumped?

Monkey picks up Ruth's computer. Eeeze-y now, he says, patting it tenderly. It wasn't dangerous; the pool was very deep. All the kids used to dive there. There were crayfish at the bottom. He closes his eyes and licks his lips. Just a bite per tail. It took lots to make a meal. But watch out! Watch out!— and suddenly his eyes are open and he's snapping his hands at me like claws. Watch out for the pincers, Soooze-un!

The next thing I know he's on his feet and walking around the table, faster and faster, on the verge of being churned into butter the way the tigers were in the book the ever alert Mrs. Koop put down our garbage disposal because she claimed it was filled with racist nonsense, even though it had been a birthday present to me from Uncle Tony.

Ruth says it was like the young man disappeared, I say.

Well sure, Monkey replies, yanking out drawers and slamming them shut. It was like that. Eeeze-y now. Eeeze-y. At last he comes to a halt, having discovered the expensive Swiss carving knife Bobby used to make a big deal out of sharpening, prior to mutilating the Sunday roast.

In the bleary nonexistent light of the kitchen the knife somehow manages to have a shine to it, not unlike the nonexistent key Ruth claimed to have seen twirling through the air above the pool, or the little red bug I saw what seems like years ago now, in the meadow. Shhh, Monkey says. He kneels on the floor and tips the carton on its side, coaxing the rabbit, calling to it—coney! coney! coney!—and extending a hand, palm up.

At first the creature hangs back, its moist nose twitching, its gray ears folded flat against the side of its beautiful sleek head. Coney! coney! coney! Monkey repeats, softly, sweetly. He has a piece of some kind of root, sort of like a carrot only redder. Little by little the rabbit creeps from the carton. Its ears lift; it takes a few small hops. And then, just as it's getting used to the idea of no longer being alone in a box but inside a kitchen with two full-grown human beings, Monkey's arm shoots out, quicker than quick, and he grabs it by the hindquarters. Eeeze-y now, he says, holding it aloft. In one precise, forceful motion, he cuts its throat.

He lays the bleeding rabbit on the cracked marble counter-top where once upon a time Mrs. Koop rolled out her famous pie dough, and makes a long cut in the soft white fur of its underside, from the throat to the genitals. Then he peels back the fur, almost like he's taking a coat off a doll. Dressing it, he explains, without a clue about how ridiculous that sounds.

The idea, he says, is that he'll show me how to cook the rabbit and then we'll eat it. The idea is that I won't be so stringy if I eat some meat. Stringy—his word. Hard times are upon us; I need to put a little meat on my bones. The older people are, the more meat they need, otherwise a strong wind can break them in two. Not a lot of meat for me, but more than what I've got. The skin he'll save to make glue. Rabbit-skin glue—the best. Don't just sit there, he orders. Get me a basin.

No, I say.

The rabbit was blind, Susan. Monkey puts out his hand and wiggles the finger. Come on come on come on, he orders. Basin. It couldn't have survived. I did it a favor.

Never let a bully see you're afraid, Bobby used to advise, it'll only make him bully you more.

I shake my head and tell Monkey he seems pretty stringy himself, whereupon he unfastens the complicated system of straps and loops that hold the top of his garment together and shows me his chest which, though narrow, also happens to be surprisingly muscular. Because he hunts, he tells me. Not an ounce of fat. Like cats, he adds; have I ever seen a fat cat?

Yes, I say. When I was a girl, I had a cat named Sammy and he was obese.

Then he couldn't have hunted, Monkey points out. Besides, he says, you *are* a girl. Correcting me, good-natured but firm —for a person who talks like he's putting quotes around almost all his words, Monkey's extremely literal. Three hunters, he says. One, two, three. Airily he waves his long pointy nail above the paper piles, and when I warn him to be careful, since, after all, hasn't he just finished murdering a rabbit, he acts like he hasn't heard me. One, he says, Carole. Two, Coleman.

Oh, come on, I say. My mother wasn't muscular. Neither was Coleman. Also, what about three? Aren't you forgetting Bobby?

For a moment he regards me wildly, the way the coypup did when I found it trapped in the pantry—I half expect him to piss all over the floor. He tells me I'm the person forgetting things, like for instance that phone booth. *You* be careful, Sooze-un, he says. You should get out more. You don't know anything.

He goes on to explain that no one noticed him leave the pool because he knew if he swam under water long enough he'd come out a mile or so downstream in a little glade just above the phone booth. The phone was ringing exactly like it had that time when Ruth went jogging by it. He was all alone and the phone kept on ringing and when he couldn't stand it a minute more he picked it up, and a man said Hull-o? Hull-o?

and guess what? It was Bobby. Naturally Bobby didn't know it was Monkey, since Monkey kept his mouth shut and dwelt in the future, but he knew it was Bobby, because of the American accent. Bobby said, don't think I'm not on to you, sweetheart. He was trying to sound tough, but he sounded miserable. Okay, Bobby said, two can play this game. He hung up and a second later the phone rang again.

Monkey begins rifling through the piles of paper on the table, impatient, making a big mess. You think you're like Carole, he says, but you're not. You're more like him. You even look like him, he says, and produces the photo taken at Tintern Abbey, Abyssinian King Bobby seated on the grass in the lengthening shadows, staring into space, emitting his usual aura of loosely banked sexual energy. A profile shot, showing the long straight nose with its commalike nostril, the heavy-lidded hazel eyes, the slightly parted lips.

When you think you're alone, Monkey persists, you look like him.

There's a blotchy full-length mirror on the second-floor landing, and while I've resisted seeing myself in the shocked woman I come face to face with there almost every day (or view her in profile, for that matter), over time I've developed a pretty good idea of what I look like, and it isn't my father. Not that we don't have other less tangible things in common. When you choose to sequester yourself like royalty, defining the mission and sending others forth to carry it out, your own power flow gets obstructed. You sit there waiting, twiddling your thumbs. You're the last person to touch the booty, hold the grail, hear the answer. Maybe it shows up in your face, a vaguely congested quality, all that power with nowhere to go swarming just under the surface—maybe that's what Monkey has in mind.

But how did he know about the phone call? He couldn't have known, since I only just read that part of the transcript the night before (QC: And your purpose in placing the call, Mr. Rose? RR: My purpose? Surveillance. No, strike that. I wanted Ruth to guess I was spying on them, and then, being Ruth, to rat on me)—unless of course Monkey has mythic attributes like a Celtic hero, permitting him to hold his breath underwater for nine days and nine nights, and granting him an unusual ability to show up where least expected.

What do you mean when I 'think' I'm alone, I ask, and he once again bursts out laughing.

You don't want to know, he replies, meanwhile restoring order to the piles, and from time to time glancing over his shoulder and out the window, the tip of his tongue poking from the corner of his mouth exactly like my mother's.

Shady breezes, the little gooseberry bushes waving their hands from the other side of the screen door. Shady floor of the garden house, and a brand-new box of markers, twenty-five colors in all including gold and silver, perfect for the Four Horsemen of the Apocalypse. The hippie gardener starting the lawn tractor, and Minnie beginning to bark, both of them faintly at first and then louder and louder, tractor and dog, approaching the studio. A gold cape for you, Mr. Horseman! Chemical smell of marker ink mixing with the shady smell of ground pigment, and the holiday smell of cloves. Ruth's small head bent over the knee of the leg she's extending straight onto the birdbath, stretching, getting ready to run. The tip of my mother's tongue, moistly pink, flickering. *Very nice work, Susan!*

Meanwhile those of us having crossed the much vaunted bridge into the twenty-first century find our day folding itself up, layer on layer, well past the six folds I remember Uncle Coleman explaining is the limit for a piece of paper, or for anything you might try folding, into a dense thick clump of dusk.

A second later the phone starts to ring, Monkey repeats, like we've never left the subject. This time he picks it up right away. Bobby again. Monkey screws his eyes shut in a good imitation of a person actually trying to retrieve a memory. Bobby wants to know if my refrigerator's running, he says.

A joke, I explain. You're supposed to say 'yes,' and the other person says 'go catch it.'

But it wasn't a joke, Monkey says. He seems troubled, vigilant, his eyeballs darting from side to side under the lids, scanning an invisible horizon for signs of movement. It wasn't funny, he says. Bobby meant I should watch out. He meant it was going to get me.

(13 June) darling—thank u! thank u! meds arrived today & so a good night for once tho moon was full & RIGHT THERE doing its best to drive me mad. bobby attentive & o so contrite. said he wanted to turn over new leaf. who needs other people as long as we have each other? life is short etc etc. not worthy (demonstrating) to lick sole of my foot & speaking of which could i have a look at his which was throbbing.

i said i love u too—meaning it but also fishing i admit since bobby usually turns over new leaves when feeling shafted & ONLY spouts platitudes when building case against shafter, turning position of weakness to his advantage (& also turning himself on in process).

afterwards we sat propped on pillows & i ate bath buns stolen from kitchen while pointedly overlooking bobby as he smoked, exhaling through open window so we wouldn't get caught. v. chummy, pillow talk. night sky magnesia bottle blue, stars (glasses-less) like dandelion fluff. bobby expansive, in alyosha-mode. welsh people salt of the earth, couldn't find better. travel broadens horizons, lends perspective, new lands new seas & so forth & so on. glad we came. i expressed relief, cautious, sizing things up. finally said (dangling least menacing hook possible & clearly miscalculating) i'd been afraid he'd been troubled by something—tho maybe just that foot.

TROUBLED? his mood not so much affronted as more

effusively large-hearted, munificent, than ever. why always look for worms? wasn't it enough roses were beautiful? worm hunts: my problem, in a nutshell.

it's oddly relaxing to be lied to by someone who doesn't know he's lying. maybe key to bobby's success. kisses & fresh air mixed with cigarette smoke, like madeleine releasing scenes of shipboard romance. we never knew what hit us — rolling around on deck between legs of striped steamer chairs, huge swells slapping prow & ship going up & down like our breathing on biggest scale possible, kissing, kissing — still a great kisser, bobby, a plus side u might say of arrested development, tho unlike most teenage boys he knows secret's not tongue but lips pressed down with enough force to convey teeth, bone . . .

SATURDAY MORNING everyone was up bright and early, having turned in the night before after a light supper of field greens and the brook trout supposedly caught by Coleman and Mr. Hsia, but which Ruth says they'd no doubt paid some local kid for "through the nose." She describes the general mood as subdued, Brenda in particular appearing listless, defeated, padding off in her aqua flip-flops, towel turban and soiled terrycloth robe to nurse her cup of coffee alone on the porch. Had she lost the latest skirmish in one of her many mysterious ongoing power struggles, Ruth wonders, or was she still feeling the effects of the whiskey? Of course with hindsight it's easy to see that Brenda Fluellen's reasons for behaving the way she did may have been much less complex than Ruth's analysis suggests. Probably she was merely experiencing morning sickness, or sick of sharing her house with nine strangers, many of them neurotic. Only David, busily overseeing the packing of the Rover, remained cheerful, buoyant even —but what else was new?

In any event, despite predictions to the contrary, the weather seemed to be holding: when the sun rose it looked unusually large and close, not celestial but like something recently launched from the woods across the road, a hot air balloon maybe, fully inflated and capable of casting its own giant shadow. They'd be traveling in caravan, David explained: he'd be driving the Rover; Brenda, the Minx, which though small could easily accommodate two other passengers, three, if thin. Ruth and Naomi? Coleman's legs were too long. Maybe Mr. Hsia? The trip would take at least five hours, not counting stops along the way; there was no reason they all had to cram themselves—forget their packs and provisions—in a single vehicle.

Ruth says she met this news with about as much enthusiasm as if David had told her she was going to be tied to the rear bumper by the ankles and dragged. Five hours in a Hillman Minx with Brenda Fluellen? No fair, she said, and when David looked taken aback she had to come up with some lame story about small cars making her nervous, to which Coleman, ever helpful, put in that that was news to him, especially given her "lifelong dream" of owning an MGB.

"It also isn't fair to segregate according to body type," advised Paula.

From her elevated position on the porch Brenda sat taking this in, grimly toweling dry her long wet hair and wagging one foot so the flip-flop made a rubbery slapping noise against it. "Do you have a better suggestion?" she said with a sigh.

Paula replied that she would've been happy to volunteer, except she'd already promised David she'd ride in the way-back with Major. How about the Kopeckys? But Magtil, who hadn't forgotten Brenda's outburst at the soup table, confessed that she got carsick in small cars.

Bobby, then? Ruth proposed. She admits that her motives were "none too pure," like the time she opened the jar of yellow jackets in Mrs. Hecht's second-grade classroom, hoping to get a rise out of the despised new girl at the exact moment when she stood to lead them in the Pledge of Allegiance, though as it turned out the plan backfired, since even then Carole had a way with bees, and she, Ruthie, ended up in the emergency room in anaphylactic shock.

"I don't believe this," Bobby said. He was leaning against the Rover's grille with his arm around Carole, his hazel eyes —saintly Alyosha eyes—radiant with hurt. "We sound like a bunch of second-graders," he added, causing Ruth briefly to entertain the terrible possibility that he'd figured out how to read her mind. Aluminum foil, she thought. I should wrap my head in aluminum foil. Was it because some new bond now existed between them, post-kiss? Was it because she was wearing black and yellow stripes?—but that didn't make any sense at all.

"Children can be spanked," Brenda said. She arose from her chair, announced that she was going inside to change, and asked that they give her a shout when things were settled.

"You should talk," Coleman said to Bobby. "Mr. Refrigerator."

"I'll ignore that," he replied.

Ruth could see him working his hand through the narrow gap between Carole's torso and her upper arm, inching the tips of his fingers into position to "cop a feel" though you'd never have known from her expression, her whole face, especially the eyes, remaining cool and opaque like an Elgin Marble's. Meanwhile David had finished loading the Rover, Paula was whistling for Major, and Mr. Hsia was consulting his mint green Swatch. If they didn't get going soon, he pointed out, they'd be right back where they were yesterday. As it was, they probably weren't going to have time to stop in Swansea for lunch.

The rear hatch of the Rover banged shut as the door to the terrace banged open, and out came Brenda, smiling widely. "Bugger Swansea," she said, her reappearance a little shocking not just because it was so sudden, but because she looked so completely transformed. Clad like a schoolgirl in a pair of very short cutoffs and what appeared to be a white cotton gym blouse, her still damp hair in a long French braid, she sailed into their midst, a stack of ordnance survey maps cradled to her chest. The food at the Queen was overpriced, she reassured Mr. Hsia. They'd be better off saving their appetites for Fairy Ring. She handed Ruth the maps and opened the passenger door of the Minx, giving a small ironic bow. Enough of this dicking around. Ruth could navigate, and Bobby and Carole—who if they'd had any objections at least had kept them to themselves—could neck in the back seat. It was a perfect day, and it would be a shame to waste it in a car.

"Now's your chance," Ruth whispered to Bobby as he climbed in behind her.

৲

The road from the Blackbrook to Chepstow was fairly narrow and followed the course of the Wye, curving when the river did through a green and claustrophobic landscape, everything moss-covered or ivy-choked, cliffs and tree trunks and cottages and walls, Wordsworth's "little lines of sportive wood run wild: these pastoral farms, green to the very door," and everywhere thick forests of ferns taller than people and thickly wooded hills, the sky visible in jigsaw-shaped pieces like it had already broken and was falling, dropping blue pieces of itself onto the unsteady golden surface of the river.

They passed Cuckoo Wood, the Devil's Pulpit, Tintern Parva. "I've been there," Bobby said, pointing at the ruined abbey, so small and remote on the far shore of the river, like a birdcage or a trap. "A million years ago," Carole answered with a sigh, and Bobby, lost in thought, echoed, "A million years." The Minx led the way, Brenda taking the curves quickly but definitely not recklessly. According to Ruth she was a better driver than her husband, who had a tendency to fly up on the Minx's tail, then veer across the center line and back again like he'd been planning to pass but changed his mind.

When Brenda pulled over at Chepstow so they could get a look at the castle, Ruth stepped out to stretch her legs and Bobby followed. The castle's limestone battlements appeared indistinguishable from the limestone cliffs they'd been built on, as if the whole thing had been heaved up that way from some place deep in the earth, crenelated and pierced with loopholes and crawling with people in hiking boots. "As far as Brenda goes," Bobby said. "Let's just say I could. Seduce her, that is. What's in it for me?"

Ruth stood on the grass verge, the mild air and the sound of the passing traffic filling her with deep happiness, like a carousel ride she could get on whenever she wanted. "My silence," she said, and Bobby shook his head.

"Carole doesn't care what I do."

"Well then, my allegiance."

"Do I look like a flag?"

They climbed back in the car, Bobby sitting closer to Carole than before, Ruth couldn't help noticing. "Better now?" Carole said, as Brenda suddenly accelerated, narrowly missing a pair of scrawny young people whose immense backpacks towered over their ponytailed heads. Dyke walkers, she explained. This was because Offa's Dyke began here, the ancient barrier between Wales and England. It used to be that a Welsh-man caught with a weapon on the British side of the dyke would have his right hand cut off.

"Given the subject," Ruth wrote, "I was keeping an eye on Brenda for any sign of a mood swing, but nope. In fact I'd have to say her mood was a little unnatural. In our car, at least, everyone seemed to be in an unnaturally good mood." *Not* due to mind-altering substances, as counsel would later try to suggest, but maybe because it was a nice day, they were headed somewhere interesting, and they'd all finally gotten a good night's sleep.

They picked up the M4 just west of Chepstow and immediately the landscape changed, spreading out around them on all sides like a fan suddenly shaken open, lifting on the right in a vast sweep of empty-looking sunlit hills, dropping on the left toward the sunlit mudflats of the Severn estuary and the bay beyond, a wide slow body of water likewise fanning out as if to suggest even greater expanses of water to come, the Bristol Channel, the green and churning sea, an endlessly evolving sense of destination.

The trip was uneventful, conversation lively if not exactly amiable. Carole read Bobby a letter from Aunt Doe. Apparently I'd overheard Uncle Tony say that he'd caught my mumps, which I took to mean I no longer had them, though I was still sick as a dog. Bobby told Carole about a recent phone conversation with Mrs. Koop. She'd caught the hippie gardener and Tony "going at it" in Carole's studio. Mumps all around, observed Brenda. Didn't they cause sterility in adult males?

Increased traffic, families on holiday, westbound lorries crazily switching lanes. Signs for Newport, Caerleon. The yellow sun bore down from behind like a hot flat hand pushing them forward—at first when Ruth twisted in her seat to address Bobby and Carole she couldn't see a thing. Some people, she informed them, claimed Caerleon was Camelot. It was one of the places Giraldus visited on his pilgrimage.

Then (still in yellow-jacket mode) she recounted a story about a young man who lived in Caerleon in the olden days, "a million years ago," back when the sea came all the way up to the city walls. One Palm Sunday, while he was embracing the pretty girl he'd always loved, he discovered that she'd suddenly turned into a hairy and hideous creature, the sight of which made him lose his mind. He didn't get it back for a long time, and when he did, he found that his years of communing with unclean spirits had turned him into a prophet. The spirits appeared to him with horns suspended from their necks, and on foot like hunters, though not of animals but of souls. Their abilities, she said, seemed aroused by places and people, making her wonder whether they'd have been able to tell the young man "about all of us."

So? Bobby said. He sounded defensive, just as Ruth knew he would. Only set his mind in motion and there it would be, the scene on the kissing rock played out over and over, an infinite ringing of infinite changes.

Let him sweat a little, she thought, it'll serve him right. Let him see he can't toy with a girl and drop her like a dog drops a bone once the marrow's gone—or *some* metaphor to that general effect. Besides, who knew how Carole would react? Don't look at me like that, Ruth added, saying that she was merely wondering whether the spirits could have predicted a dark blue Minx driving past Caerleon on a sunny summer day.

But why would anyone *want* to see the future? Carole interrupted. You'd either see something bad, which would make you give up, or something good, which would take away all the suspense. Had Ruth actually forgotten that visit to Mrs. Flower when they were girls?

A swarm of feathers hit the windshield—Brenda cursed and pulled out around a truck filled to the brim with chickens. Unless the prediction lay so far ahead, Brenda suggested, that it couldn't be taken personally; good news about the human race as a whole, something like that. Even worse, Carole replied. Minx, Bobby said. Minx. How would the dude have known what he was seeing, let alone its name?

By now Ruth was again facing forward, watching the Minx's shadow precede it like a boxy little augury with mirrors for ears. The young man's specialty, she said, was knowing when someone was telling a lie because there would be a tiny unclean spirit jumping for joy on the liar's tongue. She could feel Bobby's eyes drilling into her scalp, like having eyes in the back of her head, only they weren't hers. And if the young man were reading a book falsely written, she continued—at which point she could feel Carole's eyes join Bobby's—another tiny unclean spirit would start jumping on the page.

"Oh come on," Carole snapped. "I never said falsely. If you didn't want to hear what I thought, you shouldn't have asked. Besides, I was right, and you know it. There were no unclean spirits involved."

Bobby said nothing, but Ruth could hear him shift position, recrossing his legs, then jabbing his uninjured foot, hard, into the back of her seat.

She shut her eyes against the sun, its dazzling brightness,

only instead of shutting it out they shut it in. Hotter and hotter, the sun overhead and the car like a pot coming to a boil, and she and Carole and Brenda like eggs dropped in to poach, each in her hot funnel of water, each taking shape around the defining yolk, that stupid weakness they had in common as women, while the whites spun their confining web, Ruth's a hideous and pointless swirl of threads and strings, swirling, drifting, dizzying, dizzying . . .

Another sunny summer day and there she was, standing with Carole Ridingham on the threshold of the yellow house trailer next to the gravel pit where the fortuneteller lived — the famous Mrs. Flower, who'd turned out to be a squat puffy creature like one of the huge translucent spiders dangling from her roof. Not exactly what Ruth had expected, Mrs. Flower was wearing a pink jumpsuit and white bunny-shaped bedroom slippers, and was reclining on a chintz-covered sofa, sipping beer from a can and surrounded on all sides by her salt and pepper shaker collection.

Oooh! Oooh! Oooh! Mrs. Flower squealed as the girls came through the door, her voice high-pitched like the voice a spider would have if it could talk. Guests, darling! She rang a small silver bell previously hidden on a nearby table in a thicket of shakers — among the pairs of dice and dogs with lifted legs and shiny red fire hydrants and pouncing kittens and balls of yarn and mice. Some nice cold lemonade, Mrs. Flower squealed, also some, some — she rang the bell again, frantic — some toast! Cinnamon toast! Then suddenly her mouth widened, becoming a rectangular hatchway out of which a new voice slunk, a man's voice, thick and deep. Go away, little girls, the new voice said. You aren't welcome here. On the double. March.

Carole nudged Ruth, the companionable elbow in the ribs reserved for best friends only, which Carole definitely was not. In fact, Ruth reflected, it'd been Carole who got them into that mess in the first place, accepting Tom Savage's dare to ask Mrs. Flower if he'd ever give a shit about two fucking losers who couldn't stop kicking his fucking jacket from one side of the schoolyard to the other. Naturally Ruth had no choice but to go as well; she couldn't let Carole hog all the glory. Don't worry, Ruth said, consulting the Patek Philippe wristwatch she'd only recently filched from Mrs. Ridingham's purse. We're on our way. But you just got here, said the spider. Nice watch, said the man.

Mrs. Flower repositioned herself on the sofa, making room. Come closer, girly-girl, she wheedled, spider-voice, patting the cushion and giving Carole an encouraging nod. Yes, you — don't be shy. I won't bite. Tenderly she took Carole's hand and began to read her palm: a journey over water, a handsome dark stranger, a fruitful marriage, fame and fortune — the usual flattering nonsense, marred only by some unwillingness to elaborate on a mysterious crisis "midway along life's path" which would come to a favorable, if startling, conclusion. Such a good little girl! the spider crooned. She caressed Carole's cheek, lingeringly, almost sadly — and then it was Ruth's turn.

Of course since she'd expected more of the same, it came as a bit of a shock when the man-voice took over, judging her mound of Apollo overlarge, meaning her love of beauty might deteriorate into a craving for luxury, her noble dreams into rank ambition. She'd have two marriages, the first for love, the second, money. Also two children, though the lines were faint — miscarriages maybe, or abortions. Could it be she was an artist of some kind? Carole let out a snort and Mrs. Flower bent closer, showing the bald spot on top of her head. She picked up a rusty church key and began to drag its sharp tip across Ruth's palm. A long heart line and an equally long head line, both disrupted, breaking from their banks in midlife like brooks in spring, petering out here and here and *here* . . .

Ouch! Ruth yelped, you're hurting me.

By this time it was getting dark, the sun having plunged into a knot of clouds above the gravel pit, turning the inside of the trailer a watery shade of gray. That was what happened to bad little girls, Mrs. Flower said, the spider-voice back again and—if such a thing were possible—higher than before, rising higher and higher and higher like the sound a balloon makes when you rub it, just before it pops. Bad little girls got hurt. And Ruth was a *very* bad little girl indeed, not to mention —here Mrs. Flower began energetically working at Ruth's thumbnail with the church key—the disgusting condition of her nails.

Ruth, Carole said. Ruthie! Let's go.

But I couldn't move, Ruth remembered, couldn't then, can't now, the effort of will required to deliver myself completely into the hands of another person always leaving me will-less, impassive, propelled like a sleepwalker (or a passenger in a car) out the door and away, uphill and down, faster and faster, no heart, no head—and then all of a sudden the rain began to fall. Big drops at first, widely spaced, making tiny craters in the road's dusty surface, tiny eruptions of a fine and impervious substance like face powder. Plop. Plop-plop. Plit-plit-plit. Plitter-plitplitplitplit. Rain falling onto the leaves of the lupine, depositing in each open palm a clear bead of water.

Lupine and wild raspberry, small green palms and purple thorny shoots, everything tossing to and fro, up and down, as the rain fell harder and harder, releasing the peppery smell of the flowers, the lemony smell of the berries, even though they weren't even out yet. Well, I'm going home, Carole announced, blinking. I'm soaked. A rust-colored van approached, its single wiper blade taking slow ineffectual swipes at the rain-sheeted windshield; the minute it came level with the girls the driver downshifted, the window rolled down and out popped Mrs. Flower's face under a boatlike hat of sodden newspaper. Need a lift? she sang, but before they could answer she'd shot forth in a spray of chunky mud. A drenched bee landed on Ruth's shoulder and Carole, solicitous, brushed it away. Such nice clean nails, so neatly trimmed, the cuticles unchewed! Envy, the worst deadly sin, you couldn't even enjoy it, like sloth or lust . . .

"Hey," said Bobby. "Rise and shine." He was leaning over the headrest, giving Ruth's shoulder a little shake. "I didn't know you snored," he added, and Carole laughed, saying, "Ask Coleman. Ruth's always been a champion snorer."

They were wending their way slowly up a long steep drive toward a large stone manor house more or less hidden in a clump of trees. On either side spread fields of purplish gorse and pinkish purple thyme, dotted with wild ponies and paint-branded sheep; behind them swelled the sea. Just as in Llangleisiad, the sun came as a surprise to Ruth, though on this occasion it had lost some of its charge, a thin pale gauze-wrapped disk of a sun hanging low on the western horizon, chalky-looking and flat and basically dull, kind of like a Necco wafer.

"I'd rather not," Bobby said. "Ask Coleman, that is. I'd rather ask Ruth."

"Sure," Ruth said. "I don't know. What difference does it make?"

"A lot. Depending on your answer."

Brenda let out a sigh. "Will you look at that," she said, pointing off to the right where Magtil stood revolving slowly in the center of an uneasy-looking circle of ponies as if she were trying to interest them in a game of blindman's bluff. "What's *she* doing here?"

"They passed us at Swansea," Carole said. "When we stopped for gas."

"But I'm not done with Coleman yet," Bobby persisted. "I mean, wouldn't you say he's been under a lot of stress lately? Forget snoring. I mean, do you think of him as strong? Trustworthy?"

"I would say," said Carole, "Coleman's human. Everyone makes mistakes, right, Ruth? You should've given it back, you know. A Patek Philippe, worth a small fortune—lucky for you it was insured."

FAIRY RING was legendary. Built atop Gower's high central spine, the main house dated back to 1785; in keeping with the first Evan Griffith's plan it represented a pure example of neo-Gothic style, its stone facade interrupted by a series of ornate lancet windows, pier buttresses, crocketed doorways, and framed at each end by an imposing pinnacled tower. This should have been more than enough, but restraint was never a Griffith family trait, subsequent generations having felt compelled to add a Florentine campanile, a Burmese pagoda, and a Romanesque chapel, as well as the copper-domed orangerie, where the current Evan Griffith served his famous dinners.

Yet Fairy Ring's notoriety doesn't seem to have been due so much to its architecture and cuisine as to a mysterious event in the youth of the second Evan Griffith, who, so the story goes, set out with a friend for a day of shooting from which the friend returned alone. A common motif in Welsh tales (e.g., Manawydan returning from the caer without Pryderi), it often includes the friend's arrest and imprisonment for murder—precisely what happened in the case of David Rhys, the unfortunate friend, who would have been hanged if it hadn't been for the Griffith family nurse. Obviously her young master had been kidnaped by the fairies, she said. Everyone knew they had a ring somewhere in that part of the *rhos*, or moorland, where the two friends had been hunting. David would have to return to the ring exactly a year after Evan's disappearance. He wouldn't be able to see the fairies, but if he stood on the ring's edge, being extremely careful not to let even so much as the tip of his big toe creep inside it, and if he held out a staff of rowanwood or iron, as Evan came round in the dance he'd be able to grab hold of the staff and the spell would be broken. Was David by chance a Methodist? Fairies hated Methodists even more than they hated rowan trees.

David followed the nurse's instructions and it went as predicted. Of course Evan had no idea that any time at all had elapsed since he entered the ring. He'd been weakened by his encounter with the fairies—mortal men always were— and though he didn't flake away into dust the minute he tried to eat something, he seemed to languish in other more subtle ways, his formerly ruddy complexion growing pastier with each passing day, his delight in hunting and riding and the company of his friends replaced with a tendency to wander the *rhos* on foot and alone, straying ever farther from the house and sometimes not returning until dawn, feverish and bramble-scratched. Two years to the day after his original disappearance, Evan Griffith vanished for good. Nine months later the nurse found an infant boy in a nest of white feathers on the scullery doorstep, "the spit and image" of her young master at that age, except for the eyes, which were of unearthly size and the palest blue, "the color of whey, with pupils as big and black and shiny as salamander eggs."

Raised by his grandparents, this infant, Evan Griffith III, grew into an unusually beautiful man with a taste for music and poetry. He gave the house its name and its reputation as a gathering place for intellectuals and artists. Over the years Adelina Patti, Matthew Arnold, Lewis Carroll, Napoleon III, Queen Elizabeth of Austria, Edward Burne-Jones, the Countess Ida Hahn-Hahn, Lord Byron, and even Dylan Thomas (who claimed to have written "Altarwise by Owl-Light" after a supernatural midnight encounter) would come to drink from the Griffiths' renowned cellars and break bread "wondrously light yet uncannily filling" at their damask-naped tables. No less a luminary than J.M.W. Turner himself painted Evan Griffith III's portrait, which at the time of the walking tour was hanging in the great hall, among the portraits of all the other Evan Griffiths. My mother claimed you had only to take one look at their faces to believe the stories: fairy blood ran in those veins, increasingly dilute yet potent nonetheless, right down to the present Evan Griffith, a spindling rush of a man with long white hair and undeniably weird blue eyes, and with a length of faded gold brocade draped across his shoulders like a shawl.

It was he who greeted them at the door. "*Nos da,*" he said, "good evening," for by now the huge oaks surrounding the house were unrolling their shadows darkly back toward the east, all the way to where a violet-gray horizon intersected with a violet-gray sky, behind which the Blackbrook waited, out of sight and empty, under a pale thumbprint of a moon. "The others beat you by ten minutes," Evan Griffith added, taking Bobby's hand and holding it a little longer, clearly, than Bobby thought necessary. "I didn't know it was a race," Brenda replied.

Nightjars were swooping from their roosts on the towers,

in pursuit of the moths whose paper-thin white bodies littered the darkening sky, just as the grass at everyone's feet was littered with paper-thin white petals, drifting in a sudden humid breeze. The whitethorn had just finished blooming— "luckily," according to their host, since it was an ill-omened tree, its first flowers heralding that unluckiest month in the ancient calendar, which, incidentally, ended on June fifteenth. Some men associated the smell of the whitethorn with the smell of female arousal, he added with a shudder. "Is today the fifteenth?" my mother asked, and Bobby told her, nope, tomorrow, but at least now he knew why the place smelled like a brothel.

The wind picked up; Brenda detached herself from the group to sit on a nearby stone bench with lions' heads for arms and paws for feet, her elbows propped behind her, her legs stuck out in front of her like two-by-fours. "Go on without me," she said, staring down the long driveway to a place miles away where the sea was barely visible, a thinly dancing bracelet sporadically lit by flashes of heat lightning. "I'm not ready to come in yet."

"Are you all right?" my mother asked, and cast what Ruth thought of as her "gimlet look" at the back of Brenda's head.

"Please," Brenda said. "Just leave me be."

Nothing would keep still: nightjars and moths and petals and wind and their host's spiderwebs of hair. Nor was it any better once they finally got inside, the entry hall shot through with endlessly shifting panels of color, depending on where a person stood in relationship to the four stained-glass windows, its air swarming with hundreds of enticing yet disturbing strands of aroma, all of them—colors and aromas alike—

crisscrossing one another, tangling together, now and then tying themselves in a pungent murky knot. Ruth was still feeling unhinged from the ride, and Coleman didn't improve matters any by darting from behind the huge marble pillar she'd chosen to steady herself against and whispering *Boo!* (or maybe Roo), as if his usual stickish self had been replaced by something more in keeping with the setting, something lissome and manic and not entirely human, an offshoot of the marble vine carved around the pillar maybe, or the marble snake coiled beneath it, infused with vitality and menace.

Naturally he apologized, but his apology struck Ruth as perfunctory—indeed he seemed pleased to have startled her. He told her they'd been put in the east tower, in the Ivy Room, right below Carole and Bobby, who were in—get this —the belfry. Magtil had gone out looking for fairy rings; Tadeusz and David were unpacking the Rover. Attila the Herne and Naomi, having renewed their vows of friendship somewhere between Cardiff and Swansea, were taking Major for a walk before dinner, which would be in an hour. The house rules were simple: you could go anywhere you wanted, indoors or out, except the kitchen, which was strictly off limits. As for himself, he was supposed to be meeting Hsia in the pagoda, and was already five minutes late . . .

"I could feel a brain tumor coming on," Ruth confided to her computer. "A big one. All I wanted to do was find my bed and lie down, preferably alone, but the way between me and it was an infuriating labyrinth of stairs and hallways and paintings in gilt frames and more hallways and more stairs and large porcelain vases and dark red rooms and pale blue rooms and more and more stairs etc etc etc. I guess I got lost because at some point a very pale woman in a long gray dress popped up out of nowhere the way people seem to do in this place and, without saying a word, led me up more increasingly steep flights of stairs, and down more increasingly narrow hallways, and finally up one last insanely narrow and steep circular staircase apparently built into the wall of the tower, to deposit me at the door to my room, which is almost completely round and circled with tall thin windows. Out front I could see Magtil standing where we'd left her, still surrounded by ponies; out back I could see Tadeusz and David and the Rover, surrounded by luggage and periodically obscured by huge clouds of steam billowing from the kitchen exhaust fan.

"Of course if this were a fairy tale that's where I'd be, right there in the kitchen, doomed by my disobedience to complete some impossible task such as restoring Coleman to his normal self. But this isn't a fairy tale, and so here I sit, propped against my pillows under an oppressive ceiling fixture, a sort of ivy-twined wheel of antlers sprouting lightbulbs, trying to put my brain to work despite there being less than an hour till dinner. Like, why Coleman's sudden infatuation with Mr. Hsia? He's no Bobby, but even so he usually prefers the company of women, the kind who think they can 'bring him out of himself,' as if his rigidity is actually a plus, like an attractive suit of armor. Carole for instance. Normally he'd be all over her. Besides, I'm the one who makes friends in this couple—not to mention Coleman's fear of anyone who isn't a WASP, even though he'd be the last to admit it. No, this has to do with something else, possibly going back to that recent business at the fishing hole, or probably even further back to that famous day when dear old Mr. Snow took Coleman out on Egg Harbor Bay in their dear old cabin-cruiser and he caught his first fish, which, even though it was a disgusting bottom-feeding blowfish and he had to let it go, he will never forget as long as he lives, never forget the sheer thrill of dangling a tiny little hook baited with a tiny little minnow into a gigantic body of water and actually catching *anything* and then reeling it up out of its alien bottom-feeding world and into the polished brass and mahogany world of the boat and good old Mr. Snow looking it in its flat dull little eye and drawling at me that way the whole WASP lot of them do, so tell me my dear where are your people from . . ."

What happened next seemed so much in keeping with the manic temper of the place that it took Ruth several minutes to react. She'd been wildly typing, completely filling her sea blue screen with a white block of words exactly like the white scrim of wake she imagined filling the bay behind the boat, when suddenly the wake began receding and her words began to disappear, a line at a time, beginning at the bottom of the screen and slowly but persistently working upward, as all the while new lines of text were pouring in, ALAS ALMIGHTY GOD WOE IS ME replacing *where are your people from*

*A Fall of Mist*, Ruth thought at first—somehow her *Mist* file was leaking into her journal file. She tried pushing ENTER, then she tried pushing DELETE. Meanwhile it was becoming clear to her that whatever was going on, it bore no resemblance to anything she'd ever written, or even dreamed of writing, for that matter.

*Having attained his first goal*, the computer explained, *the warrior has three options.* Three small pictures appeared: a castle, a bird, and a sword. She tried pushing all the F controls, one after another and then in various combinations, but to no avail. CLICK ON ICON the computer suggested. YOO HOO! it beckoned. CLICK, ROO! And when at last she gave up and did as she was told, choosing the bird, the screen filled with the image of a triangular-faced man in a black cloak, standing on a hill that contained within it a skull wearing a golden crown. No sooner had he appeared than the man was set in motion, rapidly striding down the hill, where a huge red bird began pecking him to pieces.

Stop it! Ruth ordered. STOP IT! she typed, but the cursor refused to obey, merely leaping around madly before disappearing altogether. The man's cloak turned white, the screen went blank, and then the whole thing started up all over again. ALAS ALMIGHTY GOD WOE IS ME, followed by the three options, and the three small pictures. What have you done with my book? Ruth sobbed.

As if in answer a soft tapping sounded on her door. A voice piped up—my mother's voice—saying, Ruthie? Ruthie darling, are you in there? Ruth caught her breath mid-sob and held perfectly still; there was a jiggling noise, the doorknob began to turn, and then, to her dismay, the door creaked open and the next thing she knew there was Carole, her usual array of loose white garments flapping around her like sails. Why oh why, Ruth thought, did I forget to set the latch? She slammed the computer shut without turning it off, as if she hoped to squash its insane activity like a bug between the pages of a book. Now I'm going to have to devise some stupid lie about why I'm so upset, she thought, and then submit to one of those shows of deep concern Carole always mounts when she thinks she's being lied to.

Though as it turned out, Ruth needn't have worried: after warily taking a seat on the edge of the bed, Carole, herself, burst into tears. She couldn't stand the way things were going a minute longer, she said. Ruthie was her oldest friend, the only person who was nice to her back in the old days when she was a pathetic loser, inviting her home after school for milk and cookies, even playing Barbies with her when it was clear that she, Carole, whose body image wasn't merely bad but nonexistent, didn't have a clue about the vicarious thrill of endlessly dressing and undressing a doll. If it weren't for Ruth, Carole told her, she'd probably have slit her wrists ages ago. She used to like picturing her soul leaking out of her dead body and drifting to the ceiling, where it would look down on all the people who'd ever been mean to her, crying their eyes out. But then, after Ruth came along, it wasn't the same. Carole would roll the picture and everything would go as planned until she got to Ruth, and the amazing thing is, Ruth wouldn't be crying. No matter how hard Carole tried, she couldn't make Ruth cry.

"I'd cry," Ruth said, a little irritably, and Carole said that wasn't the point. What mattered was that Ruth had looked utterly unconcerned because she didn't believe Carole was dead. And since Ruth was the only person who'd ever acted like Carole existed, if Ruth believed Carole was alive, she must have been alive.

The moon had risen above the treetops to the east, and even though it was still practically full, somewhere on its way up it had gotten snagged in a web of clouds, leaving its light nebulous and bleary. Time to turn on the antlers, Ruth thought; time to join the grownups in a glass of wine. Who cared what happened over forty years ago? Or ten minutes ago, for that matter? Who cared about some ancient Welsh hero who didn't even know enough not to involve himself with a woman everyone referred to as the mare-headed-one-who-feeds-on-raw-flesh? Time to have some fun, Ruth thought, away from all this adolescent *Sturm und Drang*. Her mind drifted to her suitcase, where her black spandex dress lay dreaming of the moment it would acquire bewitching shape, thanks to her.

But when she made a move to get up, Carole blocked her way, turning to face her, removing her glasses and wiping her moist blue eyes with her fists just like she used to do forty-some-odd years ago. Whatever she'd done to hurt Ruth's feelings, Carole said, she was truly sorry. She loved Ruth, she said, sniffing noisily; she always had and always would. So what if it was Ruth's mother who'd been the driving force behind all those after-school invitations? Carole had known from day one that Ruth couldn't stand her.

A toilet flushed, a door slammed, oddly syncopated footsteps sounded on the circular staircase—boom pat, boom pat—and for a moment Ruth found herself wondering whether the next thing she'd see would be her father limping in his mismatched shoes past the doorway of her girlhood bedroom.

"I'd cry," Ruth repeated, giving Carole a long look. Go ahead, she thought, read my mind; it's your funeral. Though the harder she tried to conjure just that—Carole in a coffin, her big eyes shut forever, her slit wrists crossed over her big unbreathing chest as everyone who was anyone in the art world gathered to pay homage—the worse she felt. Poor little thing, she heard her parents saying, smug in the knowledge that *their* daughter would go far, publishing her "predictable" creative efforts in obscure literary magazines, unlike poor

Carole Ridingham, who would only just turn out to be a world-famous painter. Besides, Ruth hadn't exactly been Miss Popularity herself.

What a setup! Two outcasts breezing a popular boy's jacket across a schoolyard. Of course they could never be equal. When two people are constantly thrown together, if one of them doesn't rise to the top they'll melt together into a single monstrous creature with a single monstrous destiny, like something in a dreary Celtic tale.

Boom pat, boom pat. The footsteps approached, and came to a halt just outside the door. Carole returned Ruth's look. "You're my best friend," she whispered fiercely. "Nothing you could do could ever possibly change that. Nothing." Then she hauled herself off the bed, her white garments exuding a faint odor of sweat and something else that Ruth could never put her finger on, an unpleasantly sweet smell she thought might be a by-product of all those pills. "Including Bobby," Carole continued, her voice louder now and directed at the door. If anyone was to blame for Bobby's behavior, it wasn't Ruth. Not Bobby, either, she concluded grimly, seizing the doorknob. Not you, darling.

"Wait!" Ruth said. "What about me? Don't I get to—" But before she could complete her sentence Carole had yanked open the door, revealing, to their complete surprise, the woman in the long gray dress.

Everyone was waiting for them, the woman announced. Twould be a crime if Mr. Griffith had to hold dinner a moment longer, she added, her speech peculiarly cadenced and her words running together, a smooth river of sound breaking here and there on jagged guttural rocks.

She was younger than Ruth had first thought, younger and

less mysterious, her face a little chubby even, especially around the cheeks, her small dark eyes deeply set like the raisins in David Fluellen's Bath buns. *Everyone*, she admonished them. Then she turned on her heel and limped toward the staircase, at which point Ruth was amazed to see that the woman's left shoe had a thick heavy sole, almost two inches thicker than the right, just like her father's. How had she managed to miss it earlier?

"I'm sorry," Ruth said to Carole, once the woman was gone.

"No need to apologize," Carole replied.

"But there is," Ruth persisted. "You can't keep doing this, taking all the credit. I'm guilty too."

"It's not about guilt," Carole said. "It's about friendship." Abruptly she threw her arms around Ruth, swamping her in a wave of gauze and flesh. A shiver rippled through Carole's big fleshy body—though whether that was due to the chill of the stairwell, or to medication, or to some other less tangible cause, Ruth could only guess. It would be a bad idea, Carole sighed, to leave things unsettled between them. A person should never go to bed mad, Bobby always said. A person should never count on settling things tomorrow, because when you thought about it, who could say if there'd even be a tomorrow? And then, as abruptly as she'd grabbed Ruth, Carole released her, saying she supposed they'd better get dressed.

"Okay," Ruth said, glad to comply. "Only first, one more thing. Before. In the car. How did you do it?"

"Do what?"

"Read my mind. When I'd just been thinking about the watch. About stealing your mother's watch. You said I should give it back."

Carole laughed. She reminded Ruth that she, not Ruth, was the one who'd brought up the subject of Mrs. Flower, and that having brought it up, naturally she couldn't stop thinking about it. That awful house, that awful woman, those awful salt and pepper shakers, not to mention that idiotic name. Carole had actually thought Mrs. Flower was trying to take possession of Ruth. "I can't read minds any more than *she* could," Carole told her. "It was just a matter of reading your mood. Like you said, you were feeling guilty. 'Tweren't you?"

Later Ruth would return to this conversation, obsessively examining it from every angle. "You are all that binds me," the sinner tells his confessor in *The Brothers Karamazov.* "And if you had been at the other end of the earth, but alive, it would have been the same, the thought was unendurable that you were alive knowing everything and condemning me. I hated you as though you were the cause, as though you were to blame for everything."

That was the curse of intimacy with another human being, Ruth would think, remembering her conversation with my mother in the Ivy Room. And woe to the man or woman who denied it.

"ALAS, ALMIGHTY GOD, WOE IS ME," says Manawydan. Having attained his first goal—burying his father's head in the White Mount in London—he doesn't know how to proceed. Click on icon. Click. Click. Click.

The warrior has three options. He can return to the Isle of the Mighty and live with his cousin, who's succeeded his brother as king and can't be trusted. He can accompany his friend Pryderi to Wales, and marry Pryderi's mother, the beautiful yet bloodthirsty Rhiannon, who also can't be trusted. Or he can try staying put, which is always a bad idea, since stasis spells annihilation.

As in real life, it's never possible to halt life's steady forward motion. The warrior selects the second option, under the assumption that there's safety, if also complication, in numbers.

Click on icon. Two figures now, identical except for the color of their cloaks, Manawydan's black, Pryderi's gold. The landscape unreels before them with dizzying speed, London's confusing maze of streets replaced by an equally confusing maze of paths. The two figures proceed through forests and fells, up steep green hills and into lush green valleys, their progress impeded at every turn by obstacles, chiefly other warriors and a frightening array of birds. With each obstacle surmounted, they receive a new weapon or protective device, and their cloaks get brighter; with each wound sustained, their cloaks get paler. Pure white cloaks mean they're dead.

When at last the two warriors arrive in Wales, they find a feast has been prepared in their honor—delicacies of every kind, including roast birds, which should put Manawydan on his guard, but he's too hungry to notice. He marries Rhiannon, whose gown is red; Pryderi is reunited with Cigfa, whose gown is silver.

As in real life, it isn't always easy to keep the couples straight, especially if "no one of them chooses to be without the other, day or night," and if basically the only thing you have to go on is their outfits.

Psychological insight will just have to wait. The rules are perfectly suited to the temper of the times, with everyone either suffering from anxiety, which makes them anticipate the future with fear and trembling; or from depression, which makes them refuse to believe it exists.

Meanwhile the four friends continue feasting, oblivious to the way color is draining not only from their outfits but from everything around them, as if they've entered a perpetual twilight, or—as it so happens—a fall of mist. The mist is cold, clinging, and clearly supernatural in origin; when it evaporates, they discover that everyone aside from themselves has vanished. "And into the hall they came: not a soul was there. Into the bower and the sleeping chamber they went: not a soul could they see. In mead cellar and in kitchen there was naught but desolation . . ."

Cautiously at first, and then with growing confidence, they investigate a landscape devoid of any sign of human habitation, though otherwise teeming with wild beasts, fish, and bees. Plenty to keep them occupied and well fed, as they realize soon enough. "And in this wise they passed a year pleasantly, and a second. And at last they grew weary."

If the life of the hunter-gatherer weren't ultimately boring, we'd all still be living in caves. Obviously what the friends need is useful occupation. What they need is a business.

Three times, in three different towns, they make an attempt at starting one up, beginning with saddles, then shields, then shoes. But since in each case their workmanship is of truly fabulous quality, in no time at all they've stolen the existing businessmen's customers, and have to run away in order to avoid getting killed.

That's the problem with business: either no one pays any attention to you, meaning you're a failure; or you're a success and have to watch your back every single minute of every single day.

Bringing us back to that fall of mist, as in: who or what made it fall? And, having done so, did the mist-dropper wash his hands of all further responsibility, or (CLICK ON) water heaven with his tears? (Assuming, that is, the existence of hands and eyes.) CLICK ON: when you get married the rest of the world disappears. CLICK ON: you can only amuse yourself with fishing or hunting or beekeeping for just so long. CLICK ON: and don't forget sex.

But then what?

The landscape is rife with its own dangers, and eventually you're going to run out of options.

BENCH: On which Bible do you wish to be sworn?

PAULA HERNE: I'm an atheist.

BENCH: King James, then? For the poetry, if not the theology?

PAULA HERNE: Whatever.

BENCH: (swears her in)

QUEEN'S COUNSEL: Please make yourself comfortable, Miss Herne. Our chief concern is to learn something of events leading up to the excursion to Worms Head on 15 June.

PAULA HERNE: Fairy Ring, you mean? Or before? If you mean before, I'm afraid I won't be of much help. Gnome and I had been feuding, so I was a bit distracted.

QUEEN'S COUNSEL: Gnome?

PAULA HERNE: Naomi. Miss Westenholtz. I'd accidentally broken her glasses, and she accused me of doing it on purpose. A minor tiff.

QUEEN'S COUNSEL: A lovers' quarrel, perhaps?

COUNSEL FOR THE DEFENSE: Objection. The line of inquiry has no bearing on the situation.

BENCH: Sustained.

PAULA HERNE: But I don't mind the question in the least. To set the record straight, Naomi Westenholtz and I are not, and never have been, lovers. We are the best of friends, a category many people on tour seem not to have understood. People see two women traveling together and immediately they make assumptions. I felt responsible for her, didn't I? It was my idea that we come on the bloody tour in the first place. I thought she needed a break from Mrs. Westenholtz, who isn't —well, wasn't—as sick as everyone seemed to think. The two of us have gone on other tours together; in fact we met on one, four years ago now, in Brittany. I was still in university, and Naomi had just finished at the Slade. I was getting over a bad relationship, licking my wounds, you know, and she—

QUEEN'S COUNSEL: Miss Herne . . .

PAULA HERNE: No. Let me finish. This is important. What I'm trying to say is that I was worried about Naomi because from the beginning, even though I could tell Brenda Fluellen didn't know what she was doing, she's a beautiful woman, and Naomi's so impressionable. She's always getting crushes, you know? For instance, she had one on Ruth—Miss Farr—for the longest time.

COUNSEL FOR THE DEFENSE: Objection. Witness is hypothesizing.

BENCH: Sustained. Miss Herne, please attempt to confine yourself to the events of the evening in question. Miss Herne?

PAULA HERNE: I was merely trying to help. This is no picnic for me, you know.

QUEEN'S COUNSEL: We understand the difficulty. Do you feel competent to continue? Perhaps if you were to begin with your arrival at Fairy Ring? You and Miss Westenholtz went for a walk . . .

PAULA HERNE: We took Major. That's the Fluellens' Irish setter. A gorgeous dog, full of beans, typical of the breed. He'd been shut up in the car for hours and needed his exercise. Of course the Fluellens couldn't be bothered—David, to be fair, was busy unloading our luggage, and Brenda was in one of her moods. She's a cat person, anyway. Sneaky, secretive, you know the type. Butter wouldn't melt in her mouth. So, by the time we got to Fairy Ring it was late afternoon and Major was going mad. Mr. Griffith had recommended the footpath around the grounds as being less filled with temptations for a dog, but he couldn't have been more wrong. We hadn't even gotten out of sight of the towers when Major caught scent of something and took off like a shot. I happen to be an excellent runner, only Naomi was slowing me down, because of the broken glasses. And even though it was starting to get dark by this time—

QUEEN'S COUNSEL: Could you perhaps give us a precise idea of what time that was?

PAULA HERNE: I don't know. Six maybe. Six-thirty? Dinner was to be at eight, and I knew we had an hour or so before we had to head back. Normally, of course, it would still have been light, but the weather had already started to change—lots of clouds pouring in from the west, that kind of thing. Anyway, as I was saying, even though it was getting hard to see, I'd been doing a pretty good job of keeping Major in view, especially since he'd headed north, into open moorland. The ground up there was spongy, and there were cairns marking some sort of trail that led across the ridge. Major was barking, very excited; when I got closer I could see that what he'd been chasing was a weasel, and that he'd tracked it to its lair under one of the stone piles, where it was doing its best to defend its young. Naomi was beside herself; she's a vegan, you know, not so much for health reasons, but because she's extremely tenderhearted where animals are concerned. I urged her to return to the house, and tell Mr. Griffith he shouldn't hold dinner for me. It took some convincing. She was afraid of getting lost, but I explained it was downhill all the way. You can still see the towers, I said, just head for them and you'll be fine. That was when I gave her my binoculars, to help improve her long-range vision. Then I went after Major.

QUEEN'S COUNSEL: And Miss Westenholtz?

PAULA HERNE: She did as I said. Gnome always does. She likes being bossed—it's the way she was raised. At least I assume she did as I said, since that's where I found her when I finally got back, sitting there in the orangerie with the others, dressed to the nines and sipping her Lillet.

QUEEN'S COUNSEL: But to return to your immediate situation with the dog?

PAULA HERNE: Yes. Well. I was worried, since I knew from my work at the surgery that a weasel's bite can inflict a good deal of damage. Their saliva's highly infectious—that's why people used to think weasels were poisonous. By the time I got to the cairn, though, all that was left was the nest of babies, and Major had torn off across the ridge with the mother weasel in his mouth. I tried the standard voice commands—*halt, drop*—but needless to say the Fluellens have never gone in for obedience training. Lucky for me Major was heading more or less in the direction of the house, which luckily happened to be all lit up, since in the last ten minutes or so it had really become quite dark.

QUEEN'S COUNSEL: Again, an idea of the time?

PAULA HERNE: Seven? It was quarter past when I stopped outside the pagoda. I know because I looked at my watch.

QUEEN'S COUNSEL: And had the pagoda been on the route originally mapped out for you by Mr. Griffith?

PAULA HERNE: What?

QUEEN'S COUNSEL: Had you intended a visit to the pagoda?

PAULA HERNE: Of course not. I ended up there because that was where Major ran out of steam, next to the goldfish pool. He'd just given the weasel one good hard shake, and was preparing to tuck in. I tried distracting him with a piece of jerky, but he could've cared less, and when I began inching up on him, he snarled at me. Still, I wasn't about to go without him, was I? No, I knew I was in for a longish wait. Fortunately there isn't much meat on a weasel.

QUEEN'S COUNSEL: And that's when you found yourself in a position to eavesdrop on the exchange between Mr. Snow and Mr. Hsia in the pagoda?

PAULA HERNE: Well, I wouldn't exactly call it eavesdropping. The pagoda had a small platform, a porch of some kind, that extended out over the pool, and I figured I could sit there and bide my time watching the fish until Major had finished eating. I was feeling fairly peckish myself by then: breakfast had been hours ago, and we hadn't stopped for lunch, a fact I only bother mentioning since when I first heard the voices, I actually thought I might be having an auditory hallucination. I didn't realize I wasn't alone until I heard Mr. Hsia laugh — he has a very odd laugh, almost like a sneeze. And then I heard Coleman — Mr. Snow — say that if it were Roo's cooperation they needed, all it would take to win her over would be a little subliminal autohypnosis, but Carole was another story altogether.

QUEEN'S COUNSEL: Did it occur to you to ask the men for assistance in getting the dog back to the house?

PAULA HERNE: Maybe for a moment. But it also occurred to me that maybe I'd overheard them say things they'd have rather kept private. Really, I didn't know what to do: I couldn't leave, and I couldn't let them know I was there. I was in a quandary. Mr. Hsia laughed again, and said he thought Mrs. R wasn't so much another story as she was a koan. A woman attuned to paradox, a Buddhist by nature, he said, making her the perfect vehicle.

QUEEN'S COUNSEL: Vehicle?

PAULA HERNE: Yes, that's the word he used. I remember because it didn't make sense to me, and also because when Coleman replied, he sounded almost angry. Hsia didn't get it, he said. Carole might seem tranquil on the surface, but she would go to any lengths to protect Bobby, and if she thought she were accidentally complicit in a plan that threatened his well-being, there was no telling what she'd do. Especially if she thought she was merely serving as a pawn in someone else's game. And then Mr. Hsia said if anyone could understand Coleman's concept, Mrs. R could. And then Coleman reeled off some equation, as if to say, *I don't think so*, and Mr. Hsia launched into some abstract gibberish that I can't remember very well since it left me completely in the dark.

QUEEN'S COUNSEL: Could you perhaps give us a try?

PAULA HERNE: Not the equation — that's never been my strong suit. But as for what Mr. Hsia said? Let's see, I think it was something about how maths don't exist in time . . . that's it. About how maths preexist, and their form must be honored as absolute, completely apart from normal ideas of time. Like the ideal form preexisting in a block of marble that a sculptor tries to release, he said, and then Coleman informed him that Carole hated sculpture, which she claimed 'didn't make sense,' and Mr. Hsia said maybe Coleman should leave Carole to him, Mr. Hsia. Am I doing all right?

QUEEN'S COUNSEL: Brilliant, Miss Herne. Anything else?

PAULA HERNE: No, that was about it. The last thing I heard was Coleman saying they'd better get a move on before the others noticed they were missing. Major'd finally finished with the weasel, thank God, so I grabbed him by the collar and we made a beeline out of there, beating the other two back by at least ten minutes. When I arrived in the orangerie the maid—or Miss Griffith, or whoever she was, I've never actually been clear on that—was putting the soup on the table. It looked good enough to me, but no sooner had she set the bowls down than Mr. Griffith started removing them. He seemed flustered, saying he'd only just realized *who* he was feeding. He had something truly special saved for such an occasion, he said; if Miss Ridingham would bear with him it would be on the table in the twinkling of an eye. I was surprised, since even though Gnome had told me Carole was a famous painter, the truth is she seemed too out of it to be a famous anything. Anyway, Carole said she'd be honored, and Mr. Griffith began taking a head count, explaining he had to make absolutely sure how many we were, in case there wasn't enough. But when he started counting, for some reason he bogged down at five, and the maid had to come to his assistance. It was the fairy blood, she told us; she sounded quite proud of the fact. Everyone knew fairies couldn't count beyond five. And then Bobby, who'd obviously had a lot to drink, said, 'Fairy, sure, but who are we kidding?' and Mr. Griffith swept from the room with the maid hard on his heels, though not before she'd informed us that in case we hadn't heard, fairies also didn't have a sense of humor.

I DON'T have a sense of humor, Monkey says. One two three four five um um um . . .

He's disproving his own point, I say, and he leans back to glare at me, when all at once the lamp goes out, turning his eyes to reproachful pinpricks in the pitch-black kitchen. Mouse eyes, like the ones I just saw regarding me from behind the potato bin — both of them, Monkey and the mouse, implying I'm the interloper, and the sooner I leave them alone to steal my money and cheese, the better.

This usually happens when the seasons change: the power goes on a rolling outage schedule, and an army of mice invades the kitchen, a situation I've never really minded until now. But for some reason, maybe because I kept asking about her, Monkey's brought Netta along with him today, letting her loose on the floor where she immediately started crawling, planting her little palms in mouse droppings and then sticking her thumb in her mouth. Of course I've done what I can: set traps, swept, even tried plugging some of their more obvious holes with rags, only there are too many of them and it's too dark to see, invisible mice everywhere, nibbling, squeaking, scrabbling for purchase on the linoleum with their awful claws. It's like that scene in *The Nutcracker*, which frightened me so badly the first time I saw it that my mother had to give me half a Valium and take the other half herself.

Of course *she* never had this problem. She had an army of servants instead. Though, being Carole, she thought it was because she kept bees. According to her, mice really hated bees. A single bee could kill a mouse with a single sting in less than a minute.

Six seven eight nine ten, Monkey says. Okay? Then he puts an amiable expression on his face to let me know he bears me no hard feelings for refusing to go along with his harebrained suggestion that he's anything other than a human being, and asks which one do I really hate.

Somewhere in the vicinity of the door, meanwhile, Netta has started whimpering. Come on, I think, getting up from the table and stretching. Which what? Though it's early evening, without the lamp it feels much later.

The one *I* really hate is Paula, Monkey says. She acts like she cares about Naomi and Major, but it's all pretend. She's a selfish girl and I hate her. He pauses, keeping a bright mousy eye on me as I feel my way toward the whimpering dark lump that's Netta. I don't hate Ruth, though, he says. I could never hate Ruth. Coleman only got her because she was slack. Time for a candle, he points out, still amiable. I can feel the heft of him there in the darkness and smell his smell, like dirt and stone and meat, and hear the sound of his breath as it comes from his mouth and goes back in, shallow and moist.

Ruth, I think. Ruth Ruth Ruth. Time to eat a potato and go to bed. If only Monkey could see her now, either dead or so old she'd curdle your blood. Whittled away to nothing the way it happens with the skinny ones. Thin as a rail and living in an old people's home in New Jersey . . .

The baby's gotten herself tangled in her grubby overlarge

T-shirt; when I lift her from the floor it's obvious she needs to be changed. This is no good, I say. Where's her mother? She does have a mother, doesn't she?

You mean Peggy? Monkey asks, and begins reciting— sourly at first but with increasing dreaminess—O my darling O my pet whatever else you may forget in yonder isle beyond the sea do not forget you've married me . . .

A wall of haze blocks the moon, but enough light is coming through the door that I can get a good look at the baby's face. Or maybe what I mean to say is that the baby gets a good look at me. Those unblinking blue eyes, totally serious, that wide placid brow. Rosebud lips without a trace of a smile. Hair like the wavery white halo you see around the moon during a total eclipse. *O my darling o my pet* . . . those same words being sung somewhere nearby, and Bobby handing me a special pair of glasses so I could watch without going blind . . . but what am I thinking? That was years ago.

When you're looked at by a baby, it's like being looked at by an animal or a god. You feel yourself viewed as a thing apart from the overall cosmic plan, denied access on the basis of having had the audacity to grow up, learn to speak, become a separate human being.

Where'd you learn that song? I ask.

Learn what? I can hear Monkey rummaging in a drawer, no doubt looking for a candle, because the next thing I know a match has been struck, releasing wavery eclipse light into the room. That's for me to know and you to find out, he says.

The baby needs a bath, a sprinkling of powder, a bottle. A mother, in other words, but are there any mothers here?

Be a champ, Suze, I remember Bobby saying, lying on his

back under the strangely dark daytime sky. Sipping whiskey from a bottle, smoking, the picture of adult impregnability, he wanted me to crank up the Victrola, which was running down. Just don't stare at the sun without the glasses, he warned. Though if I wanted I could watch movies of the eclipse, hundreds of miniature versions of it playing themselves out in the puddles from last night's rain or, stranger still, in the shadows cast by plants. Careful not to scratch the record, he called out, and then the song started up again, and be so kind as tell the wind how you may be and send me words by little birds to comfort me and o my darling o my . . .

Netta's cough is getting worse, Monkey announces. It's the dampness does it. He begins digging things from pockets hidden here and there within his garment, and setting them on the table. Mrs. Koop's bifocals. My good scissors. A box of tacks. Several open bags of pigment—burnt sienna, Naples yellow, terre verte—the last of which I suddenly realize is what he's been using to powder his wig. I won't be needing these anymore, he says.

Glad to hear it, I say, and am just breaking it to him that Netta doesn't have a cough, does she, darling, when into the ensuing silence—because of course she can't say a thing—there comes the sound of grit spattering against the windows. Could it actually be a gale, headed in our direction? Not close yet but hulking in the wings, the way gales do? You should be leaving, I say, and hand him the baby. Now, before it's too late.

Monkey smiles at me and gets up from the chair. Which one do you really love? he asks Netta. Susan or Peggy? He gives her a quick kiss on the cheek, smooths her T-shirt, and begins walking toward the hallway. We'll stay, he says in a firm tone, like he's finally allowed himself to be won over. Who needs Peggy, anyway? She's a selfish girl, here today, gone tomorrow. Then he informs me that he's going to make a fire in the living room, and when I tell him he can't, he reassures me there's plenty of wood, he put it there himself only yesterday.

No, I insist. What I mean is, they can't stay. It's my house. I like living in it by myself. I don't want houseguests, I say, following him into the living room.

More grit, accompanied by greenish flashes of lightning. Off to the east a siren begins to wail, growing louder as it makes its way along the coast road. Never a good idea to get caught in a car when a gale's starting to blow. I mean it! I yell, but already I can hear the sound of kindling being snapped in two, paper being crumpled, another one of my precious matches being struck.

Paula's problem is she only likes people who are like Paula, Monkey says. The fire blazes up, turning his face golden red, creating a small warm cave in which he sits cross-legged with Netta on his lap. Susan's problem is different, he tells her. Susan's problem is she only wants to hear what she already knows. It is, he adds, putting on a length of applewood, and moving over a little to make room for me. Don't touch me, he warns. I've been sick.

Nor can you stop yourself when a cave looks so warm and inviting.

But Susan doesn't know anything, Monkey goes on. Like, where we live. She probably thinks this house is an im*prove*ment.

You live across the brook, I say, on the chautauqua grounds, right? Or at least that's where I've always imagined you living, to be close to the poppies.

Once again Monkey reaches into a hidden pocket and draws forth a shiny object, a little golden ball. I'm half right, he tells me, tossing the ball into the air and catching it; I'm also half wrong. Half right because to get to where he lives you do have to go to the chautauqua grounds. Half wrong because that's just the beginning. There's a path leading into a thicket of black willow growing behind Bobby's pavilion where the hemlock used to be; it's almost impossible to see unless you know what you're looking for. The path leads through the thicket, a very marshy and treacherous area, and continues out the other side, where suddenly the landscape changes to an expanse of delicate velvet turf, sort of like a huge putting green, perfectly smooth and flat. It looks seamless, but if you walk exactly one hundred paces from the edge of the thicket, you find a square-shaped depression in the turf—a trapdoor, in fact.

And when you open it? A steep flight of stairs leading down down down, at first to an extremely dark passageway lined with moss-covered stones oozing moisture, and finally into a most beautiful country filled with streams and meadows, woods and plains, though also extremely dark, since it has no sun or moon or stars to light it.

Acorns before oak we knew, an egg before a hen, Monkey says softly, but never the like of that. He shoots me a sly little glance, then lowers his lips to Netta's ear and whispers, Susan doesn't believe us.

By now the baby's sound asleep, the fire burning briskly. I can hear the wind wrapping itself around the house, around and around and yanking, trying to wrench it loose. I tell Monkey I'll make up a bed for him on the sofa. Netta can sleep on the floor beside him in a laundry basket. Just this one night, I say. Tomorrow it'll be back down the trapdoor for both of them.

(14 June) so sad & missing u & u so far away! my little girl my little girl my darling little girl! teacup & saucer, gravy boat & plate, break them to bits & tempt the hand of fate. 3 little chinamen fishing in the sun, 2 fell in & then there was 1. 1 little chinaman living on a dish, somebody dropped it & off swam the fish. o susan u most of all deserve explanation & not just sorry this & sorry that & even tho yr father's always tried his best to shield u i count on u to understand. 3 little chinamen walking near the sea, out came the sun & then there were 3. u know the rest thank god.

AND WASN'T IT just like Carole, Ruth thought (fondly now), to be lying flat on her back staring at the sky when she knew perfectly well it was time to eat. "Get up!" she called. "Hey, Carole, get up!"

Magtil twisted in her chair. "Mrs. Ridingham is all right?" she asked, peering at the diaphanous white bundle deposited there on the lawn like the chrysalis of a gigantic moth.

"Never better," Bobby replied. He extended his glass, and Miss Griffith (for so she'd turned out to be—their host's maiden sister) filled it with the exceptional wine he'd been happily consuming while waiting for everyone else to arrive.

The orangerie was lit by hundreds of candles, hundreds of golden flames reflected in hundreds of night-black windows, so you felt like you were voyaging through stars. Mr. Griffith had replaced the unacceptable fish stew with a huge celadon tureen, then stationed himself in a thicket of flowering plants to await the guest of honor, who was taking her own sweet time. When at last she made her appearance, drifting in on a humid gust of air, he couldn't keep his hand from trembling as he filled her bowl.

"Oh," Carole said. "Oh my!"

"*Diolch,*" replied Mr. Griffith. "Thank you." He bowed the white tuft of his head, a milkweed pod bursting with seed and pride, then abruptly vanished out the door.

Miss Griffith finished serving, limping loudly around the table to fill the remaining bowls with an almost colorless broth in which the tiniest bits of vegetation floated—a pretty bland-looking concoction, according to Ruth, though when she finally took a spoonful she couldn't believe how good it was, its flavor both complicated and deep, simple and delicate, making her feel as if she'd never actually *tasted* anything before, only gone through the motions. The room came alive with the sound of spoons chiming against porcelain, greedy slurping noises, exclamations of delight.

"Can you tell me what's in it?" Naomi asked Miss Griffith, and then, when she received no answer, asked Paula if she thought it was okay for her to eat.

"If you don't," Mr. Hsia said, "you'll be very sorry."

"If you don't," Bobby echoed, "you don't deserve to have a mouth." He turned to Carole, who'd settled herself next to him, listing slightly toward the head of the table where David sat, the elbow of her left arm planted on the tablecloth and her big drowsy head propped in the palm of her left hand, as her right hand dreamily spooned up broth. "What on earth were you doing out there?" Bobby asked, pointing at his own chin to indicate she should wipe hers with a napkin.

"Writing to Susan," Carole replied, continuing to make a mess.

She seemed drugged, Ruth thought, though maybe it was the soup or the candles, which were so slow-burning you lost all track of time. Certainly everyone was acting strange, including her own husband, who'd been seated directly across the table from her, and who appeared to have developed a sudden unexpected interest in Paula Herne. Paula was seated to his right, her skin flushed over her high flat cheekbones, her yellow hair damp and slicked back like a greaser's. "They can't be trusted," Paula was saying, and Coleman was nodding, actually drawing her out on the subject, which seemed to be weasels. *Where* exactly had she seen it? he wanted to know, and Paula infuriatingly responded with a series of ordnance survey coordinates. Of course they'd all been through a long exhausting day. Possibly it was just the wine. Ruth shot Coleman a questioning look and he shot one back, though aimed not at her but at Mr. Ilsia, who was busy masking some unspecified anxiety of his own with a show of indifference.

"Well?" Naomi persisted, and Paula reluctantly tore her attention from Coleman.

"No problem, Gnome," she said. "Whatever's in the soup, it isn't meat"—at which point Ruth saw Miss Griffith, who'd been handing round a basket of odd clamshell-shaped rolls, stifle a smirk.

"Writing a *let*ter?" Bobby said.

How sweet the room smelled! How sweet the candles, lacing the air with lucent drops of that substance the ancients called Divine Medicine, as they melted away to nothing! The night was growing cooler, a damp wind shaking the windowpanes. The moon had disappeared behind its scrim of cloud hours ago; to the east Ruth could make out the lights of the kitchen, where their host was no doubt conjuring a banquet from an eggshell, as fairies were known to do. And never shall our bounty fail till within the hall the flag-reeds tall and the long green rushes grow . . . Owls were hooting in the treetops, field mice nesting in their tidy holes, foxes sleeping in their sacks of fat and fur.

On Ruth's left, two-faced Mr. Hsia; on his left, Naomi Westenholtz, blind without her glasses. Languid Brenda at the foot of the table, slipping her bowl to Miss Griffith for a refill. Opposite Ruth, Paula Herne and Coleman, still deep in weasel talk, then sloshed Bobby and out-of-it Carole, and around to tomb-silent David, gravely eating his soup at the head of the table, followed by the evidently feuding Kopeckys, and back again to Ruth. A group in which she felt either quick-witted and glamorous, or excluded and dull, depending on how she read her dinnermates' tangled motives. Especially Bobby's, if truth were to be told.

If truth were to be told, Ruth nursed her memory of Bobby's kiss like a frail seedling that, given the proper management, might develop into a tree of truly mammoth proportion. And then? Take up residence in the shade of its boughs? Cut it into lumber for a house? I have always loved you, Ruth imagined Bobby whispering. Two versions: the first into her ear, the second, into a skillfully hidden microphone. She watched him watching Carole, then growing bored, aimlessly looking around the table, his narrow hazel eyes finally lighting on Brenda.

Those beautiful nostrils! That unruly black hair! He was a kindred spirit, hot-blooded and impetuous like herself, unlike Coleman with his phony ethics and old money, unlike Carole with her trust fund and drowsy morals.

Mr. Hsia's watch let out a little beep. *"Oy a duw!"* Miss Griffith exclaimed, consulting her own plainly watchless wrist. The next thing they knew she'd limped into the night, and they were all alone.

Immediately they began babbling, infused with that pent-up glee schoolchildren feel when the teacher's left the room. Was it only her, Naomi asked, or did anyone else find the Griffiths a bit *off-putting*, and when Magtil replied that the food was so delicious she didn't care, Tadeusz cocked his head and remarked that his ears seemed to be playing tricks on him, since he could have sworn he'd just heard his wife's voice, even though he'd watched her wander into a fairy ring earlier in the day and disappear.

"More soup?" Brenda asked, extending the ladle, clearly aware of how the blue black bodice of her pathetically out-of-date though annoyingly becoming Empire-cut dress cast enticing shadows across her skin and accentuated her cleavage. "Miss Herne?"—fakely formal—"Mr. Snow? Mr. Rose?" Bobby still hadn't taken his eyes off her, Ruth noticed, even while he was busy slopping wine into all the glasses he could reach without getting up. Come on, Bobby, she thought. Come on. Cut out the window-shopping and get to work. But did Brenda really want him? Did Brenda really want *anything*?

"*Oya do?*" Bobby said, and Coleman solemnly informed him that he could now kiss the bride.

The door swung open. The Griffiths were back, Evan Griffith bearing a platter on which reposed a huge quivering slab of what seemed to be a segment of a much larger creature, the whole thing cased in a gray tough-looking skin, its dense snow-white flesh exposed at either end, with a razor-sharp fin protruding from the top. Monstrous, Ruth thought, monstrous but marvelous, like that fairy-tale fish that granted wishes, its muscles still tense with the urge to swim—it should never have been caught, let alone cooked. Indeed it looked like the last thing in the world you'd want to put in your mouth.

As Miss Griffith removed the soup bowls, her brother set the platter in front of Carole, handed her a long sharp knife, and asked if she'd be willing to do the honors.

"Wait!" Magtil cried, "I—" Then she blushed, unsure how to continue, though, really, she was merely giving voice to everyone's misgivings. Maybe it was water from when he washed his hair, Tadeusz teased, whacking his hand against his ear, and Bobby told him to knock it off.

" 'Flounder flounder in the sea, come I pray thee here to me,' " Ruth recited.

"I love that story," Naomi said. "I always loved that story. 'For my wife, Dame Isabel—' "

"But is not so funny," Magtil interrupted, glaring at her husband. "In the ring, time isn't moving. Is gray and flat, like Eastern Europe. I am in there three hours. *Three.* But is like one second, one little blink, and poof! Now I am here. So knock it off, mister. Knock it off." She tossed her head and pouted, and suddenly Ruth realized that this was a kind of foreplay, all the more exciting for being enacted in public. Tadeusz's eyes shone, and his pink rosebud mouth glistened. *"Passt mir nicht,"* he said, turning down her trump card. *"Passt mir nicht, schatze."*

"Flounders are flat," Carole reminded Ruth. "Flat as a flounder, remember?"

Meanwhile she was expertly cutting the thing on the table in front of her into slivers, almost as if she'd performed the operation a million times before, though you didn't have to be a genius to know she hadn't. "Your plate, darling?" she asked Bobby, and Miss Griffith reminded her that the first taste was intended for her and her alone.

Utterly unadorned—no vegetables, no sauce, not even a sprig of parsley—the snow-white slices made their way around the table. "Begs a boon against my will," Naomi continued reciting. She watched—they all watched, anxious—as Carole took a bite, chewed, and swallowed. Then she dropped her fork, stared at her plate, and took a deep breath. Her eyes filled with tears. "Carole?" Ruth said, rising from her chair, but Bobby waved her back down. Blindly Carole groped for her fork, found it, and kept on eating.

Once again the Griffiths swept out the door, their exit this time heralding a strange hush. The fish—if fish it was—tasted even better than the soup, though *better* struck Ruth as barely adequate to describe the effect. It tasted like the sea, but not fishy, not salty—it tasted elemental, like the only thing you'd ever want to eat, and eating it gave you that same mysterious feeling you got in your chest when you inhaled after swimming in the ocean, a feeling of profound sorrow, like the only feeling you'd ever want to have.

"Look at you, Gnome," Paula finally said, and Naomi wiped her mouth and eyes, replying that she didn't know what had gotten into her. "I don't think we should be doing this," she added, but by then it was too late. The platter was empty and so were their plates; they'd eaten the whole thing up, skin and all.

Magtil said they had no choice, they were bewitched, and Tadeusz, finally acknowledging her presence, said at least *she* was.

"Of course we had a choice," Carole said. "Even when you're bewitched you have a choice," and she swiveled her candlelit eyeglasses toward Bobby, who froze in their glare, then stared darkly back.

Mr. Hsia tapped his wineglass with his knife. "A toast," he said. "A toast to Mr. Griffith, and to food that puts an end to craving."

"Hear, hear," Coleman said.

And it was true, Ruth thought, for not only did she feel perfectly sated, but she wasn't even remotely stuffed, her stomach replete instead with light and energy. Dessert? Coffee? Cognac? Meaningless concepts, all of them, the dinner having made her eat, literally, like there was no tomorrow, like tomorrow, too, was a meaningless concept, as well as yesterday and today. She sighed, leaning back in her chair. Mr. Hsia was right, she said. Bewitchment wasn't the problem; the problem was wanting more.

Which, when you thought about it, was exactly what happened in the story: A fisherman caught a flounder that asked to be thrown back, saying it would be unpleasant to eat since it wasn't really a fish but an enchanted prince. A talking fish, the fisherman replied, I'd throw you back anyhow. But when he returned to the pigsty where he lived with his wife, she had a fit. At least he could have asked the flounder to grant him a wish in exchange for its freedom. A nice little house, she prompted. Go back. Go back. And so he did, and this time the sea was green and yellow, and not so smooth. And he said the words "Flounder flounder in the sea, come I pray thee here to me, for my wife, Dame Isabel, begs a boon against my will." And when the fish reappeared he told it what his wife wanted, and the fish told him to go home. She had it already.

First she wanted a nice little house, then a great stone castle; then she wanted to be made king, and after that, pope. And each time the fisherman went back the water changed color, becoming wilder and wilder, until in the end, when she'd asked to be made God, the whole sea was pitch-black, with waves as high as church towers and mountains, and with frothing crests of spray at the top.

"It's human nature," Bobby said. "It's human nature to want more."

"Maybe," Carole said. "Though I'd have stopped at the house."

"It's Nature nature," Ruth added.

"But there you are wrong," admonished Mr. Hsia, the wings of his nostrils flaring slightly as he tried to hide a yawn. "The lesson Siddhartha learned under the bo tree is clear: man and nature alike are bound to the Wheel of the Law."

Siddhartha, Ruth thought—give me a break. Only suppose instead of a house the prize was a big fat business deal, what about that, Mr. Bo Tree? What about you? she asked him. If you were given the choice, what would you do? Everyone had a weak spot, she said. For some people it was greed, for others vengefulness, say, or pride. An Achilles' heel, she said, glancing at Bobby's wounded foot, which he had stuck out from under the table almost as if he was planning to trip Miss Griffith.

"Well, I know what mine is," Paula said. "Mine's—"

"No! Don't!" Naomi interrupted. "Let me guess."

But that would be too easy, Ruth objected. They already knew each other. Why not let Naomi guess at Mr. Hsia's weakness, since he obviously wasn't saying. They could make a game of it, everyone predicting how the person sitting on his right would respond to the flounder, followed by a vote. Achilles' heel, she said.

The windowpanes began shaking harder; the wind was picking up and a little rain began to fall. Naomi bit her lip and squinted in the direction of the kitchen, where the lights had suddenly gone out. Have we lost power? she asked, or . . . Don't worry, said Mr. Hsia, I assure you I'm perfectly harmless, and Paula reminded him that no one should be forced to play if they didn't feel like it. Rain outside, drenching bracken, sea shingle white, fringe of foam . . .

"For Christ sake, Paula," Naomi said. "I can fight my own battles." She scowled, tossing back her spaniel ears of russet hair, then glanced winsomely at Ruth. Mr. Hsia would probably throw the fish back before it had a chance to say a word, Naomi ventured. He liked getting a jump on things, didn't he? That way he didn't have to worry about being tempted.

The vote was almost unanimous, despite Coleman's objection that George never threw anything back, not even shoes.

*George!?* They were in an uproar. George Bernard Hsia, Mr. Hsia admitted, yawning uncontrollably now. His mother was an Anglophile.

The play moved around the table. Naomi liked to put others first, Brenda said; it made her feel good about herself. She'd probably adopt the fish, dress it in baby clothes, and give it its own room, killing it in the process. (Allowed, after heated argument culminating in Paula's angry refusal to take part in any game that was nothing more than character assassination.)

But Brenda was only expressing her own fears, Coleman said; Brenda was afraid of appearing soft, even though that was the way she was at heart—maternal, really. To hide the fact, she'd march down to the water, catch the fish, cook it, and eat it. (Disguised praise: disallowed.)

So dark the night, so wild the wind, so heedless the world and dangerous! What on earth did they think they were doing, sitting there like—well, like sitting ducks in a house of glass? Could anyone else hear it? The wrenched sound the world made as it tore through dark, wild, heedless space? For a moment Ruth could almost believe the sound was audible . . . Rain outside, need for refuge, withered hogweed, yellowed furze . . .

Coleman would mount the fish, Bobby said. Then he clammed up, ignoring the double entendres and irritated entreaties—*Because? Because?*—and grinning at Paula when she remarked that it seemed to her everyone was merely describing themselves. Oh I see, he said. That's why you backed out. Mr. Hsia's watch beeped again. Eleven o'clock? The Kopeckys took their leave, Tadeusz guiding a drunken Magtil along like a piece of wheeled luggage. "Good night, good night," she called out. "I sink is time for bed, yah?—is . . ." The door flew open, releasing a bright square of rain-spattered lawn into an otherwise coal black universe.

"I sink is time for nooky," Carole muttered, and when Naomi said she wished they'd all stop being so mean, Bobby laughed. Carole wasn't mean, he said, she was indifferent. Carole was like the Wheel of the Law, wouldn't Mr. Hsia agree? Or like the fish, he added in a burst of cheerful inspiration. But it appeared that Mr. Hsia was asleep, snoring delicately, his sleek round head tilting to the right, gradually closing in on Ruth's left shoulder.

"No fair," Paula said. "You already had your turn."

Rat-a-tat-tat went the rain on the windowpanes; Bobby stood abruptly and wandered unsteadily to the foot of the table, where Brenda seemed to be having some trouble lifting herself from her chair. Hiding the fact that she was eating for two was more like it, Ruth thought. She saw Carole frown, and then she saw David take Carole's hand and give it a consoling little squeeze. He felt worried, he confided to her in a whisper that Ruth strained to overhear. He felt worried and he wasn't sure why. Maybe there was something Carole wanted to tell him . . . Rain outside, drenches the hair, ocean pallid, dense with brine . . . Alas my lord, what dost thou here? Carole's big hand with its knobby graceless fingers sticking to the bowl and her big feet to the slab, and with that, lo, a peal of thunder over them, and a fall of mist, and no trace of the caer left behind.

"I don't need your help," Brenda complained, shaking herself free of Bobby, and David told him to leave her be. His wife was overtired, he said; it was high time for all of them to be turning in. If no one minded, he'd lead the way, since luckily he'd had the foresight to bring a torch. "Torch?" Carole repeated dreamily. "Flashlight," Paula said. "C'mon, Gnome."

Arm in arm and two by two, the proper order restored if only momentarily, they began slipping away—Brenda and David, Bobby and Carole, Coleman and Ruth—through the door and into the wet dark night. Of course the men were getting aroused by the touch of the women, by the erotic message it conveyed, whereas the women were merely bent on gathering information, a condition common to relations between the sexes, Ruth thought. Though Naomi and Paula were another matter entirely, and as for Mr. Hsia, he was sexless, like a shrub. She could hear him shuffling along in their wake, trailing his roots and humming to himself, softly, softly.

> *Rain outside, drenches the deep;*
> *Whistle of wind over reedtips;*
> *Widowed each feat, talent wanting . . .*

PART THREE

## Last Clear Chance

When all is said and done, how do we not know but that our own unreason may be better than another's truth? For it has been warmed on our hearths and in our souls, and is ready for the wild bees of truth to live in it, and make their sweet honey. Come into the world again, wild bees, wild bees!

—WILLIAM BUTLER YEATS

I WAS THIRTEEN when my parents left for Wales, just turning fourteen at the start of the trial. For a while the story was front-page news and then, like anything that's hung around too long, it vanished altogether. I was an adult by the time the case finally got settled, though to no one's satisfaction, except maybe the lawyers'.

But isn't that the way the world works? In any given situation, whoever has the most at stake usually has the least power, especially if she's a high-strung and solitary child—"your mother's own daughter," as Aunt Ruth used to prognosticate cheerfully. Which is no doubt why I was kept in the dark for at least a week after Bobby's telegram arrived, during which the only hint I had of there being anything wrong was a mysterious change in Mrs. Koop's behavior toward me, a surprising tenderness accompanied by a tendency to race for the phone whenever it rang and disappear with it into the hall closet.

And then one rainy morning toward the end of June, when she'd been strenuously ignoring my game of dress-up with a not yet (and never to be) worn Jil Sander, Uncle Tony came stumbling into the master bedroom and, collapsing drunkenly onto the sleigh bed, asked me if I didn't know it was bad luck to wear a dead person's clothes. Besides being a bad color for me, he added, given my olive complexion, which by the way had been done no favor by the mumps—it brought out the yellow tones in my skin and made me look terrible. I told him that for his information the dress belonged to my mother, mimicking the special tone of amused resignation she reserved just for him, her fucked-up little brother. No one ever took what Uncle Tony said seriously. Every now and then he'd appear out of the blue, put a big dent in Bobby's liquor supply and initiate some grandiose project, his equally sudden departure saddling us with hundreds of shrieking peachicks or shriveling apricot trees or, once, a pair of bad-tempered bison.

Tell me about it, Uncle Tony said. He sighed and rolled onto his stomach, cradling his head in his arms and peering at me out of one large blue eye that, though moist and bloodshot, looked exactly like my mother's. Honey, there've only been three women in all history who can wear that color, he told me. Jackie and Cleopatra and Carole, and two of them're dead. No, better make that three, he said in a jumpily muffled voice. It took me a while to realize he was sobbing.

Sometimes I think if it hadn't been for Uncle Tony I would never have learned the truth, but of course that's crazy. There were the newspapers, for instance; there was Bobby's telegram, followed by his letter. And finally there was my trip to London with Uncle Tony and Aunt Doe, not to mention the trial—though that came later. For the moment, all I had to go on was Uncle Tony's story, which he dispensed in short breathless bursts between long anguished sobs.

On June 15, at ten o'clock in the morning, the walking tour set out for Worms Head. The weather was "iffy" but seemed to be holding; an expected storm had apparently shifted course, and the sea, though choppy, presented no impediment to their plans. It took the group approximately an hour and a half to hike from Fairy Ring to the pillar marking the highest point on the Gower peninsula; they stopped there for a bag lunch, lingering to admire the view and chat with a pair of Irish hang glider pilots, after which they negotiated the steep bank to Rhossili Beach. The tide was out but starting to turn —the window of opportunity for reaching the Snout still open, though growing narrower by the minute.

It was about two-thirty. Everyone (except Aunt Ruth, who refused to leave the beach) got as far as the Inner Head, where a strong wind suddenly blew down on them from the north, bringing with it drizzle and dense clouds, and splitting them into two groups, the larger of which sensibly opted to go no farther. At this point my mother decided to strike off on her own, her behavior sufficiently characteristic that no one paid too much attention. Evidently she'd done the same thing several days earlier when they climbed some mountain.

According to one of the tour leaders, a Mrs. Fluellen, the last she saw of my mother she seemed to be moving in the general direction of the Devil's Bridge and, presumably, the Outer Head. She seems to have been moving quite fast, particularly in light of the slippery conditions; by the time Mrs. Fluellen managed to mobilize the smaller group (including Uncle Coleman and a large dog) there was no sign of my mother anywhere. Mrs. Fluellen led them through the Low Neck's tidal ooze and over its seaweed-draped stones with as much speed as she deemed prudent, but no sooner had they reached the Devil's Bridge than the dog got sidetracked, and in the ensuing confusion a lot of valuable time was lost while one of their group, a young British woman, chased after it.

The sky was now an ominous shade of green, and the tide coming in faster, the waves increasing in size, the Blow Hole sending up huge towers of spray that totally obscured the Snout. Mr. Snow had just finished leaping from the bridge to the Outer Head when the storm broke. There were flashes of lightning, cracks of thunder. The rain fell so hard and fast you couldn't see a thing.

"They didn't make it," Uncle Tony told me. "Mr. Snow's body washed up on Rhossili Beach the very next day. But as for your poor mother, she vanished without a trace."

I'd have given anything to believe that this was just another instance of my uncle's famous talent for melodrama, only I couldn't. I couldn't because, even if I'd been able to ignore the expression on his face, I knew that no matter how many faults he had, they'd never included cruelty, at least not toward me. I began to shiver, and he reached out and drew me onto the bed. Outside our house the rain was still coming down, a light summer rain, pattering on the windows, and I remember telling him I wanted to kill it because it was the same rain that had fallen on my mother. "You go, girl," Uncle Tony said. He had his arms around me and was stroking my hair, gently, obsessively, and I knew he was pretending it was my mother's hair, but I didn't care, since I was pretending his hand was her hand.

"Anthony!" Mrs. Koop called from the foot of the stairs. "Are you up there? Have you seen Susan? Lunch is ready."

He stopped stroking and covered my mouth. "Shh!" he said. "Let's just give her a rain check on that, shall we?" Then he rolled away from me, lifted himself heavily from the bed, and wobbled over to the closet, an enormous walk-in affair, where I could hear hangers rattling, the sound of shifting fabric, almost like the whole thing was one huge mistake and my mother had been in there all along, getting ready for a party.

But if they never found her, I asked, how did they know she was dead? Maybe a boat picked her up, or . . .

"She's gone, honey," Uncle Tony said, emerging from the closet, his arms draped with dresses. "Believe me, I know. The night it happened Carole came to me in a dream. Very shapely, the way she used to be before she married Bobby and gained all that weight. We were having a picnic in the meadow, and she leaned over and kissed me and said goodbye, and the next thing I knew she'd turned transparent like cellophane, and a gust of wind caught her and blew her away." He dumped the dresses on the bed and told me to get up. With my coloring, he said, sifting through them, definitely black. Possibly midnight blue. But the Yamamoto was way too stark—no wonder Carole never wore it. Though of course she never wore anything except those god-awful muumuus, such a waste of Bobby's great taste in clothes, not to mention all that money.

No, Uncle Tony went on, the occasion called for something more fin-de-siècle, more suited to a night of revelry and drink, loads of champagne, dancing till dawn . . . How about the Armani? He disentangled a long shimmering gown from the pile and held it up to me. Needless to say the thing was positively huge, but with a few safety pins and . . . Put it on, he urged. He promised he wouldn't look. And did I think this little Helmut Lang number would do for him?

By the time Mrs. Koop came storming into the room, we'd fallen so deeply under the spell generated by our shared misery and extravagant denial that at first we didn't notice her. I was seated at the dressing table, applying lipstick; Uncle Tony was standing behind me, teasing a few strands of blond hair from under the silvery turban he'd wrapped around his head. It didn't matter that he was a lot taller and thinner than my mother, in that getup the resemblance was uncanny—of course Mrs. Koop thought she'd seen a ghost. She let out a scream and then grew furious at having been made a fool of. "Come with me this instant, Susan Rose," she said. "Even if your uncle can't be relied on to act his age, you at least know perfectly well that closet's off-limits."

The rain continued pattering on the windows, as meanwhile a bright midday sun was doing its best to break through the clouds, splashing the walls with watery beads of light. I told Mrs. Koop I hated her. I told her I was never leaving my mother's room. I told her she was wrong not to have told me what had happened. How could she have kept it from me, I yelled. My own mother—

"Rosalinda," Uncle Tony corrected. "You'll have to excuse us, but we have a reservation at Sardi's, and they'll only hold the table just so long."

He may have been a fuckup, but if it hadn't been for Uncle Tony, I don't know what would have become of me.

It was as if my world had ended, and he was right there to supply another. The waters under the heavens gathered together into one place, and the dry land appeared.

SEEN FROM ABOVE, the promontory looked less like a sea serpent and more like an arm disappearing into a seething cloud of truly supernatural proportion, a magician's arm, long and muscular, reaching in deep to retrieve . . . what? Patrick Lynch couldn't say, though Queen's Counsel pressed him hard. By the time he was airborne the weather had already started to turn, which was why his companion, Thomas Ahearn, decided against following him off the cliff. Of course, Lynch said, that was typical of Gower. The weather there changed so quickly it made your head spin, and he was having trouble enough preventing his glider from getting swept back against the rock face, or from plunging straight into the sea. He could hardly be bothered to keep an eye on a group of tourists who'd had the bad judgment to think they could outguess the tides. The truth is, he was busy dealing with the consequences of his own bad judgment.

Earlier though, he clearly recalled a conversation up by the pillar, when he'd warned the woman who seemed to be in charge about the advisability of pursuing such a plan. Yes, that woman sitting over there, one of the two defendants, she'd seemed perhaps a bit distracted but she definitely heard what he had to say. To be sure, the storm came on suddenly, but it wasn't like there'd been no warning. And no, he had no idea the defendant might be pregnant, neither from her appearance nor from anything she let drop. In fact he'd wondered if she might be having some problem with her husband, who appeared to be giving her very little help managing the group.

And as for the others? Tommy Ahearn had taken a fancy to Miss Farr, the one tour member Lynch actually recalled seeing from the air, since she'd stayed on the beach and then at some point climbed back up the steep flight of wooden steps to the car park. He knew she'd testified that she was getting her allergy kit, and while he thought it pretty unlikely under the circumstances that there'd have been any wasps or bees down there in all that wind, who was he to say? Miss Farr had been wearing a very noticeable outfit, black and yellow stripes, sort of like a bee herself, so she was easy to keep track of. Besides which, the beach was essentially empty; when he finally landed on it there was no one else in sight. He'd swear to the fact, even though he was basically preoccupied with getting free of his harness. No one. And that was all she wrote.

But surely! . . . Think, Mr. Lynch! Close your eyes.

∽

Close your eyes and see it: the empty beach, the blowing wind, the woman like a bee . . .

See yourself soaring down through thick wet clouds, blinded at first by the mist, and then, amazingly, clear patches appear and in them the sea, as opaque as mercury, with here and there a hint of weed-laced depths, smooth rocks streaming seaweed like the hair of the drowned, a barking dog . . .

Yes! A dog, racing back and forth along the Low Neck, the sharp noise of its barks like a flurry of arrows released into the air, aimed straight at your wildly pounding heart. A fairly large dog with auburn fur and a long plume of a tail, though who can explain why you've forgotten it till now? Maybe because all you've been able to remember is your life flashing before you, your mother and father, your house and your sisters . . . Isn't that what's supposed to happen when you think you're about to die?

Lynch saw the dog only for an instant before the wind whirled him back toward the cliff and the clouds once again closed in. But while he could still see it the dog was racing along the Low Neck in ankle-deep water, and seemed to be barking at something or someone on the side of the Outer Head invisible from the beach. It seemed very agitated, then all at once it calmed down and froze in place, almost like it'd been given a voice command.

An auburn dog, and—hold on a minute!—something else, something long and narrow, a sort of cigar-shaped shadow in the water, kind of like a giant fish . . . though Lynch went on to admit that it made no sense for a fish of such size to be swimming in the shallows on the south rim of the Devil's Bridge. During a storm a human being might exercise bad judgment about the conditions surrounding Worms Head, but not a fish, unless it were injured or already dead.

Only perhaps there was another explanation? Queen's Counsel urged the witness to think carefully before answering. Could what he had seen possibly have been a boat?

Objection! Objection! Leading the witness!

Bang! Bang! Overruled.

Though, really, when you thought about it, the presence of a boat was equally implausible, if not more so.

Where had the so-called boat come from? Whose was it?

How had it gotten there, and what was preventing it from smashing into the rocks?

Not to mention the more pressing question of *why* anyone would want to feign drowning, especially if they happened to be, just for instance, the mother of a young girl whose heart could be as easily broken as the promise to come home to her all in one piece, hands and face and legs and torso, talcum powder, turpentine, and grass . . .

It wasn't until after Lynch had finally extricated himself from the glider, wrestled it into a bundle, and started lugging it toward the long flight of steps leading to the car park, that he realized anything was wrong. He saw a solitary figure, a woman in a green tent-shaped coat, obviously distraught, racing back across the mudflats in the direction of the beach, stumbling on the wet rocks and picking herself up again, waving her arms at him and shouting. By now the storm was fully upon them, a solid wall of wind and rain advancing from the sea—Lynch could hardly remain upright, let alone make out what the woman was trying to tell him. He abandoned the glider and ran to meet her, at which point she collapsed into his arms, weeping.

There had been an accident, that much he could understand. The woman was frantic and kept lapsing into some foreign language. An accident *out there* (pointing). Two? three? or maybe not a number at all but a word meaning stranded, swept away, drowned? The woman's face was as white as a sheet and slick with rain, her lips bright blue and flecked with dark grains of sand. She looked like she was going to faint, but when Lynch tried to make her wait on the beach while he went for help, she became even more hysterical. My husband!

My husband! she howled. Evidently the two of them had become separated in the confusion following the dog's disappearance, and now she couldn't help but think the worst. Really, Lynch said, if the Asian fellow with the umbrella hadn't chosen that precise moment to show up, he wasn't sure what he would have done. As it was, he had a hard enough time handing the woman over—peeling away her arms, one at a time, and then draping them around the other man's neck—not to mention his difficulty actually getting to a phone, since the climb back up from the beach was devilish steep and slippery, the visibility nil, and the Visitor Center crammed full of tourists.

Wet tourists, all of them overexcited and milling around, with the exception of Miss Farr and Tommy Ahearn, whom he discovered after he'd at last managed to place the call, sitting together on the floor in a corner under a display of Worms Head singlets, sharing a Guinness and clearly oblivious. At first when he attempted to tell them what had happened—or at least what little he knew of what had happened—Miss Farr refused to believe him. In fact she seemed pretty well smashed, and it occurred to him that maybe they'd had more than the one Guinness. She asked Tommy if his friend was always so solemn; *her* friend was that way too, she said, pulling a face.

Though even after Tommy had convinced her he was telling the truth, Lynch reflected, Miss Farr remained oddly calm, almost as if the news weren't news to her at all.

As if perhaps she expected it? But while Counsel's sly query was met, not surprisingly, with the usual firm objection, Lynch held his ground. Not like you're trying to suggest, he insisted. Miss Farr struck him as the kind of woman who tended to cast her fate to the winds. Superstitious, like his girlfriend, Moira. Brainy women often were, he'd observed, though he didn't know why. Besides, it wasn't until much later that Miss Farr actually found out what had happened. The idea that there'd been a plot or a plan, or that Miss Farr might have had a hand in it, was ludicrous.

And she was right to be fatalistic, wasn't she? Even Queen's Court could prove no match for Nature, for Nature's way of lulling human beings into thinking they'd figured her out, into believing they understood the laws governing her actions and actually striving to mimic them, only to watch powerless as she swooped down and smacked even the most airtight testimony off its pins, obscuring it like poor Mrs. Ridingham or poor Mr. Snow in a tumult of wind and water, in great billows of ocean spray and blowing sand until it had dwindled to a dot and then a pinprick and then to nothing, a poor little thing subsumed for no apparent rhyme or reason in the fury of the storm.

LISTEN TO ME, SUSAN, says my mother. *I'm worried sick about you and I don't know why.* Not talking to me but to something little, cupped in the palm of her hand.

On those rare occasions when a bad sleeper at last sleeps soundly, she tends to wake confused, her dream having leaked out around her, filling the house with long-forgotten morning sounds, Mrs. Koop's fervent nose-blowing, Bobby's dazed lunge at the coffeepot, the back door's lazy squeal followed by a bang . . . My dream mother making a dream getaway, headed for the garden house in her white veil and gloves, holding something little in the palm of her hand, maybe even a bee.

Or more likely what I heard was Monkey and Netta making a real getaway, and with them the bedding and the laundry basket and the bag of rolled oats and the half dozen or so eggs they seem to have helped themselves to before they went, as well as their bowls and spoons but not the scorched saucepan, which they left sitting beside the little gold ball—suspiciously like a gilt-coated Ping-Pong ball—in the middle of the kitchen table.

Thank you very much, I say. Eeezie now. Eeezie. Recalling Monkey's lips blowing in my ear—*pssst! pssst!*—as he tried to wake me. Kneeling beside the sleigh bed where he had no right to be but where, I admit, I was pleased to find him or even more than pleased, but when I reached out to feel his face—to reassure myself I wasn't still dreaming and felt for an instant that dull oily skin and saw the same dull oily sheen covering his eyeballs—he drew back, averted his head, and told me not to touch him, said *don't*, and then he was gone.

It's a strange morning, the knobby tops of the plant towers gleaming like scepters, the whole world bathed in a phantom version of sunrise, yellow and humming, almost like the bees are back, though it's probably just flies, eagerly rubbing their hindlegs together, or the power station beyond the chautauqua grounds, returning to speed. A smell like resin. Like burned milk.

For a while, during the period when I wanted to be a dairymaid, I think we actually had a cow. I always wanted to *be* things, based on outfits—or maybe it was because of having a name that sounded less like a particular girl than a category. Nurse. Hula dancer. Cheerleader. Susan. Which is why my mother chose the name in the first place, going on the assumption that the duller the container, the more brilliant the contents.

Every morning there'd be fresh cream in a brown pitcher, a slab of butter. The little dairymaid in a red-and-white-checked apron, her cheeks flushed, and Bobby, hidden behind his paper, mouthing something to my mother, both of them trying not to laugh. Bacon frying, that smell.

But wouldn't you know—Susan Rose is finally hungry, and there's not a thing in the place to eat.

Or maybe I'm still in the grip of my dream, ferried onward like a person with actual places to go, with a sharp yet fraudulent sense of destination—little remembered hints of houses grouped on sunny hillsides, swing sets, wash lines, walls and windows printed with the restless shadows of shade trees, white and yellow, green and blue. Lobster traps in front yards, wooden butterflies from Canada nailed to shutters. A big marmalade cat sunning itself on a welcome mat. The bright blue Volvo wagon sailing toward town, and hearing my mother say, *I'm worried sick*, and Bobby saying, *The lull before the storm.*

⁓

Once I'm finally headed east, the coast road doesn't look merely moist but is shining for a change, and far far out on the cold gray sea a circle of sun floats like a piece of gold silk, gracefully riding the swells. Once upon a time, after all, maps represented the route with a dotted green line, meaning it was exceptionally scenic.

And then, just past Penniman's Light, traffic more or less comes to its usual standstill. Horns begin to honk, and a group of enterprising Strags begins to shuttle through the flashing headlights of the oncoming cars, washing windshields the way ghetto youths used to do whenever we got stopped at an intersection in the city. Bobby always paid them, and always more than what they were demanding, going on the theory that they needed to learn how the system worked, and the sooner the better. He claimed it would be a crime against capitalism to do otherwise.

Our line of traffic inches along, the turbanlike bulge of Turk's Rock appearing ahead and to my left; a young woman approaches the Volvo and begins sponging the window, her actions brisk yet sloppy. There must have been an accident, she says. That would explain the flashing lights. Probably on the straightaway right before town, where drivers always lose their patience and try pulling out around those snail-like generator trucks. The young woman is short and built like a pony, with a long straw-colored braid down her back, wide-set pony eyes, and high pony cheekbones, and, as it turns out, absolutely no sense of humor, also like a pony, or a fairy for that matter. In honor of Bobby's memory I let her finish, though when I ask what I owe, she shakes her head. All she really needs is a ride, she explains, and then climbs in without waiting for a reply.

It takes another half hour to reach the intersection of Main and Pallas. We pass an ambulance, a fire truck, a headstrong set of tire tracks touchingly headed across the road and into thin air. The pony girl clucks her tongue like a middle-aged woman, then proceeds to hold forth on the subject of the weather. How long has it been since we've had any rain? A month? Two? Everyone's feeling pent up, on edge. At least she knows she is. And now look at it . . . She speaks tonelessly, clutching her bucket and staring straight ahead at the yellow sky through my badly washed windshield, almost like she's speaking from a script, the way Monkey used to. Oh him, she says, when I ask if she knows anyone by that name. No, not really, she adds cheerfully, then suddenly flings open the door and leaps to the curb, her landing admirably deft given the fact that we haven't quite stopped moving. As I watch her trot off down Pallas Hill, Mrs. Koop's ghost takes brief possession of my mouth. You're welcome, the ghost prompts and then departs, leaving me once again alone.

I park beneath the lobster, in the shadow cast by the larger and more menacing of its two upraised claws, and walk to the IGA. Since my last trip, a litter of those ubiquitous short-legged yellow pups has been born under the fan at the base of

the lobster's tail, the ruined sidewalk between it and the IGA
has been torn up and replaced with a slatted wooden walkway,
and the store itself is now pink and turquoise blue with faded
plastic vines stapled around its doors and windows like a store
in the tropics. Still called the IGA, though, and still run by a
tribe of teenage girls. Still uselessly stocked, but also omi-
nously in the know, pushy even, offering among piles of limp
carrots and oven mitts, sixpacks of infant formula and only
slightly damaged boxes of zwieback.

No oats, however, and as I make my way down what passes
for a central aisle, stubbing my toe on a can of tuna the size of
a hatbox, I can't say I'm surprised to find the pony girl sitting
on a drum of canola oil near the rear door, sharing a bottle of
ginger wine with the horselike cashier I remember from before. When the pony girl sees me she gives a wave, and then,
once she thinks I'm out of earshot, begins talking like a person
who's been drinking and doesn't know how loud she is. That's
the one, she says, and the horse girl replies, Shh. Keep it down,
followed by something I can't make out, a whispered string of
words including *rich* (or maybe *bitch*) and ending in a long
belch, a burst of giggles.

Should we tell Peggy? the pony girl asks, or maybe it's more
like: Should we tell, Peggy? I can't hear the horse girl's answer
since the noon whistle chooses that perverse moment to go
off, even though it's barely turned eleven.

Peggy, I think. Peggy. A selfish girl, according to Monkey,
but probably also dark and thin, since he seems to like his
women that way if his interest in Ruth Farr is any indication.
Dark thin selfish Peggy, who naturally will have made it her
business to know where I live. I picture her conspiring with

the other girls in the back of the IGA, all of them chummily hatching a plan. A robbery, no doubt; possibly even a full-scale assault and occupation. Hurry up, Susan, I tell myself. For God's sake, get moving.

On the way back the Atlantic's on my right, its surface thick, gray, rubbery. *Right*, signifying good luck, from the Latin, *dexter*. I remember Uncle Tony explaining this one night over dinner, blaming left-handedness for his latest misadventure, and Bobby saying in that case wouldn't Dexter be a bad name for a shoe store, unless of course you happened to have two right feet. Out the window the massive heads of the trees, their dark rustling, and on my plate the pair of little blue and white birds that always looked like they were about to kiss, their sudden appearance leaving me heartbroken and panic-stricken and hopeful. Leaving me in the grip of those feelings we all used to accept as the privilege of adolescence, whereas girls these days make the change from baby savage to smooth operator without missing a beat. They never know what it's like to hear in the rustling noise of summer's end the approach of a destiny so at odds with your parents' that it seems like a betrayal.

❧

When I get there the house is locked tight. No sign anywhere of vandalism or forced entry, and the day's turning out to be almost nice, the air mild and wet, a shimmery yellow-gray, making it possible to see all the way to the meadow's edge, the tangled sea of shrubs and creepers actually looking like someone grew them there on purpose. Little by little the names come back: woodbine, bishop's-weed, gill-on-the-ground, snow-berry. You want to move cautiously, though, take your time.

You want to make sure when you finally inch the door open you won't find any unpleasant surprises. Hold your breath, proceed on tiptoe. The kitchen empty but uncharacteristically astir with light and shadow, with a sense of lively activity that came to a halt only seconds earlier. The bacony smell of last night's woodsmoke. One of Netta's rusty safety pins glinting between two floorboards. On the table, in the exact place where Monkey left them, the ruined saucepan and the little gold ball.

With my arms full of packages, I kick open the pantry door and pause at the threshold, peering in. The room's lit by a single bare bulb screwed into an ornate ceiling fixture. To turn it on, you tighten it; to turn it off, you loosen it and your fingers get burnt. Even in the old days our house had a provisional look—that was the way my mother liked things—and whenever Bobby started talking about calling in a contractor, she'd throw a fit. I think the bare bulbs and cracked windowpanes and rotting sills made her think her escape routes were still open, that she was still free to come and go as she pleased. Sometimes she'd try hiding an especially bad section of wall with one of her paintings, but no sooner had she done so than a telltale heap of plaster dust would show up on the floor beneath it.

Don't be mad, Susan, Monkey says, and continues brushing the dirt from a dessert plate before slipping it into one of the house's many pillowcases monogrammed with the initials of total strangers. Then he sidles up to me, his gray eyes wide and serious, his wig sticking out in stiff strawlike tufts all around his face. Leaning so close I can smell his breath, sweetly milky and sour like a baby's—Don't be mad, Susan dearest, he whispers—and before I know what's happening he's pinching me, hard, on the arm.

He seems bigger, somehow, his shoulders broader and his chest meatier, his face no longer pale and pointy but thick-skinned, congested almost, brutal. It's your own fault, he whispers; you don't love me and your dishes are filthy, and when I say don't be ridiculous, he pinches me again. Saying, Pinch her, pinch her, pinch away! black, purple, yellow! Saying he thought everyone knew fairies hated human infidelity, squalor, lying, and inconsistency.

The plate in question belongs to the set of Blue Willow dishes my mother so enigmatically alluded to in that final letter, and which still waits under its thickening layer of grime and cobwebs and dead flies and mouse droppings, silently longing for the day when it will once more be taken from the pantry and laid on the long dining room table, the room vibrant with talk, with the flash of knives and the smell of roast meat and hot rolls—in other words for those routine pleasures we took so readily for granted and which are now gone forever, along with the greater mysteries of sex and dreams and childhood. Pay court to dreams and wake in chains, so the saying goes. One kiss, one touch, one baby too much. Nighttime sleeping, morning weeping. He who walks in the robber's shoes will never get robbed.

I tell Monkey he's a fine one to be lecturing me about truth and cleanliness. But it has nothing to do with lying, he says. He's merely obeying convention, visiting the home of his wealthy neighbor, grateful for whatever hospitality might come his way, as well as the chance to give his dear little baby a bath near a fire. Also to borrow such ordinary household items as he and his kind, in their primitive state of civilization, don't possess. Baking supplies, for example. *Dishes.* Besides, he paid me handsomely, or didn't I notice? His currency might not resemble mine but it's real, and if the ball turned to ash when I picked it up, that was merely proof of my unworthiness.

Cut it out, I say, and he makes his fingers into scissors and snips the air in front of my face. I have more dishes than I know what to do with, he reminds me, taking a pile of saucers from the shelf and dropping them carelessly into the pillowcase. What's another dish more or less? They're all the same, anyway—the same house surrounded by trees, the same path and the same fence, the same little bridge with the same three little men marching single file across it to the same little shrine, the same boat, the same island, the same birds . . .

Of course he's wrong. The plates only seem the same, but I'm not about to point that out to him in his current frame of mind. Sometimes, for instance, there aren't two but three birds, a bird love triangle, just as all the men on the bridge sometimes carry fishing poles, and sometimes only the first man, or not a pole but a stick with a bundle, like a hobo. Sometimes the willow leaves are solid blue spheres or scalloped balls outlined in blue, sometimes crosshatched eyebrow-like rows or a single broccoli-like clump. Speaking of dear little babies, I say, where's Netta?

With Peggy, Monkey replies, barely opening his mouth, the only sharp thing in his newly thick face. I think we're all getting tired of this, Susan, he adds, bending to knot the pillowcase. I know I am. Aren't you?

Tired of what? Of stealing? Of pinching? Of showing up uninvited and spouting unfathomable maledictions like the bad fairy at a christening? I only ask, I say, because I met a friend of hers—and even though it's clear he knows perfectly well who I mean, Monkey tells me babies don't have friends. Her friend told me she wanted to be remembered to you, I say. Peggy, that is.

He doesn't look so pretty anymore, I realize. That's what's different about him. Nor does it seem like the change has occurred naturally, but that he's brought it on himself by an act of will.

Another lie, he says. Why do you lie to me, Susan dearest? And he begins pinching me again, at the base of my rib cage where there's only the flimsiest layer of skin and it really hurts.

A pinch is genuinely mean-spirited. Unlike a punch, which is designed to discharge anger, a pinch reminds you that you're made of skin and bone. It's humiliating. The pincher can look you right in the eye and keep on pinching. The pincher can look you right in the eye with his cold gray eyes and check to see if you're feeling pain.

Why do you waste a sentence on a lie, Monkey asks, when there are so many true things to say and time is running out?

*One hundred paces*
*In rain or in sun*
*Leave Fairy Ring*
*And your fun's just begun.*

*White Moor to Burnt Mound*
*To Rhossili Bay*
*Left on the footpath*
*Five cairns mark the way.*

*Head for the kissing gate*
*Stop for a kiss*
*This is a chance that*
*You won't want to miss . . .*

Of course Brenda Fluellen's "maps" were never meant to be taken literally. Like clues in a treasure hunt, they were meant to contribute to a mood of adventure and mystery, to "set the tone" for the walkers, who by the time they arrived in Wales would surely have had ample opportunity to absorb the more prosaic materials in the brochure (". . . nor should you forget warm & waterproof clothing, suitable footwear, i.e. strong boots or shoes that will provide good traction over rocky terrain and on slippery slopes, a first-aid kit, torch and whistle. The Welsh landscape may look innocuous enough, but it must be treated with respect. Even on the loveliest summer day conditions can quickly deteriorate, transforming a verdant hillside into dangerous wilderness . . .").

I remember the first (and only) time I saw Brenda Fluellen; I remember thinking she was like a snake, which is odd, since she didn't seem all that thin, or slithery, or even poisonous for that matter. Not a trace of make-up on her face, and the skin tan and unlined except for deep grooves on either side of her mouth that might have been dimples. Her wide tan brow, her dark brown eyes, her gleaming teeth! Nor was she especially beautiful or psychologically complex, as some people, i.e., Aunt Ruth, seemed to want to think. In fact I suspect Bobby was right about her from the start, though he may have been overstating the case to divert suspicion: Brenda Fluellen seems to have been a basically unimaginative and practical woman.

When I saw her it actually *was* a lovely summer day. Conditions, legally at least, had only just started to deteriorate. Uncle Tony and Aunt Doe each held one of my hands and were leading me up the Strand, Uncle Tony languid, Aunt Doe at a brisker pace, stretching me between them like taffy. So far from home, so strange, so strange!—the trees darker green and the shadows they cast bigger, blacker. Uncle Tony had been crying and blamed Waterloo Bridge, which we'd caught a glimpse of down a side street and which he said also was the name of the saddest movie ever made. Stopping to remove a tissue from the pocket of his blue seersucker jacket—"Take your time, why don't you?" Aunt Doe said—he reminded her the trial had already been going on for a week with no end in sight.

Indeed the way things were going, it might never end. Uncle Tony sighed. A simple case of negligence—a tragic accident, but an accident nonetheless—was being turned to courtroom melodrama just because one of the victims happened to be a famous painter, and the other a former CEO of a major corporation. Not to mention the confusing array of possible charges, including "contributory negligence," for instance, where the victim's own failure to meet standards of prudent behavior somehow contributed to her injury or death. "Carole Ridingham. Failed to meet standards of prudent behavior," Uncle Tony said. "Doesn't that say it all?"

"Oh for God's sake, Tony." Aunt Doe put her arm around me, staking a claim.

"And how about 'last clear chance'?" Uncle Tony added. "Don't you just love it? How about all the people who had a chance to jump in and stop the tragedy before it happened and stood around like bumps on a log? How about them? Though who's to say when there's a tragedy in the making? Except you, of course," he said. "You know everything."

They'd never gotten along, Uncle Tony and Aunt Doe, and now she was furious that he'd had the bad judgment to involve me in what she referred to as a media circus (SECONDHAND ROSE read the caption under *The Independent*'s pathetic photo in which I peered yearningly off into space), though she certainly seemed to be enjoying herself. Schoolmarm Doe, with her striped Victorian blouse and wire-rimmed glasses, her soft freckled face and round blue eyes. I think the main reason Uncle Tony hated her was because she looked so much like my mother, which is to say like him.

By the time we got to the Royal Courts of Justice, the two

of them were openly squabbling and I was literally dragging my feet. A fine day in mid-July, puffy white clouds slipping quickly past like suds toward a drain, and at the edge of a shallow deep green lawn the courthouse, an array of turrets and spires and towers and buttresses and steeples like a castle pieced together by a lunatic out of soot-stained brick, and presided over by Jesus and Solomon and King Alfred. *Unless you want*, I heard a familiar voice say. *Go on forever*—and there was Bobby, off to one side and partly hidden by a shrub, talking with a woman I'd never seen before, their two dark heads bent close together.

"How was I to know?" the woman was asking. Dressed in a white linen suit, lizard-skin shoes, and matching purse, she looked as elegant and unflappable as Bobby looked like he was about to fly into pieces. He rubbed his neck, twisted it this way and that, glanced up at the sky, down at his shoes, back up at the sky, past the shrub's gently nodding branches and then, suddenly, straight at me, at which point he flinched and averted his face like a person who'd been slapped.

"Just a sec," he said, briefly resting his hand on the woman's elegant shoulder. I may only have been a fourteen-year-old girl, young for my age and socially oblivious, but I could tell there was *some*thing going on between them. "Suze, my God," Bobby said, and he opened his arms wide to take me in. "Baby," he said, "oh baby."

I was so relieved I started to cry, and then so embarrassed I had to insult him. I told him his breath was bad; he held me tighter and asked me what I was doing there. Wasn't I supposed to be at home with Mrs. Koop? I couldn't see a thing except his white shirt, which since my face was pressed into it actually looked black. He seemed to be sweating, a smell I liked, mixed with the smell of ironed cotton, the thick sweaty feel of his skin—his flesh, really—sliding around under the fabric, and under it the bones, the big sloppy heart.

"Uncle Tony brought me," I said, and I could tell Bobby was looking for him, or maybe looking over at Snake Woman, twisting slightly in any case before letting me go. And then boom! it was like an explosion, the sun so bright, and all at once Aunt Doe came back to claim me, squinting her round blue eyes as she wildly swatted at a bee that kept knocking on her head.

Knock knock. Who's there? Orange juice.

Bobby told her he was happy to see her, but Aunt Doe just squinted past him and put out her hand. "Come on, Susan," she said, though she wasn't exactly looking at me, either. Orange juice sorry I made you cry? The bee's legs were heavy with pollen as it went buzzing on its way. A sign, of course, a sign from my mother, as if I'd ever had any choice. I leaned against Bobby, stuck my thumb in my mouth, dumb little bunny that I was, just try and pry me loose. At first I thought Aunt Doe was going to hit me, she looked so mad. "Suit yourself," she said and followed Uncle Tony into the building, swinging her hips, such a saucy schoolmarm.

I would cry for you, lie for you, die for you. Snuggling under Bobby's arm, where the good smell was. He ruffled my hair, but that was about it, because all of a sudden Snake Woman came untwined from the shrub and approached him as if I wasn't there, though not like Aunt Doe since she didn't take her eyes off him, not even for a second, not even when she raised one arm to point dramatically up at the clock tower.

He told me they had to go back inside; the recess was almost over. George Hsia was testifying; next would be Mrs. Fluellen's husband, David. No harm in my hearing their testimony, didn't Brenda agree, though I'd probably think it was boring as hell. But where were his manners? Susan, meet Brenda. Brenda, Susan. Then he started to cry. My God, Suze. My God. Brenda glared at him and headed for the entrance.

We walked in under the footless stone bodies of Jesus and Solomon and King Alfred. Cameras flashed and then they couldn't anymore because we were in the great hall, which was enormous and filled with activity like a train station and solemn like a church and where cameras were forbidden. "That must be the daughter," I heard someone say. Footless living men floated past in triangular crimson robes with broad ermine collars, their faces like tiny eggs in huge nests of curling gray or white hair. Wigs, Bobby told me, judges—though I already knew that from *Alice*. Brenda Fluellen preceded us up the stairs, and I could just make out Aunt Doe's striped blouse at the end of a long stone hallway, Uncle Tony's blue seersucker jacket.

But as for the man who was in the process of testifying as we passed through a green-draped alcove and into the courtroom —do I really remember seeing his round pale face, as inexpressive as a button or a frozen pond and set atop a cherry red bow tie, or is it merely another "memory" concocted from photographs and stereotypes? Is it possible he actually said "Confucius say"?

You've got to have more to go on than a red bow tie and a white face—you need the smell of a person, the feel of him. The tender stalk of his neck and a place where the barber missed several black hairs, longish and curved like eyelashes. Except that isn't Mr. Hsia. That's Bobby.

Bobby, who I *know* I remember, who I can still picture pausing like an usher at the foot of a bench, indicating that I should slide in ahead of him and take a seat next to Aunt Ruth. No, I indicate back. You go first. Even though he needs a haircut and a shave and his shirttail's come undone, he looks like someone you'd want to sit next to, a real flesh-and-blood person, as opposed to Aunt Ruth, who has that vee of chest that's the hallmark of all stylish fin-de-siècle women, flat and tan and ridged like a washboard. Not so much a snake, Aunt Ruth, as a woman being swallowed by a snake, her head still visible within the giant maw of her clavicles. Meanwhile Brenda has gone to join her husband and their lawyer.

Pay attention now, Bobby's telling me. He takes my hand and squeezes it. I can smell the bittersweet smell of varnish grown tacky in the heat. A chandelier hangs directly overhead, and for a moment I think a crystal drop from it has landed on Bobby's cheek. The tall guy with the nose, he's explaining, the one in the black robe and gray wig, is Counsel for the Defense. He wipes away the drop. No, that one. Shh, he whispers, handing me a beat-up pair of binoculars with a fox face scratched into the paint near the focus knob. Listen, he says.

☙

GEORGE HSIA: Confucius say, in business as in Buddhism, absolute purity required. Mr. Snow and I see eye to eye from start. Very well named, Mr. Snow. Velly.

COUNSEL FOR THE DEFENSE: Might we infer that Mr. Snow and Mr. Rose had *not* seen eye to eye, at least insofar as their business was concerned?

(Bobby's mouth at my ear, so close I can feel him blinking. *Leading*, he's whispering, *Counsel's leading the witness*, and Aunt Ruth whispering back, *But why's he pretending to talk like that? He speaks English better than you and me* . . . Focusing in on the man's not so very apricotlike left ear. A diamond stud in the lobe, and his red bow tie, printed all over with tiny black Scottie dogs.)

GEORGE HSIA: Sure thing. What Mr. Rose never understand is business is entity unto itself. Five years ago when Mr. Snow say 'sell,' Mr. Rose take it personal. Nothing to do with me. Not then.

COUNSEL FOR THE DEFENSE: Can you tell us at what point you actually did become involved in this affair?

GEORGE HSIA: Sure thing. Weekend of March twenty-second, Year of Pig. I am walking down Madison Avenue when I see painting in gallery window. Mrs. R's show just opening, lucky me.

(and *What!?* Bobby is saying.)

COUNSEL FOR THE DEFENSE: That would be the year you went to Wales? You were in the States on business, is that correct?

GEORGE HSIA: Yes, business. I am on my way from coast to UK, stop over in Manhattan. So far from the rim, say Mrs. R, you have fallen in bowl with the rest of the noodles and now you will be eaten.

(and *Puhleez*, Ruth is saying . . .)

BENCH: Confine yourself, if you will, to answering the question, Mr. Hsia.

GEORGE HSIA: So solly.

BENCH: Mr. Hsia?

GEORGE HSIA: Only trying to explain. Only trying to show before she die Mrs. R advance further than most on eightfold path. Maybe even all the way . . .

(and *You were at the opening, Suze, do you remember this clown?*)

But that must be some other little girl he's thinking of, the one who didn't routinely get left behind with Mrs. Koop. No, Dad, I wasn't at the opening. I was home—re*mem*ber?— which is why I have no memory of the "clown" or of his purchase of *Hive #11* or of any part of the transaction whatsoever, at least as the clown described it to the court in an increasingly bad imitation of Charlie Chan.

෴

It seems George Hsia was attracted to my mother's painting not so much because he was an art lover, or even because he was a bee lover, but because he was a man of business.

When George Hsia walked down Madison Avenue on that fateful spring day in the Year of the Pig, his eye may first have been caught by the image of the hive on the canvas in the gallery window, but what prompted him to go in and buy the painting was the peculiar elongated object my mother had painted with gold leaf in the blue sky just above the hive, which one critic suggested was the "wafer-cake" described in Charles Butler's famous treatise on bees, "The Feminine Monarchy," but which George Hsia immediately recognized —even before he'd had a chance to view it through a corrective lens—as an anamorphic projection of a computer program board unlike anything he'd ever seen before.

Of course my mother didn't have a clue how it worked—or even what it was, for that matter—but from the moment

Uncle Coleman showed her the prototype and told her it possessed "a radical new architecture," she hadn't been able to stop thinking of Butler's story, famous among beekeepers, of the woman who put a consecrated Host in the hive where her bees were mysteriously dying, and when she opened the hive later to see how they were doing, not only were the bees once again busy making honey, but they'd also built a miniature chapel "with an altar in it, the wals adorned by marvellous skill of Architecture, with windowes conveniently set in their places; also a doore and a steeple with bells. And the Host being laid upon the altar, the Bees making a sweet noise, flew around it."

A perfect metaphor, according to my mother, especially since the board, as painted, looked just like a side view of a communion wafer. A perfect addition to her Hive Series.

Mr. Hsia said that by the time he wandered through the door, the opening was going full swing. No one seems to have noticed him, but then he'd always been good at vanishing in crowds. It took him several minutes to track down the artist, who apparently shared his ability to vanish; eventually he found her in an unlit storage room, drinking wine straight from the bottle. She was a big woman, he said, dressed all in white. Her eyes were very unusual, like a carp's.

According to Mr. Hsia, Mrs. R was pleased to hear that he was a fellow beekeeper, delighted that he was familiar with the writings of Charles Butler. In fact she seemed to be in such a friendly mood, repeatedly offering him swigs from the bottle, that pretty soon he felt bold enough to ask her where she got her ideas. Ideas? she said. Oh I never have *them*, and when he persisted, saying, the wafer for instance, she grew quite emotional. The wafer had nothing to do with her. No, that was Hans Holbein and Coleman. Coleman who? Mr. Hsia continued, trying for an offhand tone, but by now the mood was broken. She completely "clammed up."

When at last Mr. Hsia finally located him, Mr. Snow was on his way to Wales. Moderately interested in striking a deal of some sort, though it would have to be on the sly, he said, he'd promised Carole. Ever since they sold the business Bobby had been at loose ends. A person could only buy so many expensive shirts, after all, only so many silk ties, and according to Mr. Snow, whatever advance the new board represented, it far exceeded anything Bobby was capable of understanding, let alone imagining.

And when a man, even a very smart one, messed with things beyond the realm of his imagination, he ran the risk of corrupting either the things being messed with or the people they affected or, more often, himself.

The lights went out. A slide of the painting appeared as, simultaneously, the painting itself was offered in as evidence. Even by my mother's fanatic standards *Hive #11* was excessively realistic, a canvas roughly three feet by four feet showing a straw skep, the dome-shaped object most people picture when they hear the word *beehive*. A straw skep on a field of green that, looked at more closely, proved to be an actual landscape with the skep rising above it like a mountain. Tiny fields and rivers and roads and bridges, a hint of coastline running from the upper to lower right-hand corner. A lighthouse. A pavilion. A white farmhouse. A sky the pale yet saturated blue of a forget-me-not; a cloudless sky infused with a sense of heat and light, of a hot yellow sun just out of reach. A gold wafer floating through it . . . But that was our house, I suddenly realized. *Our house!*

"Oh yeah," Bobby was saying. "I'm real smart." He was getting more and more agitated, balling and unballing his fists, the vein in his temple that usually remained hidden and threadlike filling disgustingly, suggestively, with blood. "So smart I forgot to think," he said, and Aunt Ruth shushed him, telling him to listen up for once.

The next slide appeared, a no longer distorted view of the golden object, which looked like the floor plan of the kind of gigantic building you find yourself trying to get out of in a bad dream.

Yes, Mr. Hsia confirmed, that was Mr. Snow's brilliantly conceived program board, the very object Mrs. R had so cunningly concealed in *Hive #11*. Indeed Mr. Snow had accomplished the impossible, what scientists had been trying to do for years. He'd created a board with more memory links than there were molecules in the universe. Any computer installed with Mr. Snow's board would possess something not unlike actual human consciousness. It would be able to make the wildest imaginative leaps, to daydream even. It would be able to nurture a grudge, experience paranoia. In time it might even be able to learn to love and hate. Mrs. R was right. In the wrong hands—her husband's, for instance—it wouldn't merely be corruptive. It would be dangerous.

You could say the purchase price of the painting was, in a sense, an earnest of his intention to put Snow's design in production. And yes, that was why he signed up for the tour. No, he had absolutely no interest in Wales or King Arthur. In fact he disliked King Arthur, who struck him as a bully. But he'd hoped that under the right circumstances he might be able to convince Mr. Snow to agree to such a project. What he hadn't counted on was the immense force of Mrs. R's personality, her fierce conviction that when you found yourself in possession of something dangerous there was really only one thing to do, and that was to lock the dangerous thing up in a work of art.

Large wooden fans revolved high overhead. The chandeliers glittered. I could see the back of Brenda Fluellen's head, the nape of her neck, which for some reason filled me with rage. *I don't believe this,* said Aunt Ruth, and Bobby laconically replied *Listen up,* or words to that effect. Really, I'm not sure what I remember, only that they made me think of the bad kids who always sat together in the last row in school, their constant sparring theoretically a sign of how much they liked one another.

The testimony concludes with the Fluellens' lawyer trying unsuccessfully to get Mr. Hsia to admit that neither Brenda nor David was in a position to assist my mother at the moment when she was swept into the sea, or to give a hand to Uncle Coleman when he finally took off after her. But the most he can recall is seeing Mrs. Fluellen and Mr. Rose standing together on the Low Neck, Mr. Rose reaching out as if to restrain Mrs. Fluellen. Furthermore, he has no idea when he saw this—or even *if* he saw it.

Mrs. R was, as usual, dressed completely in white. It was impossible to tell her from the spray and the foam. The human mind, Mr. Hsia said, made mischief like a monkey. For all he knew, Mrs. R was still standing there on the Snout, biding her time. Immediate awareness was the same as in dreams. By the time immediate awareness arose, seeing and its object were already nonexistent.

How could anyone think, Mr. Hsia asked, that there was such a thing as perception? The human mind, galloping like horses, swarming like bees, all over the place?

CLICK ON ICON:

A single bee, leaving the hive. Another. Another.

The hive's full of bees; you can't see them but you know they're in there. You think they're making honey, but guess again. They're building a church.

Like the nursery game where you clasp your hands and then open them and see all the people. As if something like your hands, something that's actually part of you, could suddenly divide itself into separate pieces: church, steeple, people. As if your own mother could decide to leave you and walk off the edge of the world.

CLICK.

And lo! the clock strikes twelve and all at once the greatest commotion in the world has erupted in the croft. The greatest host of mice in the world, so that neither number nor measure might be set to them. And before Manawydan knows what's happened, the mice have fallen upon the croft, a mouse climbing up along each stalk of wheat and bending it down and breaking off the ear and making off with the ears and leaving the stalks and there's not a single stalk that doesn't have a mouse climbing up it.

CLICK.

Stop doing that, I tell Monkey, but he ignores me. We have to hurry, he says. Listen, he says, cocking his head. But I can't hear anything except the delicate stuttering noise the computer makes as it ransacks its doddering memory bank.

Hello, Roo! Anybody there? Roo sweetheart . . .

CLICK.

At some point a majority of the old bees in any given hive, together with the queen and a few of the younger bees as well, will pour forth in a dark buzzing cloud, at which point they are said to be a "swarm." No one's sure what makes them do this, though it's generally understood there's a crown princess waiting in the wings, snugly nestled in her cell, dining on royal jelly. The bees shoot from the entrance of the hive like water from the nozzle of a hose, each of them filled with honey and euphoria. Usually they choose a sunny day in late spring or early summer, departing between the hours of ten in the morning and three in the afternoon. The queen may be the first out or she may be the last; in any case she's the key player, having changed just for a moment from a stern destiny-maker into an aboriginal bee-woman, pleasure-loving and improvident. *Zeep zeep*, she goes, to stir things up.

Carole Ridingham, in her blowsy white garments, making her way to the nethermost tip of the Outer Head.

But come on. My mother didn't go to Wales because she was swarming. People aren't bees, I tell Monkey, who's sitting at the kitchen table, stabbing at the keyboard of Ruth's notebook.

No, he says, agreeably enough. We're the ones who're swarming.

And then in wrath and anger Manawydan rushed in amid the mice, but he could no more keep an eye on them than on the bees or the birds in the air; but one he could see was very heavy, so that he judged it incapable of any fleetness of foot.

He went after that one, and caught it, and put it in his glove, and tied up the mouth of the glove with a string, and kept it with him, and made for the court.

The most foolproof method of preventing your bees from swarming is to "de-queen" the hive.

Like this, Monkey says. CLICK CLICK CLICK, he goes, and suddenly wherever the word *queen* was there's nothing.

Like this, he says, and strides into the pantry. He removes the largest of the Blue Willow serving platters from its place on the bottom shelf, returns to the kitchen, lifts it over his head, and drops it.

Like this, he says, and hands me a blue-and-gray-striped work glove, the kind the hippie gardener used to wear in the olden days.

Thanks but no thanks, I say, watching the glove wiggle like there's something trapped inside it, trying to get out.

I give up, Monkey says, again cocking his head, glancing out the window. He puts his arm around me and looks in my ear. What are you, deaf? he says. I didn't think you were that old.

And suddenly I can almost hear it, a slow rumbling, like something thick and heavy, a chain with huge iron links being unreeled down a mountain.

Consider the plight of the bees, how the very force that drives them is the force that kills them, each of them a victim of their investment in a future they will never live to see: the worker dying as he stings, the drone dying as he mates, the queen dying of sheer exhaustion, having laid one too many eggs.

I stand next to Monkey and together we look out across the meadow.

A summer meadow, a beautiful dream that waits up ahead, the white clover only just starting to come into flower and the worker's legs heavy with pollen, the drone with sexual energy, and the queen a princess again, throbbing with anticipation in her sweet golden cell.

IT WAS A TERRIBLE STORM. The worst David Fluellen had ever seen, though perhaps only because it came on so suddenly, and, no, he wasn't trying to suggest he'd been taken by surprise, because he hadn't, he thought Miss Westenholtz had already made that abundantly clear. He heard the weather report but he chose to ignore it, his first mistake.

Or maybe you could say that happened four years ago, when Brenda started talking about making money off the tourists and he didn't say no but went along as usual, even though he was, frankly, appalled at the idea of filling his house with total strangers. The truth is, he'd do anything to please her, from the moment he sent out that fateful plate of oysters to her table in the seaside restaurant where he was working as a sous-chef, and then watched, love-struck, as she ate them greedily, completely unconcerned about where they'd come from or who sent them, tilting back her head to get every last bit of the liquor. Showing her neck, the way it rippled when she swallowed.

He could never get over how beautiful she was, but you wouldn't call that a mistake, would you? Just as you wouldn't call it a mistake that he'd always trusted her and always would. If Bren said there was nothing she could have done to prevent the tragedy, there wasn't. She never lied; she didn't know how.

Besides, you had to understand: it was raining so hard that

day it was like the air had turned to water and was being churned to a frenzy by the wind—like being inside a blender or a washing machine. You could barely see the hand in front of your face, which is why even though he'd swear Bren was telling the truth, he didn't think it necessarily followed that Mr. Hsia wasn't when he said he saw her on the Low Neck with Mr. Rose at the same time she said she was on the Devil's Bridge. Worms Head was huge, the whole thing almost two kilometers long, the cliff at the western tip of the Outer Head lifting steeply from the water, higher at its peak than the cross on top of St. Paul's Cathedral. Very steep and very slippery, the rocks slimy with tidal ooze, gull droppings, and seaweed.

Of course the Gower peninsula had been officially designated an area of Outstanding Natural Beauty, but didn't that usually spell danger? *Outstanding* beauty was rarely safe, after all: no sweeping vistas without vertiginous drops, no wind-scoured coasts without extremes of weather. Worms Head was the kind of place most people would prefer to view safely from afar, through one of those coin-operated telescopes in the car park outside the Visitor Center, or from a blanket on Rhossili Beach. Which was the very thing Bren had wanted to avoid when she originally conceived of the idea for the tour.

She had no sense of danger, David said. He was the domestic one in the couple. According to Bren, soon enough it'd be the same as it was in the States everywhere, with warning signs all over the place and guardrails, maybe a chain-link fence to keep you off except on nice days and only when the tide was all the way out. For now they should thank God they were still treated like adults. And he agreed. When Mrs. Ridingham went out onto that promontory, she went of her own free will. No one forced her.

Though, really, when he thought about it, maybe you had to go back even further, years and years ago, to that moment in the kitchen when his mother showed him how to knead dough and then singled him out for special praise from among all her other children, dubbing him Sir Baker with a thumbprint of flour . . .

Because if you were going to talk about "last clear chance," shouldn't you begin at the beginning, which in the case of a moral decision would have to begin with that first budding of the ego? How could you know whether you'd acted bravely or morally or like a Good Samaritan if you couldn't trace back to the very beginning of whatever path you'd chosen, the one that had led you to the place where you ultimately got put to the test?

If you couldn't trace all the way back, how would you ever reach an understanding of your original design, without which you could never hope to recognize the precise moment before the worst actually happened? The moment before the cream turned to butter, for example, or the custard curdled. You wouldn't have a prayer if you didn't know what it was you were hoping to make, as well as what temperature the eggs were before you started adding the milk, or how thoroughly they'd been beaten, or how hot the milk was. The law was right in thinking that without taking "foreseeability" into account, it was impossible to assign blame.

David admitted it: he wanted to be special, he wanted to be loved. Specifically he wanted to be loved for his cooking. And yes, he could foresee how such a wish might have led him to act less than morally, that it even might have kept him from acting as the *bonus paterfamilias* or "reasonable man" dictated by the law. Because sometimes the law ruled as negligent errors that even a reasonable man might make. Meaning sometimes the law encouraged a man to take the easy way out and avoid litigation, to use cornstarch and end up with a custard as glutinous and heavy as lead. Okay, it wouldn't have curdled, but it wouldn't have tasted very good, either.

So, yes. He'd been flattered by Mrs. Ridingham's attention, and had gone to great lengths to reciprocate, saving her the best cut of meat or the featheriest pastry, letting her sit in the passenger seat of the Rover, dancing with her and choosing her as his partner in the Kopeckys' ongoing skat game, despite her basic clumsiness and bad card sense. She was an unusual woman, Carole, a woman of tremendous stamina and will; when she singled you out it made you feel you were better than everyone else, since clearly she didn't suffer fools gladly. Well, fools and women—not to equate the two, but she also seemed to be a "man's woman," meaning she preferred the company of men. Even her friendship with Miss Farr, which clearly went way back, didn't seem to be without its troubles, and Bren had found Carole "cold."

In fact that was one reason why he'd remained on the Inner Head with Miss Westenholtz and Mr. Hsia and the Kopeckys. He and Bren had been feuding on and off ever since dinner the night before when she accused him of "two-timing" her with Mrs. Ridingham, and he knew it was incumbent upon him to prove otherwise. And since someone had to stay behind with the less adventurous members of the tour, and since that particular lot didn't include Mrs. Ridingham, it seemed prudent that it be he.

But it was perfectly chaste, his attention.

He had genuinely liked Mrs. Ridingham; he was devastated by her death.

And no, he didn't think there was anything "suspicious" about it—for instance that she might have committed suicide, if that was what counsel was trying to suggest.

Though to be fair, he also had to confess that their last conversation had left him troubled. On the way down the steep hillside from the car park to the beach: he'd caught up to Carole at the point where the wooden staircase suddenly ended and she'd been left to her own devices, the limestone crumbling beneath her feet and the season's new lambs cavorting on either side as if to emphasize her pitiful lack of skill. It was at precisely that point, where the steps ended and the limestone began, that the wind hit them square in the face like a mallet. One of the young Irishmen had just leapt off the cliff, and even from that distance David could tell he was in trouble, whereas Carole had seemed oblivious, plunging down the hillside in a big hurry, that confounded gauzy clothing she wore flapping around her, and the look in her eyes, when she glanced back—to make sure he was following? he couldn't tell—completely hidden by a pair of huge tortoiseshell shades.

She said she'd really enjoyed knowing him, which he first assumed was one of those remarks people make playfully, pretending they've finally been forced to tell the truth in the face of certain death. She said she hoped he'd find a worthier skat partner in the future. She handed him a jack of clubs, which she evidently had hidden somewhere in her clothes, and told him she'd been cheating all along and hoped he'd forgive her, but could he please not rat on her to the Kopeckys, especially Magtil. Null Ouvert, she said, I win. Then, after they'd more or less slid down the last twenty or so feet of disintegrating hillside to land in a heap on the beach, she turned to him and, checking to make sure the others were still reasonably far behind, took off her shades, grabbed him by the wrists, pulled him to her, and kissed him.

Not passionately, though not exactly platonically, either. Do me a favor, she said, looking back toward the car park, where Mr. Hsia could be seen waving down at them, his umbrella tipped geisha-fashion over one shoulder. Let's keep this to ourselves, okay? Let's not tell anyone, especially not that vulture. And when David asked who, she said she trusted him to figure that out for himself. Then she got up, brushing away the sand that clung wetly, heavily to her skirt, and was off again, picking her way with surprising deftness over the slick green rocks and through the tide-pocked ooze between Kitchen Corner and the Inner Head.

By now the rain had started in earnest, and the wind was blowing a gale; as David recalled, Major and Miss Herne were the next to hit the beach, followed by Mr. Kopecky, and then, after a minute or two, everyone else. Noisy, arguing: should they stay where they were or proceed to the tip of the head as planned? Have lunch in the village of Rhossili or return to Fairy Ring? But then we would return in disgrace, said Miss Westenholtz, who paused to snap a picture of Mr. Snow snapping a picture of his wife, the last one down. Anything but that, said Mr. Hsia, with heavy irony.

Uncouth and savage, the rain and the wind, without flesh, without bone, without vein, without blood . . . wide as the earth, never born nor yet seen . . . creature from before the flood.

On the Inner Head, no sign of Mrs. Ridingham.

But she'd seemed happy. Despite the somewhat ominous tone of what she'd said before running off, she didn't seem like a person contemplating suicide. She'd seemed *very* happy, in fact. And yes, David had known about her mental condition. Her husband had told Bren, who'd told him.

It was an accident. No one could have prevented it, unless you blamed him for ignoring the weather report, or for listening to Bren. Or God for creating a world with bad weather in it.

And as for that talk about a boat? Insane. Crazy. More likely a submerged rock, or some sort of skate, or ray. Possibly an eel —it would be the right time of year, when they ventured close to shore, sometimes even leaving the water altogether in their quest for food, because they were so ravenous.

*uncouth and savage,*
*without flesh, without bone,*
*am I not a candidate for fame*
*to be heard in the song?*

*in caer sidi*
*four times revolving*
*the first word from the cauldron*
*when was it spoken?*

*am I not a candidate for fame,*
*to be heard in the song?*
*no word for the coward*
*from the pearl-edged cauldron.*

*incomprehensible numbers there were*
*maintained in a chilly hell*
*except two none returned*
*from four-sided caer sidi.*

—c.r.

Turn it off, dear Susan, Monkey says. It's time to turn it off. Holding the metal box above his head—wigless for once —and shaking it. There's nothing left inside, he says. It's empty. Squinting into the port, taking a deep breath and blowing into it—*pssst! pssst!*—before dropping the whole thing scornfully to the table. Retard, he says. Then he kneels on the floor and starts rolling up the last of the old Hamadans, the one with a yellow dog in the central medallion, like the dogs of Pallas, short-legged and fierce.

CLICK. CLICK.

Empty, Monkey repeats. If you're looking for help you'll have to look elsewhere. He's almost bald without the wig, his dark hair sparsely plastered to his skull. Grass never grows on a busy street, as Uncle Coleman used to say. But *not there*, Monkey yells; stay away from the window. It's not safe. Surely even a retard like you can see that much. He reaches in a pocket and produces a pair of binoculars identical to the ones Bobby had during the trial, the same scratch like a fox face near the focus knob. Maybe these'll help, he says, and I find myself wondering—briefly, idly—not so much when Monkey "appropriated" them, but what Bobby was doing with Paula Herne's binoculars in the first place.

What I see, I say, is that it's finally nice out. A nice day. There are people walking along the drive, fairly far off, near where it meets the road. Visitors, I say, and Monkey gives me a look. Some visitors, he replies, and the way he says it makes me remind him I came by this house fair and square. In Bobby's will, still hidden behind the complete works of Robert Louis Stevenson that he bought in Wales so many years ago, before his life changed forever. First beneficiary, Carole Ridingham. And if she were no longer alive, the house would go to me, along with the proceeds from the Ridingham estate. Not to mention Ruth's "wrongful death settlement."

Poor Susan, Monkey says.

The meadow's never looked more beautiful, every hideous shrub and vile bramble seeming lit from within like it's the source of the light, the tip of each thorn, the rim of each leaf, glowing, shivering slightly in a tepid breeze. Shrubs and brambles, flies and gulls, everything in the meadow outlined in yellow light and shivering, unable to hold still, and the sky like a gold bowl upended over it to catch all that light and movement and reflect it back in a continuous rippling like the skin of a horse shaking off flies.

There seem to be six or seven people. I can see that even before looking through Paula Herne's binoculars. One of them holds a young child, another a large box, and all of them keep glancing up toward the house, or maybe toward the sky. It's hard to say. Dressed normally, which is to say not like Strags, though that could be a ruse. But when I finally try using the binoculars, it's amazing how hard it is to catch a single face — or a single anything for that matter, given how fast they're moving, and the restless quality of the world outdoors today. No sooner have I focused on one forehead (belonging to a woman about my age with black chenille-thick eyebrows and a thin wash of gray frothy hair) than it's gone, replaced by a blur of shrub and bramble, wobbly yellow light and a pair of scaly bird feet gripping a branch that's bobbing up and down, and then a man's ear with black hair growing out of it, meaning he's more or less my age as well, above a neck that has the kind of navy blue bandanna around it everyone used to wear because it was what they sold at the general store, and then a brown pigtail, a red bow, a red jacket.

Paula Herne was a young woman at the time of the tour. If sickness or routine catastrophe haven't caught up with her she's probably still alive and living somewhere in the British Isles, a full-fledged veterinarian by now, sadly watching the population of this breed of dog or that breed of cow gradually shrink, while other populations, notably insect and human, somehow keep getting bigger. Monkey was wrong about Paula, I think: it wasn't so much that she was a selfish girl, but that she never especially liked people. These days she probably wouldn't want her binoculars. She wouldn't want to see that rabbits are being born blind, or dogs with shorter and shorter legs until they have almost no legs at all, or eels with leg buds and wings.

Though maybe the rumors are false. People love hearing about catastrophes, and then passing the news on to their friends.

Nice day? Monkey says. What nice day? You're the limit, Susan. You call that sunshine? If that's sunshine, he says, where are the shadows? He's dumping the contents of a kitchen drawer onto the rug he's already piled into a duffle bag with C.H.S. scrawled on it in black marker. Coleman H. Snow. The house is thick with ghosts today, and all at once I'm back there in the meadow again, watching the robber bee and my mother's worried expression and Uncle Coleman unzipping this exact bag and taking out a needle and jabbing it right into Aunt Ruth's upper arm. Jabbing it in hard, which I thought at the time meant he was mad at her.

The people have disappeared behind a clump of plant towers. I can tell they're there because the towers are shaking, and I can see bursts of color from time to time between the stalks. Yellow, blue, red, the primary colors by which all things were made. It's noon, I say. The sun's directly overhead. It's driven the shadows straight into the ground.

But Monkey's right. It isn't noon, and though the wind isn't very strong yet, it's the wind, not the light, that's set everything in motion. The same wind that swept down on my mother, hectoring her the way wind does, heedless of her ability to withstand its force, oblivious to her state of mind. The same wind that's been with us since the beginning— because, really, it's not like it ever gets used up or added to. The same wind that passed over the face of the earth when the fountains of the deep and the windows of heaven were stopped . . . a fresh breeze rippling the surface of the water, and the paired creatures twining their necks together, kissing . . .

Because it's not like we've ever gotten or ever will get *more* of the things crucial to our survival.

The only things we get more of are the things that kill us.

Move, Susan, Monkey says, and he pushes me roughly to one side before I have a chance to do as he's said. Opening the cupboard door I was leaning against and removing a skillet.

You think I'm going to just stand here and let you get away with this? Thief. Thief.

You think I'm going to just stand here? Monkey mocks. He opens the refrigerator and though it's dark inside I can see an egg on one shelf, a baby bottle on another, both of them white, practically glowing. So much for that, he says. He removes the egg and cracks it onto the floor, one-handed, like a chef, releasing an unspeakable odor. There's a sheen of moisture on his face, and I realize how moist and sticky I am too. How I barely have the energy to slide Ruth's computer into the duffle bag, or follow Monkey to the door, or close the door behind me as I follow him onto the piazza, where for some reason he's taken off to, pausing for a moment, the duffle bag cradled in his arms like a person.

Is your refrigerator running, he says. The tiniest of dust dervishes are whisking along the cracks between the fieldstones like baby tornadoes, and there's an enormous hush, the kind of hush that used to fall over the dinner table whenever my mother asked Bobby where he'd been and he'd say, making money to keep you in pills, my darling.

Oh, the force that drives a man and a woman together is a mysterious thing, often resembling violence when it's nothing of the kind. Not gentle, not timid, but love just the same—a child has no business watching such a thing and being expected to understand.

And now it's clear that the yellow light that seemed to be sun is really the base of a cloud, a huge restless cloud that can't stop rippling, gold and gray and green and silver, no longer bowl-like but aqueous and billowing like the open sea, with who knows what hiding inside.

Is your refrigerator running? Monkey says again. Well, then catch it, Susan. Catch it! Shoving his way through the plant towers toward the windowpaneless garden house where the goose on the roof is whirling around and around like there's no such thing as direction. Uh oh, Monkey says. The swells at the base of the cloud are starting to change shape, becoming thick and bulbous and opaque, like the yellow substance in the lava lamp. A break in the atmosphere, he says. Finally.

But at what exact moment did the garden house cease to be a studio and turn into a dreary outbuilding, a few paint smudges on its disintegrating stucco walls the sole sign that an artist used to work there? Green smears and red, still visible through the paneless windows after all these years. Red-haired Mrs. Renfrew and her squirming red-haired litter. A smell like mulled cider. Oil of cloves, without which the paint dries too quickly; Paris green, a deadly poison . . . for God's sake, Susan, watch what you put in your mouth! As meanwhile the base of the cloud is developing more and more bulbs, and the bulbs themselves growing rounder and rounder and appearing at more and more regular intervals, their color darkening, no longer gold but an orange verging on brown that first looks heraldic, then spoiled, like old cheese.

A crowd of people clusters near the foot of the drive, the smaller group from before starting to move up it. The man with the bandanna and the woman with the eyebrows. The girl with pigtails. A tall young woman with sloping shoulders —but is her hair really white and stiff like that or is she wearing a wig? And is that thing glinting in the man's hand a knife, or maybe just a tool of some sort? A screwdriver or a trowel?

Hurry up, Susan, Monkey says, heading into the thicket of plant towers on the right side of the garden house, the side away from the drive.

Where are we going?

But he only points across the meadow.

Wouldn't we be safer in the house? In the cellar?

No one's forcing you to come, he replies.

Of course I know where's he's taking me. We're headed through the vile gray brambles and ash-pale vines and endless interlocking shrubs of what used to be the meadow, past the ruined bee boxes and across the streambed's jumble of sludge-coated pebbles where the same wrapper with the same insipid little blond girl on it which Bobby crumpled up and threw *right there* under the far side of the bridge so many years ago is still faintly trembling in what passes for a current, though of course it can't be the same or even a snack cake wrapper at all but just a crumpled sheet of scum, and that sound not Bobby's old Victrola or even the wind but something rising and falling deep inside *and o my darling o my pet whatever else you may forget in yonder isle beyond the sea do not forget you've married me* and past the gulls' disgusting nests atop the moldering pillars of Bobby's office and around the leaf-clogged fountain's now armless and headless naiad still exposing her large breasts to the no longer bright blue sky and onto the path leading through willow and reed-studded marshland, mucky and over-sweet and squelching underfoot, until up ahead through the black meshes of the willow boughs a chink of swirling brownish light and the landscape suddenly spreading out in an expanse of what Monkey once referred to as putting-green-like turf.

Duck down, will you, Monkey says.

By now I can barely see the hand in front of my face, but he refuses to be reassured, since he's heard something too, though not that music Bobby so unaccountably adored, that sound of the nineteenth century shining through to the twentieth and beyond, into a future William Schwenck Gilbert couldn't even have remotely imagined . . .

We'll have to move quickly, Monkey says. One. Two. A faint jagged noise, like paper being ripped or nails being filed or bees. The sky lowering, thickening, several of the largest cloud bulbs slowly detaching and dropping toward the ground. Three. Four. Stepping across the smooth green turf, which on closer look seems to be a dense mat of some kind of moss, springy and soft like a mattress. Five. Six. Seven. Eight.

It turns out to be exactly a hundred paces to the trapdoor, exactly as Monkey described it, though he left out the part about it being metal and printed with the old Civil Air Defense symbol of a triangle in a circle, as well as not having been exactly on the up and up about what I'd find inside, since it's nothing like "a most beautiful country" and more like a dark cramped cellar filled with the smell of spices and urine and a loud screaming noise, lined on three sides with metal shelving, and the shelves with things he's stolen from the house.

Bobby's bomb shelter, of course. Alluded to by Mrs. Koop all throughout my childhood in such hushed censorious tones that it's no surprise, really, that I've never been here before. As if the shelter itself could be held accountable for all the things Bobby did in it, the ghost of each amorous move still palpable, a mysterious shadow rising and lowering above the foldout cot in the corner, a sudden humid draft.

A big-boned young woman on her hands and knees, her rump to the staircase, staring into the laundry basket.

Peggy, Monkey says. Get up. Meet Susan.

And on the fourth wall? Paintings. Ridinghams, by the look of them, though there's only one I actually remember.

The young woman turns and she's the horselike cashier from the IGA. It's about time, she says, reaching into the laundry basket and picking up Netta, whose outraged red face is piteously complemented by my mother's peau de soie bed jacket. Peggy. Maybe a little less horselike than I first imagined, staring over the top of the baby's head, her wide-set eyes dark and strangely dull, like marbles that rolled under a bed and got dusty.

But where on earth did the paintings come from? And if they are my mother's—which they certainly seem to be—when on earth did she paint them? Because there are things in them, certain people and places and objects, that she couldn't possibly have known about before she went to Wales.

Impossible, I think. My mother! After all these years. Not like Bobby. Not like seeing a ghost, but finding the person herself right there in the room with me, the whole living human weight of her, smelling faintly, the way she always did, of turpentine. Do you know—I begin, and then just as suddenly as I felt it quicken, my heart turns to stone. No, I think. It would be too cruel of her to have lied to me like that, too cruel of me to think her capable of such a thing.

I'm going nuts, Peggy says. The baby hasn't stopped crying since you left. Here, she says, shoving Netta in my arms and handing me a can of formula. You might as well make yourself useful, she says. I mean, he's only being nice because he wants something. No offense. It isn't like he likes you.

Monkey meanwhile is busy unloading the duffle bag, carefully removing the things he dumped in so carelessly. The tendons of his neck straining as he bends and then Peggy joining him, laying her hand on his bent lower back, whispering in his ear.

A total of five paintings: four small canvases, one large. And apart from *Opera Cloak*—the rondel Bobby bought at the show where he rediscovered Carole, and which used to hang in his office—the small paintings are in varying stages of completion and seem to be studies, unlike the large one, which takes up most of the wall, measures about five feet by seven, and is undeniably finished, a masterpiece in fact. All of them, however, display the artist's signature touches, her use of a highly dilute egg tempera underpainting in shades of terre verte and umber, for example, or of rabbit-skin glue mixed with red gesso as a base for the gold leaf she so lavishly employed.

Standing there's not getting the baby fed, Peggy says, then nudges Monkey, and says, I *told* you. She's no help at all. She's way too old.

She's not so old, Monkey says. He lights one of his long gray cigarettes and takes a drag, the smell of the smoke mixing unpleasantly with the smell of cloves and sweat. What do you think? he asks, nodding at the paintings. Surprised?

They give *me* the creeps, Peggy says. You could never say they're not good, but still.

Two of the studies aren't much more than sketches: Worms Head seen from the sea, in repose and with a human face (the artist's?) emerging from a fan of spume; wingless bees riding winged mice across a landscape of miniature houses and fields and roads. In both cases a sky of the astonishing shade and buttery consistency critics called "Ridingham blue," with touches of gold leaf here and there, as well as my mother's impeccable draftsmanship and her uncanny sense of perspective, her way of making it impossible to tell, for instance, if the mice are unusually big, or the objects in the landscape, unusually tiny.

The third study, on the other hand, seems almost complete, a group portrait of sorts, twelve pairs of feet and shoes on a dark green ground—the lawn in front of the Blackbrook in fact, every individual grass blade outlined with deadly Paris green. In the lower left-hand corner a pair of empty red high heels beside a pair of running shoes with Aunt Ruth's skinny legs rising from them, cut off just above the knee by the top of the canvas. In the right foreground, Uncle Coleman's scuffed Hush Puppies and rumpled chino pant legs and Mr. Hsia's glistening hip-waders, and peeking from behind them Naomi's unlaced combat boots, Brenda's aqua flip-flops, David's orange high-tops, the Kopeckys' four matching plimsolls, and Major's four matching paws. Dead center, Bobby's hairy muscular legs from the calf down and facing away from the viewer to show the wound on his left heel, the most worked-over and frighteningly graphic part of the painting, like an open mouth, trailing an ornate speech banner with MOST UNKINDEST CUT painted across it in gold leaf. The artist nowhere to be seen.

Someone's banging on the trapdoor, but I'm pretty sure the hatch is secure. Banging and banging, but they'll never get in, no matter how desperate they are. The woman with the chenille eyebrows, the man with the bandanna, the child with the red bow—they won't get in because under certain circumstances you have to harden your heart, which is why Bobby had Uncle Coleman design the hatch to work that way back in the days when the sky itself wasn't the enemy but just a conduit.

Back in the days when the sky was always blue. A blue sky, Ridingham blue, dotted with small white clouds. Pretty au pairs traipsing across the meadow in their summer dresses. Pretty au pairs drawn across the meadow like iron filings to the magnet that was Bobby, who waited for them down here with his hard hard heart.

Most unkindest cut, Monkey says. That's the title.

How do you know? I ask, and Peggy points at the top of the large canvas, where another speech banner issues from the mouth of the hang glider pilot hovering above the water like a black and yellow bee. The banner likewise ornate, and the words WHAT'S WRONG WITH THIS PICTURE painted on in gold leaf.

What are you, blind? Peggy says. Of course he knows.

WORMS HEAD, viewed from Rhossili Beach, everything equally vivid and detailed as if the normal rules of perspective don't apply. Aunt Ruth in profile in the right foreground, sitting cross-legged on the sand in her black-and-yellow-striped halter top and her black-and-yellow-plaid shorts, looking to the left, her hand cupped above her eyes like a visor to ward off the rain that's falling in millions of perfect drop-shaped drops. Skin white as snow and hair black as ebony—slightly prettier perhaps than Aunt Ruth ever really was, though painted with typical Ridingham precision, right down to the little beige beauty mark on her upper lip, and the long black eyelashes I know were fake because I remember her gluing them on and telling me it wasn't fair my father's lashes were thick and curly like a girl's.

Aunt Ruth is the first thing your eye travels to when you look at the painting, and then, because she looks left, you do too, though not at the Outer Head where the action supposedly is, but at the Low Neck, where Bobby and Brenda stand facing each other, Bobby with his back to the sea, Brenda, the beach. They're considerably smaller than Aunt Ruth but just as meticulously rendered, meaning you can make out every last strand of hair in Brenda's French braid, every last whisker in Bobby's three o'clock shadow. Smiling, not yet touching but reaching for each other like they're about to touch; having been the one who put Bobby up to Brenda's seduction in the first place, Aunt Ruth is monitoring his progress from her place on the beach, happy to see that it's proceeding nicely.

Though it's also possible that neither "smiling" nor "three o'clock" nor "about to touch" nor "happy" is entirely accurate, despite the growth of Bobby's beard and the position of the hands on Ruth's Patek Philippe and Brenda's arms and all their lips. It's possible that none of this is accurate because of repentance, referring in this case not to a spiritual act but to a physical problem confronting the painter in oils.

Repentance occurs when the last application of paint— which usually happens to be thick and opaque and is, consequently, the one used for the face of things such as people or watches—begins to turn transparent, and ghosts begin leaking through. The paint loses its opacity: the teeth are shown to be gritted. Clockworks appear, the clenched fist lifts. In the woman's belly a little baby, under the thick swirling clouds a shining sun.

Of course the sun's always there; it's not like it isn't shining just because we can't see it. Just as each time someone lifts a hand to touch your face he could just as easily strike it, or the promontory could turn out not to be rock but skin, reptilian and black and glistening, with hints here and there of a skeleton beneath.

To the left of Bobby and Brenda, about half their size and walking single file along the boulder-strewn base of the Inner Head, Naomi Westenholtz, Magtil Kopecky, and Mr. Hsia. Naomi shuffling in her unlaced boots, studying Ruth adoringly through Paula Herne's binoculars. Magtil's mouth wide open, a perfect O of either horror or amazement, as Mr. Hsia, clad in yellow rain gear, points his umbrella toward the Outer Head, and a ghost Naomi swivels Paula Herne's binoculars to see exactly what it is he's pointing at.

They haven't even crossed to the Low Neck. And you know what? They're not going to. They're going to keep walking single file like the three Chinamen on the Blue Willow dishes, never getting anywhere. No one ever gets anywhere in a painting (or on a plate, for that matter), not even the dog, who's been depicted in a touchingly disembodied way, not like a material being but a funnel of wind similar to a dust dervish that leaves a little furrowed trail behind it as it tears from the Low Neck and across the Devil's Bridge to the Outer Head, where it meets up with the larger dervish that is David Fluellen and where superficially at least it becomes a dog again, ecstatic, unrepentant, and panting heavily, its auburn ears blown back all the way to show the pink insides like the inside of a conch shell.

My mother poised at the very tip of the promontory, just beyond the Blow Hole, which is sending up its own funnel of furious white spray. Slightly bigger than Brenda and Bobby and a lot bigger than the threesome on the Inner Head, my mother is poised there in her white draperies like the Nike of Samothrace, ever so delicately sticking out her shell pink tongue and ever so boldly wearing her shell pink heart on her sleeve. Uncle Coleman at her side, the two of them holding hands like children preparing to jump into the water, only they don't really seem to be thinking of jumping, or at least not into the sea, which is itself a deep mysterious emerald green, the result of multiple glazes, one atop another atop another etc. etc., with who knows what at the bottom, maybe

Neptune's face, or the artist's, because clearly *something's* doing its best to rise to the surface.

When you use poppy oil as a medium, the paint is slow to dry and quick to crack, but there's no tendency for the white to yellow. My mother's face and draperies. Uncle Coleman's hair. The funnel of spray . . .

Major? Major? A pair of whistling lips swimming into view on the serpent's forehead, like a message in a Magic 8 Ball: MOST DEFINITELY. Paula Herne scrambling up the Outer Head on her hands and knees, then losing her balance and slipping backward. Major. Major! Bad boy.

And tumbling through the sky a million perfect drop-shaped raindrops that when followed to their source tower upward into anvils of electricity. An infinite number of drops of rain and between each one an infinite number of possibilities. Only fools make plans.

If your mother dies when you're still a young girl, then you haven't got a prayer.

The white highlights on her draperies still slightly moist, still smelling faintly sweet, like poppies. The raindrops, too, and the dots of light in her eyes—wet, still wet, avid, alive . . .

She went all the way to the edge of the world without looking back because it was the only way she knew to return to me.

Smiling, almost gleeful, her expression one I've never seen on her face before, either in life or on a canvas.

Though, really, it isn't only *her* face that seems unfamiliar. No, there's a quality of psychological complexity to all the faces that I don't remember seeing in my mother's paintings, since to be perfectly honest, she was never especially interested in people except as elements in a composition, or textures, or colors. It isn't so much that Aunt Ruth is prettier as that her face is animated by a delight in seeing her own motives played out in the world, just as the tension in Bobby's jaw bespeaks an underlying weakness akin to cruelty.

Precise, luminous, the same yet not the same. The key details implied rather than explicit; the glazes thinner, the underpainting doing most of the work. My mother's sensibility recognized and honored, adored even, yet transfigured. Which is the only way the dead come back in *this* world.

As meanwhile the artist's face continues to rise toward me, gray-eyed, delphic.

THERE WAS never any question, said Brenda Fluellen. The Americans came because of Mrs. Ridingham. It was she who made the initial contact. Miss Farr didn't get involved until much later, and the deposit check was signed by poor Mr. Snow, who'd been, incidentally, captain of the swimming team at university. It was always the best swimmers who drowned, everyone knew that.

In all honesty, though, Brenda had to admit that she'd never been sure *why* Mrs. Ridingham wanted to come to Wales in the first place. Later, when she asked her what had attracted her to the Blackbrook, she came up with something about the way the brochure described past, present, and future as blending together into one, but the truth is she sounded anything but enthusiastic. Maybe she did it to please Miss Farr?

Her husband, David, had always been an admirer of Mrs. Ridingham's painting, but once they'd actually met he'd taken a real liking to her. Brenda confessed that she'd been jealous; David was correct when he said they'd been feuding the day of the accident. Nor had it escaped her notice that David didn't run after Mrs. Ridingham when she took off in the direction of the Outer Head, as he might have done if he hadn't known Brenda would object. If that meant she contributed, however inadvertently, to Mrs. Ridingham's death, she was very sorry. She'd never felt particularly close to Mrs. Ridingham, but that didn't mean she was a "tort-feasor," or that she ever in a million years would have wished her dead.

So David on the Inner Head, then, together with Mr. Hsia and Magtil Kopecky, and Naomi Westenholtz. Miss Westenholtz had lent Mr. Rose Miss Herne's binoculars, which he was wearing around his neck when she, Brenda, met up with him on the Low Neck on her way back to fetch David. She'd gotten as far as the Devil's Bridge before changing her mind. Even though it was extremely windy and rainy and the footing was bad, these weren't the worst conditions Brenda had ever seen. Off Skye once, for instance, she'd been caught in a white squall, but at the time of the walking tour she had to think twice before taking any risks since it was two lives she'd be risking.

Of course as the court was no doubt aware, she needn't have bothered. She miscarried almost two weeks to the day after the excursion to Worms Head. A letter from her doctor had already been sworn in as evidence in case there was any doubt that she'd been pregnant in the first place. And yes, she would never get over the loss. It was a life, after all. No less important for being infinitely younger than Mrs. Ridingham or Mr. Snow, though she didn't see anyone trying to bring *them* to court.

But so much for her sorrows. So much for her . . .

To return to the Devil's Bridge: Mr. Rose seemed somewhat distracted, and at first she thought it had something to do with Miss Farr, who'd remained behind on the beach, and whom he was staring at through the binoculars.

He waved to her, and Miss Farr waved back.

And no, Brenda didn't think there was anything odd about

Miss Farr's decision to stay on the beach. Miss Farr frequently hung back; in Brenda's experience—no offense—Jews generally tended to be less adventuresome, less athletic perhaps, than their other guests. Though to be fair, when she'd first arrived in Wales, Miss Farr had seemed enormously excited to hear that they'd be visiting Gower, which she said related to some book she was working on.

She was very clever, Miss Farr. Very quick-witted. Brenda suspected that Miss Farr found her dull. All of the Americans did, no doubt—Americans in general.

Which was why Brenda found Mr. Rose's interest in her all the more surprising.

She hadn't been feeling well. The weather was bad. She'd been sick again that morning. And to top it off, Major had bolted and wasn't responding to her whistle. Granted, Miss Herne was on top of the situation. Or at least Brenda had thought she was. As David said, you couldn't see from one end of the promontory to the other.

When she tried to make her way around him, Mr. Rose put out a hand and stopped her. He said he wanted to play a little trick on Ruthie. Miss Farr. Pretend to kiss me, he said, and when Brenda asked why, he shook his head. It'll serve her right, he said. Ruthie's always trashing you, in case you didn't know. Besides, he said, Brenda *wanted* to kiss him, and no matter how fervently she insisted he was wrong—and she wanted the court to know that she did insist, and quite vociferously at that—he refused to believe her.

There wasn't much room along the base of the Low Neck. The only way Brenda could get past Bobby would be if he'd stepped to one side. That or climb off the rocks and into the water, but the tide had been coming in fast for a while now, and already it was too deep and rough to consider doing such a thing.

Bobby had just put his hands around her waist. A word to the wise, sweetheart, he was saying. Don't make me any angrier than I already am. And then she heard loud splashing and far-off barking and the sound of footsteps, and all of a sudden there was Tadeusz Kopecky, her blue-eyed guardian angel, as gentle and determined to make life easier for her as Mr. Rose was not. Almost as if he'd appeared out of nowhere, though it had to have been from behind her, Brenda said; otherwise she would have seen him coming.

Mr. Kopecky was looking past her, toward the end of the promontory. Very agitated, and when Brenda happened to look back at Miss Farr, she saw that she was standing, waving her arms, shouting and gesturing, at which point Bobby again lifted the binoculars to his face and aimed them at the Outer Head.

Of course, Mrs. Ridingham had her share of problems. David said she was a schizophrenic, though as far as Brenda could tell there'd only been the one of her. Maybe it was her evil self who jumped? But if you were divided into many selves, how would you ever know which one of them was at fault in any given situation? It made it difficult to assign blame, or understand intention, or evaluate how prudent one's behavior had been—though maybe she was getting it mixed up with multiple personality like that poor girl in the movie who'd been thrown down a well and when they hauled her back up there were lots more of her.

Mrs. Ridingham either jumped or fell or was pushed. Brenda

had no more idea of what actually went on out there than she had of why Bobby wanted to kiss her. She didn't know then, she didn't know now, and she probably never would. What she did know was that the last thing she remembered seeing was Bobby dropping the binoculars and shouldering past her. He said he was going to kill that goddamn dog and Brenda said, Major? What did he ever do?

Of course it was natural that Bobby would want someone to blame, though by the time of the accident, Major was nowhere near Mrs. Ridingham. And really, even if he had been, he never could have knocked her over. She was way too big.

Get out of my way, Bobby said, but Brenda didn't budge.

For God's sake, she told him, it's not like it's the end of the world.

© Marion Ettlinger

⌒♪⌒

KATHRYN DAVIS is the author of three other novels, *The Girl Who Trod on a Loaf*, *Hell*, and *Labrador*. She has received the Kafka Prize for fiction by an American woman and the 1999 Morton Dauwen Zabel Award from the American Academy and Institute of Arts and Letters. A Guggenheim Fellow for 2000, she teaches at Skidmore College in Saratoga Springs, New York, and lives with her husband and their daughter in Vermont.